THE SPRING SONG

by

FORREST REID

'I am a little world made cunningly
Of elements, and an angelic sprite.'
—DONNE

With a new introduction by

MARK VALENTINE

𝕶𝖆𝖓𝖘𝖆𝖘 𝕮𝖎𝖙𝖞:

VALANCOURT BOOKS

2013

The Spring Song by Forrest Reid
First published London: Edward Arnold, 1916
First Valancourt Books edition 2013

Published by Valancourt Books, Kansas City, Missouri
Publisher & Editor: JAMES D. JENKINS
20th Century Series Editor: SIMON STERN, University of Toronto
http://www.valancourtbooks.com

Library of Congress Cataloging-in-Publication Data

Reid, Forrest, 1875-1947.
The Spring Song / by Forrest Reid ; with a new introduction
by Mark Valentine. – First Valancourt Books edition.
pages cm. – (20th Century Series)
ISBN 978-1-939140-22-7 (acid-free paper)
I. Title.
PR6035.E43S86 2013
823'.912–dc23

2013007044

Design and typography by James D. Jenkins
Set in Dante MT 11/13.5

10 9 8 7 6 5 4 3 2 1

INTRODUCTION

Forrest Reid's novels and two fine volumes of autobiography include beautiful evocations of the country in his lifelong home, Ulster, especially the Mourne Mountains and the coast of Antrim. His books are also delicately laced with fantasy and hints of the supernatural. His youthful interest in classical paganism is a prevailing theme, and echoes of Pan, Hermes, and other Greek deities and spirits are to be found in many of his works. All these characteristics are especially to the fore in *The Spring Song* (1916), where hints of Arcadia linger in the local country, and the youthful dreamer Grif catches glimpses of the god of the flute and the fields.

Reid's books share some of the qualities seen also in the work of his literary friends, including W. B. Yeats, the mystic poet A.E. (George Russell) and Walter de la Mare, such as a preoccupation with the otherworldly and an urge to express a spiritual sensibility. But Reid was also a man who enjoyed such simple recreations as stamp-collecting and jigsaws, and his books are full of quiet insight into both the finer feelings and the failings of his very human characters.

Forrest Reid was born in Belfast on 24 June 1875, the youngest of a large family. His father's family was prosperous and eminent in the professions: his mother was descended from the Shropshire family of Parr, and her ancestors included Katherine Parr, one of Henry VIII's more fortunate wives. His father died when he was still a young child, and much of his upbringing therefore fell to his rather conventional mother and his elder sisters. As a youth he felt ill at ease with what seemed the narrow piety of his family's Presbyterian faith, and their solid middle-class values.

After a local schooling, he was apprenticed at age eighteen to the tea trade. The work was not demanding, and Reid coped with the tedium of commercial life by retreating into a dream world of wonder and beauty, inspired by his reading of the Greek classics. He soon identified himself as a natural pagan. He was particularly influenced by a mystical experience close to his sixteenth birth-day when he lay studying by the banks of the River Lagan near Belfast.

He recalls this vividly in his first memoir, *Apostate* (1926). There was an unnatural, breathless silence "like a bridge that reached straight back into the heart of some dim antiquity". He experi-enced "a feeling that some veil might be drawn away, that there might come to me something, someone . . . either with the winged feet of Hermes, or the thyrsus of Dionysus, or maybe only hairy-shanked Pan of the Goats". Expectation reached the point where he was convinced the woodland before him would split into two, but then "I hesitated, blundered, drew back, failed", the moment was lost, and gradually the scene returned to normality. This almost-vision remained important for Reid for the rest of his life and moments like it are evoked in many of his works. It pervades *The Spring Song*, where Grif also senses the nearness of the old gods and the possibility of a realm just beyond reach.

Reid's first book, *The Kingdom of Twilight* (1904), had been much influenced by the style and themes of the Eighteen Nineties, with a hero who is a misunderstood aesthete, reads Verlaine, and con-verts to Roman Catholicism. The plot is a romantic melodrama and the prose is ornate and highly coloured. Reid later rejected it entirely: "I hate this book; I am glad it is forgotten; and when I could do so with safety I have destroyed any copies I could lay my hands on." Perhaps unsurprisingly, it is now difficult to find.

A second, much slimmer novel, *The Garden God* (also available from Valancourt) followed in 1905. Here, Reid achieved more con-trol of the rather 'precious' Nineties prose style. But the theme of the close comradeship of two boys in an idyllic summer by the sea, and the hints of lingering unseen pagan presences, were enough to offend some contemporaries.

After Reid's mother died in 1901, a legacy left him with moder-ate private means. He left the tea trade and pursued the university education he had missed, attending Christ's College, Cambridge from 1905-8. He toured Europe during the long vacation of 1907. But after he returned to Ulster in 1908, he spent most of the rest of his life there, apart from holiday visits to friends in England. The leisure of his new life in Belfast, without the pressing need to earn money, soon enabled him to resume writing.

His next novel, *The Bracknels* (1911; a revised version was published in 1947 as *Denis Bracknel*), shows a maturer, more personal style. It combines a realistic portrayal of a smug and rather Philistine Belfast family, with a supernatural theme, involving the sensitive younger son's obsession with the moon, a form of possession which ends in tragedy. At least one critic thought the story comparable with Henry James's classic chiller *The Turn of the Screw*. The book also attracted the admiration of E.M. Forster, whose *The Celestial Omnibus* (1911) has some things in common with Reid's themes, and of Walter de la Mare, also a master of the supernatural. Both writers were to become close friends. Forster devoted an essay to Reid in his collection *Abinger Harvest*, while de la Mare dedicated his short story collection *On the Edge* to him.

Reid's next novel, *Following Darkness* (1912) was one of the earliest novels to deal with the psychological tensions and confused emotions of adolescence. Although it includes many fine descriptions of days in the countryside of County Down, the book also realistically depicts the lack of sympathy between the young protagonist, Peter Waring, and his fundamentalist father, and has some bitter scenes in a dreary and sordid quarter of Belfast. Though respected when it first appeared, *Following Darkness* was not a success with the public. The book was much better received twenty-five years later when it was rewritten and retitled *Peter Waring*.

Reid's next two novels show him still uncertain about the direction of his work. *The Gentle Lover* (1913), subtitled "A Comedy of Middle Age", was purposefully written with the aim of excluding all harshness and ugliness from the theme. In essence a holiday romance in the ancient city of Bruges with its air of quiet melancholy, it is so carefully crafted and thoughtful in tone that its qualities are apt to be overlooked a little. *At the Door of the Gate* (1915), by contrast, is a more stormy romantic tragedy, full of incident and uneven in tone. Both make use of characters with an interest in the supernatural but these are incidental and do not pervade the whole atmosphere of the book in the way Reid achieved elsewhere.

Meanwhile, the novelist had written a critical study of the greatest Irish literary figure of his time, W. B. Yeats. He had met Yeats while at Cambridge, when the Dublin Abbey Theatre players, accompanied by Yeats and his patron Lady Gregory, gave a performance there. He remained in contact with the poet, and other figures of the Irish literary renaissance were also friends and correspondents. His personal version of the old pagan faith and indifference to politics left him impervious to the sectarian divisions in Ireland.

The Spring Song was Reid's next novel, and it is one of his most distinctive. One critic declaimed, "It is impossible to give an idea of this uncommon book in a few words. It is not a novel; it is a picture of the Spirit of Youth . . .". Set in the Ballinderry district of County Antrim, where Reid holidayed as a boy, it portrays a young family on a long visit to their grandfather and aunt: one of them, the boy, Grif Weston, feels wakened to the real meaning of spring, and seems to hear the pipes of Pan. Supernatural incidents and other adventures follow and the book moves more definitely into the realm of the unseen. Yet there are also fine evocations of landscape, and well-observed, subtle portrayals of character, especially those of the children.

Reid achieves an exceptional sympathy with the intensity and individuality of the child's view of the world. While Grif shares some typical traits and attitudes with his more practical, prosaic siblings, he also has qualities that make him seem different, just as Reid himself evidently felt different in his own family. The boy has a keen affinity with trees and nature, and a sensitivity to an unseen world, so that we understand him to be an instinctive pagan, and a dreamer of other domains: he several times seems to be on the verge of encountering another, rarer world. There is little doubt that Reid expresses through Grif his own emotions and experiences in childhood and youth, and the convictions he sustained as an adult.

The book is significant in Reid's work as the harbinger of his most fully achieved creation, the *Tom Barber* trilogy (also available from Valancourt). Grif is in many ways a first, slightly more tentative, version of Tom. But already here Reid shows his ability to depict boyhood in a fully realised way, respecting both the intense inner life of his character and the simple physical excitement found in holidays, games, pets, playmates and adventure.

The character of Palmer Dorset, an older boy, resourceful and alert, and something of an amateur detective and philosopher, provides a charming counterpoint to Grif's dreamier qualities, and some of his good sense and intelligence probably also contributed to Reid's development of Tom. Reid later gave Palmer Dorset his own novel, *Pirates of the Spring* (1919), about the dawning of friendship, and shared struggles, among four schoolboys.

The way that Reid drew, in *The Spring Song*, upon his own early inner life is clear from his burningly vivid recollection of his childhood, *Apostate* (1926). "The title was intended to indicate a state of mind," he later recalled, implying "nothing more alarming than the reluctance of a small boy to go to church, and his 'passion for humanizing things', his pleasure in discovering river-gods, tree-spirits, and the divinities of sun and moon." It is more like a spiritual autobiography than a memoir of childhood events, as Reid bears witness to the "subconscious lyrical emotions" he felt as a boy. Alongside the games and hobbies of a typical twelve year old, he also led "a private life haunted by visions of beauty and the longing for an ideal companion": the natural world of trees, rivers, the sea were "reflections of a divine world existing beyond the flux of time and fate and change". All his best work was therefore to reflect this vision, a kind of "crying for Elysium".

In *Apostate*, Reid often evokes his sense of a nameless presence like the one he had nearly encountered when he was sixteen, and which haunts many of his books, but particularly *The Spring Song*. For his next book, *Demophon* (1927), which he described as "a kind of adventure story, with the scene laid in an ancient and imaginary Greece", he identified the presence with the god Hermes, guide of souls, god of dreams and protector of youth. In his second volume of autobiography, he recalled how "late at night I wrote the last words of *Demophon* with a strange emotion and excitement, a persuasion that some intelligence outside my own was impressing itself upon me."

The strange, charged atmosphere which had accompanied the

writing of *Apostate* and *Demophon* returned as Reid worked on his next novel, *Uncle Stephen* (1931), the first of the Tom Barber trilogy, and rightly regarded as one of his major works. The title character is a recluse who has returned to his ancestral home in rural Ulster after a life of wandering, some of it spent studying the arts of magic. He is seen through the eyes of the teenage Tom Barber, his sole blood relation, who feels impelled to run away to him to escape the tawdriness of life with his narrow, materialistic stepfamily. The relationship between the boy and his scholarly, serene uncle is subtly and finely handled. Tom's arrival sparks both social and supernatural complications and Reid deftly conveys both without any sign of forcing the plot. Tom's room in his uncle's house is guarded by an image of Hermes, and the patron god of magicians is a pervasive presence throughout, just as Pan is in *The Spring Song*.

So strong was the hold that the character of Tom held for him that Reid subsequently wrote two further novels about him, going backwards in years. These are *The Retreat* (1936) and *Young Tom* (1944). Both are also highly regarded and the latter was awarded the James Tait Black Memorial Prize for the best work of fiction published in 1944. *The Retreat* is set in scenery very close to one of Reid's favourite holiday resorts, Greencastle, on the coast of Donegal and this is described so naturally and well that the supernatural incidents, including Tom's encounters with an angel playmate and a sorcerous cat, seem to grow out of the scene quite harmoniously. In *Young Tom* there are fewer overtly supernatural incidents but the same clear-eyed understanding of the intensity of feeling in childhood and the way in which what may seem small incidents all contribute to the slow awakening to maturity and independence of thought.

The only other new novel outside this trilogy which Reid completed after *Uncle Stephen* was more emotionally fraught. *Brian Westby* (1934) depicts the doomed relationship between a desolate, convalescing novelist and his rediscovered son from a broken marriage. There is tension throughout the story, since the novelist cannot tell the boy he is his father. The novel is in one sense the obverse of *Uncle Stephen*. Its predominant theme is that of estrangement and misunderstanding rather than homecoming and growing rapport.

In 1940, Reid published a second volume of autobiography, *Private Road*. This is more factual and at the same time more discursive than *Apostate*. It still records some of Reid's inner life, including the emotions and impressions which contributed to his writing, but it also has a rather brisk and cheery chapter on his pet dogs and cats. There are recollections of A.E., Forster, and de la Mare, and of other less renowned friends. It is a highly readable volume which lacks the dreamy atmosphere and simple artistic unity of *Apostate* but is full of other interest.

Forrest Reid died at the age of 71 on 4 January 1947 and was buried in the local cemetery close to his home for over twenty years in Ormiston Crescent, Belfast. He had begun to win admiration in the last years of his writing career and was recognised as the first Ulster novelist of European reputation.

There is much that is attractive in Reid's work: the very personal impressions of the supernatural or mystical, the beauty of the Ulster countryside, the affinity with youth and childhood, the refusal always to concoct conclusive or happy endings. But sympathetic readers will particularly appreciate his subtle expression of an allegiance to pantheism, to Pan and Hermes, to the moon and to nature spirits. And in *The Spring Song*, Forrest Reid evokes the old gods and their secret domains with a rare lyrical gift and a fine sensibility. Perhaps Walter de la Mare identified best that these ardent allegiances are Forrest Reid's strongest qualities: "He loved this earthly life, and no less fully and fervently that of the imagination and the spirit".

MARK VALENTINE

February 16, 2013

NOTE ON THE TEXT

The Spring Song was published by Edward Arnold of London in 1916. It was issued in crown octavo format, bound in green cloth, and sold for six shillings. The following year, it appeared in America, published by the Houghton Mifflin Company of Boston and New York, with identical pagination but a different title page.

The present edition, the first ever reprint of the novel, follows the original text verbatim with the exception of a handful of obvious printer's errors, such as "robbin" for "robin" and "genni" for "genii", which have been silently corrected.

THE SPRING SONG

CONTENTS

CHAP.		PAGE
I	THE BEGINNING OF THE ADVENTURE	5
II	IN THE LANE	9
III	NEW ARRIVALS	15
IV	AT THE WINDOW	26
V	THE GARDEN DOOR	31
VI	MUSIC	43
VII	QUESTIONS AND ANSWERS	48
VIII	GREY WEATHER	53
IX	POUNCER	67
X	THROUGH THE DARKNESS	76
XI	INSPECTOR DORSET	80
XII	THE SPRING SONG	97
XIII	THE PERFUMES OF ARABIA	102
XIV	THE RECOGNITION	107
XV	DANGER	113
XVI	GRIF RECEIVES A VISITOR	122
XVII	FANTASY	128
XVIII	GRIF AWAKENS	133
XIX	DOCTOR O'NEILL CALLS IN A SPECIALIST	135
XX	MISS JOHNSON'S BIRTHDAY	142
XXI	PALMER AT WORK	148
XXII	FIRE	160
XXIII	THE GLITTERING NET	167
XXIV	GRIF FALLS ASLEEP	174

CONTENTS

I.
II.
III.
IV.
V.
VI.
VII.
VIII.
IX.
X.
XI.
XII.
XIII.
XIV.
XV.
XVI.
XVII.
XVIII.
XIX.
XX.
XXI.
XXII.
XXIII.
XXIV.

THE SPRING SONG

CHAPTER I

THE BEGINNING OF THE ADVENTURE

'So fair a summer look for never more.'
—*Thomas Nashe.*

L EANING back against the leather cushion of the railway car-riage, Griffith Weston was conscious of an endless panorama of fields and meadows, of green hedges and white hawthorn, and blazing, yellow furze. The whole landscape was bathed in a crude glare of June sunlight, and the heat, and the vivid glittering light, and the rushing train, made his head ache.

He wore a light, loose, flannel suit, without a waistcoat, and his wide short trousers left his knees bare. A dark olive-green silk tie brought out unnecessarily the sallowness of his complexion; his straw hat lay on the seat beside him. He was not in the least a hand-some boy, but his expression was pleasing. He looked quiet rather than shy; he looked intelligent, sensitive, and sweet-tempered. His eyes, beneath their drooping lids, had something of that sleepy gentleness which characterizes the angels and youths of Perugino, but the wide space between them gave the whole countenance, with its beautiful forehead, a kind of grave nobility and innocence.

A more brilliant colour glowed clearly enough in the fresh, ruddy cheeks of the sisters and brother who sat opposite him—Barbara, Ann, and Jim. Miss Johnson also sat on that side of the carriage, and Pouncer was at present invisible, somewhere under the seat.

The little boy's position, in its comparative isolation, was char-acteristic; also the attitude of a watchful, listening silence he maintained amid the chatter of the others. His tutor had left a day or two ago, and he was now more or less independent, travelling by the same train as Miss Johnson and her pupils, but distinctly not of their party.

The eldest of these pupils, Barbara, dressed in white muslin, with slim, black, neatly-stockinged legs, and folded hands, looked demure and slightly priggish. Ann, who was fat, and had reddish hair and freckles, looked only very simple and plain. Her mouth was, as usual, slightly open, her hot little hands were not folded, and in no way did she present so lady-like an appearance as Barbara. One cannot be lady-like and breathe through one's mouth, Miss Johnson had told her that very day, and poor Ann had felt at once that she was doomed. Jim, in his white sailor-suit, was fidgety and vivacious, hovering perilously on the obscure borderline which, in Miss Johnson's opinion, separated the lively from the naughty.

It was not till the train drew in at a station that Pouncer made an appearance. He did so suddenly, like a jack-in-the-box, and rushed to the window to look out, breathing noisily on the glass, and pushing aside Ann, who got in his way. There he remained, a ridiculous leather muzzle dangling under one ear, till the guard arrived with a basin of water. Pouncer lapped up the water with a big splashing red tongue, stopping every now and then to roll his round eyes and give a wag of his tail. With the amazing popularity of all bulldogs, he had managed in the space of some two minutes to attract the charmed attention of quite a group of persons. The group included the station-master, several boys, a postman, one or two porters, a sporting gentleman, and a lady who played the mandoline. Intending travellers, however, passed on in search of another compartment. . . .

Again they tore through the glare and the heat. Jim's black head was nodding now against Miss Johnson's very angular elbow, and Grif, too, began to grow drowsy. He wondered what it would be like at grandpapa's. Only Edward—who was to come on later from school—and Barbara had been there before. Edward and Barbara had given innumerable accounts of their previous visit, entering into all details, but things for Grif often had a mysterious way of turning out to be quite different from other people's descriptions of them. *His* things were rarely *their* things; and it came into his sleepy head that everybody's things must be unlike everybody else's. *His* trees, for instance, were not Jim's or Barbara's, or Ann's or Edward's. They were just *his*—or *were* they his? Was he not rather theirs? Why, if he was not, did they stoop down with long green arms to catch him? and why was there such a roaring in their branches as he had never heard before? He tried to escape, to run away, but they closed him in on every side; they clutched him, and he tore at their green, shadowy embrace, scattering the leaves in showers. . . .

"By Jove, I've been asleep!" he thought, as the crash of another train whizzing by awoke him with a start. He smiled at Miss Johnson, whose glittering pince-nez was fixed upon him with an expression at once severe and anxious.

His smile was intended to be reassuring, but he knew from past experience that Miss Johnson would not be reassured. If she took nothing to do with his education, she had, since his father and mother were started on their travels in the East, taken a great deal to do with him in other ways. It was rather a bore, of course, but then it would soon be over, for in the autumn he was going to school—to the same school as Edward. Miss Johnson had remarked that it would remove a load from her mind when he actually went, and he knew he should have gone a year ago had his people only been able to convince themselves that he was strong enough. This, in fact—this question of his strength—was just the mental load Miss Johnson had alluded to. For that matter, he couldn't remember a time when it *wasn't* there for some one—a thing to be discussed and described—discussed even with Grif himself. If they would only let him alone, he thought, he would be all right. But they never would. Miss Johnson, indeed, made more fuss than anybody else ever had. She did nothing but fuss. She was fussing now because he had fallen asleep, just as she had fussed at other times because he had remained awake. You would think from what she said that he could *help* being liable to catch colds which passed almost immediately into high fevers; could help a nocturnal restlessness which led him fine dances in dreamland, and sometimes, though not lately, had even led him from the safety of bed. Then, out of blind wanderings, he had awakened, bewildered and cold, recognizing nothing about him in the darkness except that he was not where he ought to be, tucked up, snugly and warmly, between his blankets. . . .

The engine whistled and began to slow down. Miss Johnson removed her glasses and began to polish them. Pouncer again appeared.

"Here we are, children! Get everything ready. Ann, don't forget your parcels!"

There was haste, excitement, and some unnecessary zeal, to which Pouncer contributed. Overcoats and bundles were pulled down from the racks on to the seats, and also on to the floor. Miss Johnson dropped first her umbrella and then her bag, and Pouncer found them both.

"There's Aunt Caroline!" screamed Ann from the window, pushing back Jim and Barbara with a vigorous elbow. "Stop! Oh, don't crush so!"

Pouncer was making frantic efforts to oust Ann from her position, while Grif fumbled with the leash. Aunt Caroline, tall and fair and smiling, stood on the platform. A porter swung open the door and Pouncer was first out after all, though his victory caused the overturning of Ann, who had become amazingly entangled with the leash.

"Oh, Bouncer, you're awful!" poor Ann breathed plaintively, as she sat enmeshed on the floor of the railway-carriage. She arose, to be scolded by Miss Johnson for having dirtied her muslin.

Aunt Caroline was talking.

"Well, chicks, you're not roasted alive, are you? How do you do, Miss Johnson? Ann, dear, you look positively boiling! Don't bother about your gloves: nobody wears gloves here."

Ann stuffed them back into her pocket with a sigh of relief.

"We must go and help Miss Johnson to see about the luggage. There's a man waiting for it with a cart. There's the trap, too, but it won't hold us all I'm afraid. Somebody will have to walk and keep me company."

CHAPTER II

IN THE LANE

'Straight mine eye hath caught new pleasures,
Whilst the landscape round it measures;
Russet lawns, and fallows gray,
Where the nibbling flocks do stray;

. . . .

Meadows trim with daisies pied;
Shallow brooks, and rivers wide;
Towers and battlements it sees
Bosom'd high in tufted trees,
Where perhaps some Beauty lies.'

—*Milton.*

ANN decided to walk also, and followed Grif and Aunt Caroline out of the station. From the first she made the mistake of adapting her pace to that of Pouncer, instead of stimulating him to greater efforts. But it seemed to her that Aunt Caroline simply floated over the ground, and that it was useless to try to emulate such speed. She was like a tall white yacht on a green sea, and Grif was a little boat she had in tow. Ann and Pouncer dropped farther and farther behind.

They passed along a crooked, hilly street—the main street of the town—and on to the high road. A duck waddled by, quacking discontentedly of family matters. Grave, mild-eyed cows, black and brown and white, looked at them solemnly, and a boy stood rattling a pail against a wooden trough. He smiled at Ann.

Ann was interested in the boy, and Pouncer in the cows, but both were obliged to hurry after Aunt Caroline and Grif, who were now fifty yards ahead. They turned to the right, down a green beechen lane, and Ann and Pouncer straggled behind. There were cool green places under the hedges, with thick long grass for resting on; there were cool bluish shadows under the dark, pink-flowered chestnut-trees; but Grif and Aunt Caroline passed them by. And one of Ann's bootlaces was draggling on the ground, and Pouncer's tongue was lolling out.

9

It seemed to Ann that Aunt Caroline was simply flying. Grif was big and could keep up with her, but Ann felt that she was getting hotter and hotter and would soon have to stop. The difficulty was that Aunt Caroline never looked behind. Grif, who was usually so quiet, was talking to her just as if he were trying to make up for all his past silences. Ann might have attracted their attention by a vocal appeal, but for a long time she could not summon up courage to make the attempt. "Grif!" she at last piped plaintively in a very small voice, smaller even than usual, and Grif did not hear.

The corners of Ann's mouth drooped. Her other lace had become untied. Her fat legs dragged with increasing slowness. Pouncer, suddenly forgetting his own fatigue, began to worry her laces, to get in her way, to pretend her laces were rats; and Ann's tears were welling dangerously near the surface when Aunt Caroline turned round.

She stopped at once. "Good gracious, child, whatever's the matter?"

"I'm so hot!" Ann quavered.

Aunt Caroline laughed, but it was a comfortable, pleasant laugh, and Ann, who never counted much on sympathy, didn't mind it.

"We can rest here, if you like," Aunt Caroline said, sitting down under the thick hedge. "And we've only a very little farther to go now."

"You *would* walk," cried Grif. "You always will do things."

"I wanted to walk," Ann replied. "Why shouldn't I walk as well as you?"

"But you see you can't."

"I can."

Her plaintive note had slipped already into the firmer tone of argument. Grif shrugged his shoulders. He knelt down and tied her laces for her, while Pouncer, seeing how things were going, dropped into a doze.

The air was a floating haze of dusty gold, which turned to green among the trees. The bees boomed in the dog-roses: the sky was cloudless. The tree-trunks showed almost black in the hot light, and the leaves, pale and semi-transparent, quivered, altered, taking strange forms, so that what Grif saw was now a tree, now a spirit. In the green grass the shadows made islands of a deeper green.

Presently, coming along the road in the direction of the town, they saw an odd-looking person dressed in black, with very tight trousers and a large black cravat. He walked quickly, with a curious, springy, almost dancing step, while he swung a gold-headed ebony stick. His clothes were shiny and worn, yet he presented the figure of a dandy; and as he raised his broad-brimmed hat with a fine flourish, and bowed to Aunt Caroline, he revealed a soft profusion of silky white hair, unexpected, because nothing else about him suggested age. His face was smooth, his complexion fresh and clear, his eyes extremely bright, and rather restless. His features were unusually refined, yet with a great boldness in the well-arched, predatory nose.

Aunt Caroline introduced him to Grif and Ann as Mr. Clement Bradley, and Mr. Bradley acknowledged the introduction with high formality. "On my way to the post-office, Miss Annesley. Can I do anything for you in the town? . . . The fact is, I'm expecting important letters. I should be sorry to think that the postmistress had kept them back on purpose, but it is odd, very odd, that they have not reached me before this." He spoke in a soft, clear voice, a little slowly, and with a somewhat pedantic nicety of enunciation. He had strange, sly eyes, Grif thought, and as he talked of his letters having been kept back they suddenly altered in expression, and became clear and shining like the eyes of a cat.

When presently he stepped daintily on down the lane the others gazed after him, the children doubtfully, Aunt Caroline thoughtfully, Pouncer with unwonted hostility. "How funny he looks!" Ann declared. "And did you hear Bouncer growl?"

Aunt Caroline still watched the retreating figure. "Bouncer was very naughty," she murmured absently.

"It's not Bouncer, Aunt Caroline. It's Pouncer. Ann can't say words beginning with 'p.'"

"Who is he?" Ann questioned, with a curiosity that seldom failed her. "Is he a friend of yours?"

"Yes. He's grandpapa's organist. I don't know that he's a very great friend exactly, but he's been here for a good many years."

"*I* think he must be rather eccentric," Ann decided, after some pondering.

"I quite agree with you," Aunt Caroline laughed. "You'll hear him playing in church on Sunday. His playing is rather eccentric too."

"Why? Does he makes mistakes?"

"Oh, no, it's not that. It's only that he occasionally makes a good deal of noise. And then, he likes to practise at all kinds of queer hours—sometimes in the middle of the night."

There was a pause, and Ann said, "I'm not tired any longer."

"We might take a short-cut across the fields," Aunt Caroline suggested.

She moved on, this time quite slowly, and with Ann's hot hand firmly clasped in her cool one.

"Look at Bouncer! Isn't he a silly old thing!" cried Ann.

The bulldog, who had seen a fox-terrier running on three legs, with the fourth tucked up, was at that moment making clumsy and unsuccessful experiments in this novel style of locomotion. In the sunshine brilliantly orange and white, with his black nose and kinky tail, he looked so bright and coloured that a wandering butterfly hovered about him, as if mistaking him for a gigantic bunch of flowers.

"Does grandpapa like having us?" Ann inquired, but only with a view to making conversation. "Grandpapa's a clergyman," she presently observed. "And father's a doctor—a specialist—eyes and ears. . . . Why hasn't he many patients?"

Aunt Caroline laughed. "I suppose because he goes away so much. He's really a traveller more than a doctor."

"Does he go away because he hasn't patients, or does he not have patients because he goes away?"

"It sounds like a riddle," Aunt Caroline replied; "and if it is, I give it up."

"It's not a riddle," Ann assured her. "It's just an ordinary question. Shall we see grandpapa as soon as we arrive?"

"I don't know. He was very busy when I left."

"Father's always busy too. So is mother. . . . What's grandpapa busy about?"

"He's writing a book."

"What sort of book?"

"A book about fairies."

Ann seemed doubtful. "*Mother* didn't call it that," she said reflectively, and was immediately reproved by Grif.

"What did mother call it? Folk-lore perhaps?" Aunt Caroline suggested.

"Does he tell the stories to you?"

"Sometimes."

"Will he tell them to us?"

"I dare say. . . . And this is the side gate. Our journey is over. By the way, what time do you all go to bed?"

"Jim and me at half-past eight: Grif and Barbara at nine."

"I don't go at nine when I'm on a visit," said Grif.

As they emerged from the shrubbery the glebe house stood low and square before them. It was half covered with ivy, the young leaves just now of a pale and tender green. In front of the house was a croquet-lawn, sheltered on the farther side by trees, and beyond that the ground sloped gradually down to the road. There were few flowers and no flower-garden.

Behind the house and the stables was a low stone wall, on the other side of which was a wood. The grounds had evidently once formed part of this wood, which pressed up so close to the wall that the trees leaning over seemed trying to force an entrance. With the exception of the levelling of the croquet-court, and the cutting down of a certain quantity of timber, nothing in the way of alteration or of laying out had been attempted.

"Where are the others?" Aunt Caroline inquired as they came into the hall, where Bridget and Hannah, the two servants, stood wreathed in smiles.

"The children's round in the stables, Miss Caroline."

Just then Miss Johnson appeared, and instantly, like a genii in the *Arabian Nights*, pounced upon Ann, who it seemed was disgracefully untidy.

"I can't help it. I'm so hot!" Ann sighed.

Aunt Caroline took charge of Grif, while Pouncer followed at their heels.

They climbed two wide flights of stairs. "This is where I am

going to put you and Edward and Jim," Aunt Caroline said, opening the door of a large bedroom, whose three windows overlooked
the croquet-lawn.

Grif surveyed it quietly. Already it showed abundant signs of
occupation. Jim, in a moment of enthusiasm, must have begun to
unpack, for his own and Grif's things were scattered broadcast on
the beds and the chairs and the floor.

"May I look at the other rooms too, Aunt Caroline?" he asked
politely, after a moment's pause.

Aunt Caroline seemed rather puzzled. "Don't you like it? I
thought you'd rather not be separated, and this is the biggest room
in the house."

"Oh yes, I like it very much. It's not that."

"What is it, then?"

"It's just that I love looking round. Are any of the rooms near
the wood?"

She led him along a passage, through a swing-door, up a flight
of three stairs, and then along another passage at the end of which
she opened a door.

Grif walked straight to the window. As he leaned out he could
see the wood. It was quite close to him indeed, and he could hear
the faint murmur it made, as of many whispering voices. He stood
there dumb, and Aunt Caroline guessed that she had made a mistake. She watched him struggle against a desire to tell her that he
preferred this room, but his natural politeness conquered. "Thank
you very much," he said, turning to go out.

"Would you like to sleep here?" she asked, half laughing.

He looked up quickly. "With Pouncer? Would you let me?"

"But surely Pouncer sleeps outside?"

"Yes. . . . Would you allow him to sleep here with me?"

There was no importunity in his words, but she knew he was
hanging eagerly on what she should say. "You're the queerest little
fish! Of course you can please yourself. It doesn't matter in the
least what room you choose. Only, you will be all alone here: no
one else is on this side of the house."

"I like the trees," he apologized, "and I shall be able to watch
them in the mornings."

Aunt Caroline too came to the window. "The trees are just what I don't like," she said. "Sometimes, in the autumn and the winter, when it's really stormy, they make a tremendous noise, and it sounds so dismal at night. However, I don't suppose we shall have much wind during the summer, and of course if you find you are being kept awake you can always change your quarters."

CHAPTER III

NEW ARRIVALS

'Boys are for the most part cattle of this colour.'
—*Shakespeare.*

GRIF wandered out on to the croquet-lawn, where the others were knocking balls against hoops in a desultory fashion, all playing at once, and arguing at the tops of their voices.

"Where have *you* been?" asked Jim, trying to stand on the winning-peg, which at once sank over sideways, levering up a portion of the ground.

"Oh Jim, see what you've done!" Ann exclaimed in dismay.

"Well, I can stamp it down again."

"I've been choosing my room," answered Grif.

"What room?" With the handle of his mallet passed under his armpit and projecting well above his shoulder—for it was nearly as tall as himself—Jim took aim at a ball. "Shaved it! Shaved it!"

Ann was indignant. "No you didn't, Jim; you never touched it."

"I did. I shaved it."

"You can't see it from here," Grif went on. "And there's a swallow's nest under the window-sill."

"I don't know what you're talking about. That's our room up there, just over the porch. It's yours and mine, and Edward's when he comes. . . . Clear out of the light. . . . Oh, rotten luck! My mallet turned! . . . I've bagged the bed near the window."

"You can bag as many beds as you like. I'm going to have a room to myself."

"But why?"

"I'm going to have Pouncer with me. . . . Who brought out the croquet-things?"

"We brought them out ourselves."

"Why aren't you playing properly, then?"

"Because Barbara said she'd go first, after Ann and I had bagged the blue and red balls. She's yellow, and yellow has to play last."

"I called out 'first' before you ever got the balls," said Barbara, loftily.

"So nobody could be first," Jim went on, "and we all had to play together."

"Little silly!" Barbara threw down her mallet and walked away.

"Aunt Caroline says we're to be good till dinner-time," said Ann, meekly. "And we're not to go to the kitchen, because Hannah and Bridget are busy."

"Who wants to go to the kitchen?"

"I'm afraid *I* do," sighed truthful Ann. "Hannah's going to let Barbara and me make shortbread the first wet day."

"I say; let's play a proper game now there's four of us," Jim proposed. "Grif and me'll play you two."

But at that moment Aunt Caroline, waving a letter in her hand, came from the house. "Do you know what's happened?" she cried. "You'll never guess!"

"I've guessed already," murmured Jim, modestly.

Aunt Caroline shook her letter at him. "What have you guessed? I've a good mind not to tell you."

"Edward's coming to-day instead of next month."

Aunt Caroline was somewhat taken aback. "Nonsense! How did you know? What's the use of my trying to give you surprises?"

"The surprise was a very good one," Jim hastened to console her. "All the others are surprised. I only guessed because I'm good at riddles. I'm making one up at this moment."

"Well, that's what it is anyway. And grandpapa knew all about it this morning, and thought he had told me. What do you say to that?"

"It wasn't very clever," Ann admitted.

"It certainly wasn't. Can you guess *why* he is coming?" she laughed, turning again to Jim.

The little boy hesitated. "I'd rather not, Aunt Caroline."

"What does that mean, I wonder? I'm afraid you're a humbug." Jim paused. "It would be better for you to surprise us, I think."

Aunt Caroline laughed once more. "Do you think I'd be disappointed again? Well, it's because diphtheria has broken out at school. And Edward is bringing a friend with him—I expect you guessed that too?"

"We *knew* that," said Ann. "He wrote to Barbara and told her ages ago. It's a boy called Palmer Dorset. But of course we didn't know they'd be coming so soon."

"Well I must say you all seem to be a great deal more behind the scenes than I am. This is the first I've heard of Master Dorset's existence, let alone of his intention to pay us a visit."

"We can tell you about him, Aunt Caroline; and I know Edward *was* going to write to you, but I suppose he hadn't time. He's frightfully clever, Edward says. He knows all about airioplanes and wireless telegraphy and things of that sort. And he's won crowds of competitions in papers, and he invented a system of writing six lines at a time, only it takes longer than to do them in the ordinary way. Of course all the lines have to be the same, and you write with a penholder he invented, with branches out of it into which you stick reservoir nibs. They must be reservoir nibs, because it takes so long to fix them and get them all dipped in the ink that it wouldn't be worth while using any other kind."

"Didn't Edward even mention him in grandpapa's letter?" asked Barbara.

"Oh yes, he mentioned him there, and grandpapa sent a telegram telling him to bring him. But when he had done that he forgot all about the whole thing, so how was I to know?"

"It *does* seem rather a mix up," murmured Ann.

"I wish he wasn't coming," said Jim, gloomily. "I know what he'll be like if he's a friend of Edward's."

"I'll tell Edward you said that," whispered Barbara.

"Edward's a nut," replied Jim. "You can tell him that too."

"He's not; and you aren't allowed to make personal remarks." She glanced at Aunt Caroline for approval—an action which provoked a hideous grimace from her young brother, who was standing out of his aunt's observation.

"He is. You should see the ties and socks he wears, Aunt Caroline, and the way he does his hair. You'd think it was painted on the top of his head, it sticks so close. If you want to make him mad all you've got to do is to ruffle it. Only it's not worth while, because you get your hands all over oil."

"Hadn't you better go to meet them?" Aunt Caroline suggested, feebly. "I'm afraid you won't be able to do more than meet them on their way, for the train must be nearly here by this time; but I expect they'll walk. Ann needn't go unless she likes."

"I must go," Ann declared. "I'm the only one who really knows Balmer. I was with him and Edward one day."

"Why does she call Palmer Balmer, Aunt Caroline?" Jim asked. "This isn't personal, it's a riddle. . . . Do you give it up? . . . Because Pouncer bounces, and there's a 'b' in both."

"I'm afraid it isn't very fresh," he added apologetically.

And they set out, though without evincing any undue hurry.

"Perhaps we ought to wait for them here," said Ann, at the turning of the lane.

Jim had dropped down on the dusty road, and lay with his ear to the ground.

"Jim, get up at once!" Barbara commanded; but the scout remained motionless.

"I can't hear anything," he whispered.

Grif poked him gently with his foot. "What do you expect to hear? An earthquake?"

"Look at the mess you're in!" Barbara went on officiously.

"Oh, leave me alone. It's the way Indians always listen. You can hear for miles if there's anybody on the road."

He got up and brushed some of the dust from his clothes, while Pouncer, who thought he had been looking for rats, proceeded to investigate further.

"I can see them!" piped Ann from the top of the bank. "They're walking."

There was a sudden rush, with shouts and halloes, even the correct Barbara joining in. The two schoolboys they had come to meet, however, displayed less enthusiasm. Edward merely waved a lordly hand. "These are the kids," he said, presenting his brothers and sisters *en masse* to Palmer Dorset. "I dare say you'll get used to them in time."

"How do you do, Balmer?" murmured Ann, holding out her hand shyly. But the greetings of the others were merely vocal, and Barbara gave none at all, being offended at the manner of Edward's introduction.

Edward bore little resemblance either to Grif or to Jim. He was big for his age, and distinctly the best-looking of the family; very fair, with blue eyes and a pointed chin. One noticed that his clothes hung well upon him. Palmer Dorset, though six months older, was nearly a head shorter. Palmer was very sturdily built, and had bright red hair, dry, crisp, and wavy, and strong as wire. He had a fair, fine skin, much freckled, and his eyes, of a reddish brown, were small, with almost no white showing. When he laughed they lit up and his whole face displayed an extraordinary animation: at other times his expression was grave and uncommunicative. His forehead was broad, his eyebrows nearly invisible, his mouth unusually small and delicately shaped.

"When did you get down?" asked Edward, patronizingly.

"To-day. Just by the train before yours."

"Aunt Caroline says we'll see grandpapa to-night at dinner," Ann murmured in her queer, half plaintive little voice.

"Naturally."

"After to-night we're all to have dinner in the middle of the day—all of *us*, I mean. I'm rather afraid of grandpapa."

Jim, who had been lost in thought for some five minutes, began suddenly: "My first is in 'bat' but not in 'cat.' My second's in 'uncle' but not in 'aunt.' My third is in 'night' but not in 'day.' My whole was in me this afternoon at tea-time. What is it?" He glanced with a quick smile at Palmer.

"Oh, dry up. I warned you what they were like, Dorset, so don't blame me. Just smack their heads now and then."

"No, but guess," cried Jim, indignantly. "You might guess! . . . Do you give it up?" He smiled again. "Do you give it up, Palmer?"

"Yes."

"It's my own, you know," Jim told him.

"All right: fire ahead."

"'Bun,'" Jim announced complacently. "B—U—N."

Edward laughed: everybody laughed except Ann.

"What are you all grinning at?" asked Jim, uneasily. "My first is 'B'—'B' in 'bat' but not in 'cat.' My second is 'U'—in 'uncle' but not in 'aunt.'"

"'U' *is* in 'aunt,' silly."

"How is it in 'aunt'?"

"A—U—N—T! That's how it's in it."

Jim blushed. "It's not A—U—N—T, is it Ann?"

"I don't know," Ann whispered.

"Is it, Grif?"

"Jim, don't contradict," said Barbara, primly.

But Jim was getting annoyed. "I'll contradict if I like."

"You won't. And if you're rude I'll tell Miss Johnson."

"Tell away. I don't care."

"Don't care came to a bad end."

"I *don't* think."

"And you know you're not allowed to say that. Miss Johnson told you you weren't to."

Jim put out his tongue. With that simplicity in the expression of preferences which characterizes all dogs and most little boys, he moved away from Edward and Barbara and walked beside Palmer Dorset.

They turned in at the gate. "The birds here seem jolly tame," Edward muttered, as an adventurous robin hopped up almost to their feet. "I wish I had my air-gun. We must get some elastic and make caties."

"Oh, Edward, how can you be so cruel?" exclaimed Ann. "Aunt Caroline feeds the birds every day, and she says they come right up to her when she calls them."

"That'll be all the better."

"Are you fond of Edna Lyall's books?" whispered Barbara, addressing Palmer for the first time.

Edward laughed. "As if he reads rot like that!" He had been fumbling in his pockets, and now brought out a half-used packet of cigarettes. "We'll not be able to smoke in the house, Dorset, so we may as well have one while we can."

There was a silence.

"I'm afraid he's showing off a little," murmured Grif, addressing no one in particular, unless it were the robin, who continued to flutter on their path in the most friendly way possible.

Edward coloured as he struck a match.

"One for you, Angelina!" chuckled Palmer appreciatively.

Edward walked on in offended dignity.

"Why do you call him Angelina, Balmer?"

The remorseless and inevitable question came in Ann's gentle voice. She had even ventured to take Balmer's hand, on the strength of their previous acquaintance.

"Oh, I don't know. He's always called that." He glanced at Edward apologetically, the name having slipped out by accident. But Edward, with heightened colour, and staring straight before him, maintained his attitude of indifference.

"It's a very nice name," Ann reflected. "I like it. I shall call him Angelina too."

"If you do, you won't do it a second time," her brother mentioned in accents of quiet rage.

Ann was astonished. "Don't you like it? Why do people call you it then?"

"Nobody calls me it, except a lot of fools who think they're being funny."

"Angelina——" meditated Jim. "I say!—let go—you're hurting me!"

Edward had caught his ear and was twisting it viciously.

"Ouu!" Jim squealed; and promptly kicked his brother on the shins.

Edward flung him away and pulled up the leg of his trousers. "Little brute!" he spluttered. "Look what he's done!" He made another rush, but Jim darted behind Palmer, who held the aggressor at arm's length.

"I say; let him alone; you hurt him first."

Edward hesitated. Then, with a limp suggesting that each step cost him untold agony, he stalked on alone to the house.

"I'm afraid we've made him really angry," said Ann, cheerfully. "It was your fault, Balmer, too, because you must have known he would get cross. I didn't. It was you and Jim."

"He can swear all right," put in Jim. "Can't he, Palmer?"

"He never *could* stand being ragged," said Palmer dispassionately. "I didn't mean to call him Angelina—it just slipped out. You'd think he'd have got used to it, considering he hears it about a thousand times a day."

But by dinner-time Edward had quite recovered his good-humour.

With a round black velvet cap on his bald head Canon Annesley, thin and bent and wrinkled, though intensely alive, sat at the top of the table, having Jim, in a spotlessly-white sailor suit, at his right hand. Jim, at first very quiet and solemn, ventured at length to put his riddle, in an emended form, to grandpapa, substituting "nephew" for "aunt" in the second clause; and grandpapa guessed it.

"Perhaps you have some riddles you would like to ask *me?*" Jim murmured insinuatingly, his bright untroubled eyes fixed upon grandpapa's wrinkled visage.

Grandpapa only shook his head. "Look not for whales in the Euxine sea, nor expect great matters where they are not to be found."

This reply, which was in itself a kind of riddle, did not satisfy Jim. "Are there none in your book?" he questioned.

"In *my* book?"

"The book you're writing."

"Oh, I see. I don't remember any. I might introduce a few."

"Miss Johnson is writing a novel."

The clear voice of the little boy was definite as a publisher's announcement, and Miss Johnson became covered with confusion.

"It's called *Be True, Fond Heart*," Jim pursued calmly, "and the hero's twenty-seven years old, and the heroine's twenty-two. It's *his* heart that is fond. He's called Reginald. She doesn't find out about it till he's dying—I mean about his heart. He gets wounded out shooting, and she nurses him, but it's no use. And then he tells her that he never told her, because she was an heiress; and she tells him that she was sure all along he was in love with her friend; and a specialist comes from London to see him, and he dies."

"The accident due to an explosion of his gun, I suppose?"

Jim did not know. "*Was* it that, Miss Johnson?" he asked.

"You are talking too much, Jim," the authoress replied. "No; that is not the solution," she continued after a moment, her pince-nez fixed dreamily on the opposite wall. "I'm afraid it is rather difficult to explain, as the plot is a little complex. It is really his friend who shoots him; though he takes this secret with him to the grave. And almost his last words are, "Be kind to Victor"—that is, his friend, who is a cavalry officer with a somewhat violent temper. Of course I've only told the children little bits here and there, bits I thought they could understand."

"I hope you've brought the manuscript with you," said the canon gallantly. "After hearing so much of the story it would be tantalizing not to know the rest."

"I believe it *is* somewhere in my trunk," the governess admitted. "I am sure I should be only too delighted if you would give me the benefit of your criticism. I have had so little experience. This is my first work. The idea was suggested to me by a very beautiful paint-ing in the Royal Academy, entitled *To Err is Human*. I am sure you remember it. It created a great deal of interest at the time, because nobody could be quite sure which of the persons in the picture had erred, or in what way."

She paused, and a small voice broke in softly. "The heroine's name is Angelina. . . . I'm very sorry, Edward."

Edward turned crimson, and darted an angry glance at his younger sister. The other boys laughed.

The French windows were thrown open to the warm summer night, and the drawn curtains now were seen to bulge out with stealthy, uncertain movements.

"By Jove! It looks like a burglar," said the canon. "He must have the deuce of a cold in his head too!"

For the swaying of the curtains was supplemented by consid-erable snufflings and snortings, which, to the majority of those present, had a very familiar sound. There was a moment of inter-ested waiting: then Pouncer, who was supposed to be shut up in the kitchen with Bridget and Hannah, stepped self-consciously into the room.

"And to whom does *this* king of dogs belong?" asked the canon gaily.

"He's Grif's," said Jim. "Mother says Grif takes after you, and that he will always be unpractical."

"Why such pessimistic views on mother's part?" the canon wondered, regarding Pouncer's master with a new interest.

Miss Johnson apologized profusely. "I think it will be some people's bedtime as soon as dinner is over," she remarked unkindly.

"That's me and Ann," Jim whispered to his grandfather. "Say, because it's our first night here you want us to sit up to have just one game. I mean an intellectual game—one that you can play too, you know—with pencils and bits of paper, writing things down. You choose twelve things—like a flower, or an animal, or a book—and then somebody says a letter, and you write down the names of things beginning with it. You know what I mean? If it was a flower and the letter was D you could write down daisy; and for the animal, dog; and for the book—any book that begins with D. It's just the sort of game you would love. Besides, I'm awfully good at it and can help you. . . . Say you want it—quick—quick, or Miss Johnson won't let us have it." He clutched grandpapa's hand vigorously under the table, jigging up and down on his chair, while his eyes shone.

Grandpapa coughed, and with a fine assumption of spontaneity proposed the game. Miss Johnson's objections were gently waved aside.

"Thanks *fearfully*," Jim whispered. "I like you awfully. You're not a bit like what I was led to expect."

"I wasn't led to expect anything like you either," the canon confessed in return.

Jim gazed at him.

"Why are you laughing?"

"With anticipated pleasure. You must remember I hardly ever play games."

"You can now. We can play every evening—and all day if it's wet. I'll try to think of other games you would like."

"Would you mind telling me how old you are? I know I ought to know, but I've forgotten."

"Nine. Ann's ten; Barbara's twelve; Grif's thirteen; and Edward's fifteen. I don't know how old Palmer is, but I expect he's about the same as Edward. . . . What made you ask?"

"I was trying to think what I was like at nine. I can't remember."

"You were like Grif. Mother says so."

"I don't believe I was; and anyway I don't know Grif very well. Tell me about him."

Jim was silenced, while he stared hard at his brother. "*I* don't think he's like you," he declared at last.

"Not in appearance, certainly," the canon agreed.

"Not in any way. . . . I can't tell you about Grif. . . . I could tell you more about Edward and Barbara and Ann. Edward's called Angelina at school, and he hates it. That's why we laughed when Ann said that about the heroine of Miss Johnson's novel. I expect he's called it because he thinks such a lot about his clothes and all that. I can beat him at this game we're going to play."

"And can you beat the others?"

Jim hesitated. "I don't think I can beat Palmer."

"Perhaps you and I together could."

"Oh, easily. But then—that mightn't be fair. . . . You see, he's your guest. . . . I mean, he doesn't belong to you the way we do. I think we'd better let Palmer win if he can."

"Then you're not going to help me after all?"

"Well—if you aren't getting on very well—I might help you a little."

"I tell you what we'll do. You and I'll challenge any other pair to a game of croquet."

Jim turned over this proposition thoughtfully. "Yes—we could do that. . . . But don't you think we'd be beaten?"

"I see you're doubtful. I'm quite good you know—far better than you'd believe."

"But *I'm* not very good, and Edward's awfully good at all games—I mean outdoor games. He's splendid at cricket."

"I dare say; but I shouldn't mind betting that he hasn't played much croquet:—not nearly so much as I have. What do you think?"

"We'll take them on anyway," said Jim, generously.

CHAPTER IV

AT THE WINDOW

And a boy leans over a lighted window-sill,
.   .   .   .   . his head on his arm.
Like a white moth his thought flies into the night.
—*John Alford.*

THERE was no moon, and the last faint glimmer of a prolonged twilight concealed more than it revealed.

Pan and Syrinx, the two stable cats, glided like ghosts from their hiding-place, pausing guiltily, every yard or two, as they crossed the lawn, bent on secret deeds that would never be divulged, seeking the shadows and moving forward stealthily, vanishing at last into the darkness. Presently from that darkness there arose two unearthly screams—blood-chilling, horrible:—then silence, sinister and profound. Those dreadful shrieks had brought a watchful, astonished Pouncer to the window. Indignant at suspected immoralities, and lawless, possibly criminal joys, his round eyes searched the night but could discover nothing. Pouncer was on the side of respectability and the police: he could never have even superficial dealings with Pan or Syrinx. . . .

Light shone in the windows of three rooms, two on the ground floor, and one higher up. It was not the blazing light of gas, but the subdued, ruddy glow of shaded lamps. In one of these lower rooms Canon Annesley sat at a table littered with books and papers. Before him was a volume of *The Golden Bough*, and he turned the leaves rapidly, looking for a marked passage which, when he found it, was not the one he wanted. . . .

In another room Aunt Caroline was writing a letter to her sister, telling of the arrival of the children, of all the events of the past day. Her pen raced on almost without a pause, and sometimes a smile flickered across her face. She enjoyed writing letters, and made a hobby of it. Certain of her correspondents were even slightly irritated by the promptitude with which she replied to their epistles—a promptitude that left them in the perpetual condition of 'owing Caroline a letter,' no matter how frequently they might discharge their debt. . . .

The third lighted room was that of Miss Johnson, and Miss Johnson was in bed. Beside her on a table was a large pile of manuscript. The manuscript was entitled *Be True, Fond Heart*, and Miss Johnson was lingering over that portion of it which dealt with the final explosion of the long-concealed passion of her hero. Miss Johnson, deeply attached to propriety, was indeed wondering if Reginald were not a little *too* passionate. Of course, he was dying, and on death-beds, if anywhere, surely one might let oneself go. But what would Canon Annesley think? Miss Johnson turned again to the passages which had awakened these doubts, and the only drawback to her enjoyment was the fact that the lamp was smelling. . . .

Barbara and Ann were asleep, but in the boys' room Edward lay on his back and talked into the darkness. To him out of the darkness came the reluctant voice of Palmer, growing drowsier and drowsier, and sometimes ceasing altogether.

"I wonder if they'd allow us to have a little cricket practice on the lawn? We might be able to rig up some kind of net—what?"

"Um—ff."

"What do you say?"

"Nothing. . . . Spoil—ground. . . ."

"I say, Dorset."

No answer.

"Dorset—Palmer! Wake up!"

"Not asleep. What d'you want?"

"Lazy brute! I don't feel a bit sleepy. I'm going to have a smoke." There was a scratching sound, the flare of a match, and then the red glow of a cigarette.

"What about slinging hammocks and sleeping outside if this

weather keeps up? Rather a lark, don't you think? . . . I say, you *are* a rotter! I believe you've gone off to sleep again. . . . Oh, of course if you don't want to talk! . . ."

In the room from which Pouncer had looked out a minute or two ago Grif now was at the window. He leaned across the sill, listening to the strange sounds of the night. From somewhere far away came the harsh, monotonous cry of a corncrake. There was a slight rustle in the ivy below him—perhaps a bird—perhaps a rat. Then came a low whisper that might have been the wind, but that seemed to come from miles and miles away. It was like the sigh of a sleeper bound by enchantment, scarce distinguishable from silence.

Grif was extraordinarily sensitive to sounds. The whole of life seemed to come to him in a woven pattern of music. Even through sleep the slightest noise could reach him, and a very little noise would awaken him. The values of these sounds altered. Now and then they ceased to be mere patterns, became articulate, and he listened to what they said. Words that were not actual words, but only the spirits of words, for he could never have written them down, impressed themselves, as if secretly, upon a portion of his brain, and gave birth to all kinds of thoughts.

And now, when every one had gone to bed, the old house had awakened, and he could hear it creaking and murmuring, as if each brick and board had found a restless tongue. Outside there were other voices, weaving thin, whistling tunes, which detached themselves from the low ground hum that never ceased. That flapping, leathery noise came from the wings of a bat. It was very low, but, while it lasted, it was loud enough to blot out completely this other ghostly sound moving in the air about him, now high up, now passing close to the ground, now receding, and again drawing near. And at last he could make out many voices singing together, the green, slender voices of the wood, and this is what they seemed to say:

> What is this coming that troubles our ancient peace
> With faint thrillings of spring, of music and joy?
> Who has found old-time power to awake, to release
> The spirits of earth? Who is this human boy—

He who would lead us to shake off old memories of grief,
  And a life that had wavered and sunk, like a failing well,
Back in the darkness of earth, like the sap in the leaf
  That yellows and withers in autumn? What is the spell

He has found? Ancient gods of dim woodland places,
  Rise from your long, sad sleep; ye spirits of water and land!
Shake out the dead leaves from your hair; rise and unveil your faces.
  The frozen winter is past; the spring is at hand.

Not these dull words certainly, but something of which they are but a weak and uncouth symbol, he heard; though whether the voices were within him or without he did not know.

Pouncer, who had already retired to bed half a dozen times and made a great show of falling asleep, was secretly intrigued by this curious vigil of his master, and came again to the window. He, also, leaned over the sill, but there was really nothing to be seen. He gave a very small bark in order to scare away imaginary robbers should Grif be thinking of that; then returned to his slumbers, sleeping with eyes and mouth and nose, but with ears wide enough awake.

A clock chimed midnight, and Grif, he knew not why, began to think of Mr. Bradley. He wondered if he were playing now in the church, and he could see him, in imagination, his wild silver hair floating loose in the starlight, while the organ sang and thundered. The idea appealed to him. If only he had been certain that Mr. Bradley was really there, he would have crept out of the house at once. The thought stirred in him a spirit of adventure which the plans of Edward, Jim, and the others, left cold. He was haunted by something vaguely sinister, something fantastic and a little mad which the organist's appearance had suggested to him. What it was he could not tell, but that afternoon it had made him uneasy—a very little uneasy—without being actually afraid.

He felt wakeful and rather restless. He had a curious, excited sense of being surrounded by marvellous things. If Pouncer had begun to talk, if the mirror on the wall, which still glimmered dimly in the half-darkness, had begun to sing its reedy silvery rhymes, he would perhaps not have been greatly astonished.

At any rate, he thought he would not. The cool summer night seemed to stream into his soul. He loved it. He loved the dim shadowy trees, the stars, the sky—loved them in a way he loved people at certain moments, with a desire to put his arms about them and kiss them. Unconsciously, he loved the spirit that was behind them—that great eternal mother who sang to him while he was waking, and through his dreams.

He knew the story of Tobias and his dog and the angel, and he longed for the angel to come. The angel, with a great rustling of splendid wings! But he would rather have a smaller angel, one about his own size, one like Tobias himself in the Perugino picture at home, from which he had learned the story. He would play on his silver flute for a signal, and Grif would go down to meet him. He wondered what his name would be? The only angel names he knew were Michael and Raphael and Gabriel. It was Raphael who had come to Tobias. *His* angel would perhaps be Michael. The story was written somewhere in the Bible, though he had never been able to find it. His mother had told him that it was only in old Bibles, and he had never found one old enough. To be sure, his dog was not a bit like the dog in the picture, and *he* was not like Tobias: but what matter? He wondered if the angel would be frightened of Pouncer, supposing he were a very young angel. Most people *were*, at first: and he laughed a little as he imagined their meeting, for Pouncer would be sure to want to examine the wings. Then he yawned, stretched himself, and making a bound on to the bed slid between the cool white sheets.

Next moment there was another bound, and a dull thud.

"Oh!" said Grif, for most of the breath had been knocked out of him.

"You can't get under, you know," he expostulated, as Pouncer pulled at the bed-clothes with his fore-paws, "we'll be far too hot!" A compromise was effected by everything but a sheet sliding on to the floor.

And very soon Grif grew drowsy. The wind had arisen a little, and he could hear the faint soughing of the trees—a lulling, dreamy music. Then, just as he was dropping asleep, he heard another music quite distinctly, and if it had not been that something seemed to hold him back he would have sprung out of bed. For what he had heard—whether dreaming or waking—was the low clear note of a flute.

CHAPTER V

THE GARDEN DOOR

'I have been here before,
But when or how I cannot tell:
I know the grass beyond the door,
The sweet keen smell,
The sighing sound, the lights around the shore.'
—*Rossetti.*

'He that hath found some fledg'd bird's nest may know,
At first sight, if the bird be flown;
But what fair Well or Grove he sings in now,
That is to him unknown.'
—*Henry Vaughan.*

AT breakfast Jim issued his croquet challenge, which was immediately taken up by Edward and Palmer, with the natural result that all the others wanted to play too.

"Why not let them have a tournament?" said Aunt Caroline. "I'm sure they'd like that."

"Capital idea, if everybody is willing to join in."

Jim was already counting up the possible entries, nodding at each person as he mentally ticked him off. "There's nine here," he said.

"That won't do—unless you're going to play singles. I wonder if we could get anybody else?"

"I'm sure Mr. Drummond would play. He's always most obliging."

The canon chuckled. "You'd better send a deputation to wait upon him then. He ought to be told what he's letting himself in for."

"Who's Mr. Drummond?" asked Jim.

"He's grandpapa's curate, dear; and if he comes you must all be very nice to him."

"Why? Is he ill?" Jim wondered.

"No; but it is possible to be nice to people even when they're well."

"Oh yes; I thought you meant——"

"I shall choose Balmer," Ann declared.

"You won't do anything of the sort," answered Edward. "You've just heard us arrange to play together."

"Partners will be drawn for," Aunt Caroline decided. "That avoids all difficulties and disputes."

"We'll stick our names down on bits of paper and put them in a hat!" cried Jim. He jumped up from the table to put this plan into instant execution, but was called back by Miss Johnson.

Reluctantly he returned to his chair. "Bags I to be drawer," he murmured; and watching till he saw Miss Johnson's attention diverted he gave his grandfather a slight nudge. "*You* write the names down." He felt in his trouser pockets and produced a stump of pencil.

Grandpapa, having sampled it, dipped his fingers in hot water and preferred to use his own. He tore up a long blue envelope and wrote the names as Jim called them out.

"It had better be an American tournament; each pair to play every other pair: and those who get most points of course win the prize."

"Will we begin to-day?" asked Jim, dropping a spoonful of marmalade on the table-cloth. "Oh, sorry, frightfully!"

"Jim! I *never* saw you behaving so badly!"

The remark came from Miss Johnson, but Jim, secure in his grandfather's protection, remained unperturbed.

"Yes, you can begin to-day. I must make out a card—for keeping the scores on, you know. Five entries:—that will mean ten games altogether." He explained how the points were to be counted.

The signal of release came at last, and Jim flew into the hall for a hat, while grandpapa mixed up the little folded slips of paper. Then, the centre of an eager circle, Jim drew out the first name. "Edward," he read aloud, diving his hand in for the next.

He unfolded it excitedly. "Barbara."

"Oh, I say!" growled Edward. "I think we'd better choose our partners."

Barbara glared at him. "In that case I certainly shan't choose you."

"There must be no grumbling," said Aunt Caroline quickly. "Those who don't wish to play can scratch; or if you like we needn't have a tournament at all."

"Edward, you're awful!" murmured Ann.

Edward apologized, and the ballot continued.

The next name to appear was Ann's own. "Oh!" she whispered; "I *hope* it will be Balmer!"

Balmer it was, and the canon might almost have been suspected of wizardry, for Jim and he were drawn as partners, Grif and Aunt Caroline, Miss Johnson and Mr. Drummond.

"Matches to be played in the afternoon," said Aunt Caroline,— "for grown-ups, at any rate. The only handicaps need be that grandpapa and Jim give eight bisques, and Grif and I will give five."

"Shall we do that, partner?" grandpapa inquired.

"Yes, yes. What are they?"

"It means we give them eight extra turns."

"Oh!" Jim's face grew grave. But the implied superiority was seductive, and he yielded.

"We might play our match off now, Dorset?" Edward proposed.

"If you like."

There was a rush for mallets and balls, in which Ann, as usual, was left in the rear. "Balmer, don't let them take the little mallet," she squealed, "the one with the string round it. I want it."

"I think you'd better go and see that they start properly, papa," said Aunt Caroline. "Remember," she called out, "if there's any squabbling neither side gets a point."

Out of doors, the smooth sunlit lawn looked very attractive, and when the clips were put on the first hoop, and the balls were gathered behind the starting-peg, Jim was assailed by a passionate longing for the afternoon. The fact that he was to act as referee only partially consoled him.

"You shout!" cried Edward, tossing up a coin.

"Tails! . . . Good man! Will you go first, partner?"

"No, you. . . . Oh, Balmer! *what* are you doing?" For Ann's partner had hit the blue ball straight up the ground and off the top boundary.

"He's all right," said grandpapa. "You seem to understand the game, Palmer."

"My pater is rather keen on it," Palmer admitted, "and I play a bit when I'm at home."

"You ought to have said that sooner," grumbled Edward. "You should be giving us a handicap." He tried for the first hoop and missed it.

Palmer looked inquiringly at Canon Annesley.

"Perhaps you'd better give them something. I'll wait and see you take a turn."

"Shall I try for the hoop, too, Balmer?" Ann called out.

"No; come up to me."

Ann made a valiant attempt, landing some three yards from her partner's ball.

"I don't know what they think they're doing," exclaimed Edward discontentedly. "Oh, rotten shot!" as Barbara failed to hit.

"Your own wasn't so splendid!" Barbara replied.

"Good, Balmer!" squealed Ann. "Now he'll come down and get the hoop. No—he's bringing me down! He'll knock the others away, and then I'll get the hoop next time. . . . There goes Edward. . . . Good-bye, Edward. . . . Good-bye, Barbara."

"I think you'd better give them four bisques," said the canon, turning back to the house.

The game, which had been far from silent before, immediately relapsed, so far as Edward and Barbara were concerned, into a perpetual argument about who should take the bisques and when, interspersed with erratic shots that produced expressions of commiseration from Ann. She and Palmer were getting on swimmingly, but Edward's face was like a thundercloud.

"We ought to have a bigger handicap. Barbara's rotten; she's not as good as Ann."

"I'm better than Ann," said Barbara, coldly.

"You're not; you're worse. Ann does what her partner tells her."

"You forget that Ann's partner knows how to play."

Edward took aim and missed a ball a couple of yards away.

"Damn."

"Edward, if you say that again, I'll tell Aunt Caroline."

"I didn't say anything."

"You did."

"I said 'dash.'"

"It wasn't 'dash.'"

"Oh, Balmer, I'm so sorry!" cried Ann penitently, as her ball, with the mallet firmly adhering to it, jammed tight against the wire of the hoop.

"It doesn't matter. I'm afraid it would have been a foul anyway. You're not allowed to push, you know."

"But you can't get through from the side that way unless you *do* push—a little."

"Here, I'm going to play again," cried Edward.

"Why should *you* play? You missed the last time, and it was closer than it is now."

"I'm captain of the side and the captain settles who's to play. I only missed because you put me off."

"You're not captain, and it's my turn."

"There's no turns in it, silly. The same ball can go on playing all the time."

"Well, then, I'll go on playing. Besides, I'm wired, and can go into baulk."

"Referee!" shouted Jim, rushing on to the ground.

Edward caught him by the arm. "Here, you clear out."

"I'm referee," gasped Jim, struggling to free himself. "Amn't I, Palmer? . . . Now;—Palmer says I am!" He lay down on his stomach on the grass, and examined the balls at considerable length. "You're *not* wired, Barbara," he decided. Everybody gathered round to offer an opinion.

"Hang it all, there's Pouncer running away with the blue ball! What a mouth! How on earth did he——" There was a wild chase, and Pouncer, still with the ball, disappeared into the shrubbery.

It was at this point that Grif came to the conclusion that he had watched the game long enough. Palmer had offered to lend him his butterfly-net, and now he went into the hall to get it. Shouts and laughter still came from the shrubbery, where evidently the ball had not yet been found, but Grif did not go to the searchers' assistance. Instead, he ran round behind the stables, climbed the low wall beyond, and dropped down into the wood.

It was not that he wanted to be unsociable, but something in the morning called to him, something in the bright clear air, the radiant sunshine, the rapturous singing of a lark. His blood was stirred, and a restlessness had entered into him. He must run and shout and roll in the grass like a colt. If Jim wanted to come it would be all right, but he could not wait for him. He would leave plenty of tracks that the scout would be able to follow.

He made his way through the trees and the thick undergrowth, blundering at length upon a kind of path, or what had once been a path, for it was now overgrown with brambles. The voices of the croquet-players grew fainter and fainter in the distance, the quiet of the wood deeper and deeper, till at last he felt he was alone.

Simultaneously with this he became aware of a new sound, the low cool noise of running water. It seemed quite close, and he paused, trying to get the direction. Then he forced a passage through the bushes on the right, sliding downhill, his feet sinking in loose mould and beds of withered leaves. Dry sticks snapped under his tread, brambles and trailing creepers clutched at his knickerbockers. But the farther he went, the thinner the trees grew, and the easier he found it to walk, till by the time he reached the grassy margin of the stream he was out again in the sunlight.

On the opposite bank the ground was marshy, with beds of irises in full bloom. The purple flowers, smoked with a delicate grey, shone vividly amid their green spiked leaves, and Grif sat down to wait for Jim in case he should be following.

The wood just here was no denser than a park. To right and left of the iris-swamp it stretched away in a grassy valley, bathed in sunlight. Then, where the slope began on either side, the trees grew thicker, towering to the sky and shutting out all view of what lay beyond.

It was intensely quiet. He could hardly believe he was not more than five minutes' walk from home, so solitary and undisturbed the spot seemed, so remote from human habitation. The tall feathery mountain-ashes, which looked as if a breath could bend them to the ground, stood motionless; the dark beech-leaves shone like polished jewels. Clumps of anemone-leaves grew in the shadow cast by old silver-grey roots, and the fallen tree on which he sat was festooned with the leaves of a nightshade, whose spiked flowers, purple and yellow, dropped down to the surface of the water.

But Jim did not come, and presently he wandered on, keeping to the stream's edge, his butterfly-net over his shoulder. He had gathered a bunch of irises for Aunt Caroline, but soon they began to droop in the hot sun and in his hot hand, and he threw them away.

He began to sing. His clear fresh treble voice seemed, like the skylark's song, a part of the morning. It rose above the prattle of the stream, wordless, in a simple tune, simple as all the other tunes of nature. And then, quite suddenly, he came to the end of his path.

He had reached a fence of barbed wire, beyond which stretched a meadow, where lazy cows stood patiently switching the flies from their backs. Grif, after tearing his jacket, managed to climb the fence. He ran across the meadow and up a daisied bank, on the top of which grew a hawthorn hedge. He squeezed himself through a gap and dropped down on the other side.

He was on a road now, but he had not the faintest idea where it led to, nor how far he was from home. Right in front of him was a high brick wall, with a green wooden door in it; but the door looked as if it was not meant to be opened, and the wall was uncommonly like the back wall of a garden. As he paused, undecided whether to return to the wood or not, a tortoiseshell butterfly flitted over the hedge. It hovered above him; alighted for a moment on the wall, spreading its delicate wings flat against the warm brick; then flew over and disappeared.

Grif's net was in his hand, and he became aware that he had lost an opportunity. It is true, tortoiseshell butterflies are not uncommon, but this one seemed larger than usual, and at any rate Grif's collection, if it were ever to come into existence, ought to contain

one or two. The fact was that he had an unconquerable aversion
to killing things. At breakfast, and under the influence of Palmer's
conversation, a collection of butterflies had seemed a highly desirable affair. But when the time came, his hunting in the wood had
been lamentably half-hearted, and the solitary captive that had
fluttered helplessly in his gauze net had been released.

He approached the garden door, feeling sure it would be locked.
There was a tuft of grass growing below it, which must mean that
it was rarely used. But the door, to his surprise, was open, or rather
it opened when he pushed it, giving out, as it turned on its hinges,
a single clear note, that sounded to Grif's fancy like the sound of
his name.

And on the threshold, as he stood net in hand, hatless, dishev-
elled, one stocking sagging down over his ankle, he was confronted
by a lady who walked slowly towards him, a bunch of roses in her
hand. She looked, he imagined, almost as if she had expected him.
Very much abashed, his first impulse was to take to his heels, and
he would doubtless have done so had not the lady smiled at him
and seemed in every way as kind as possible.

"If you are coming in, shut the door behind you, like a good
boy. William must have left it unbolted."

Grif came in. He pushed, with some difficulty, the stiff bolt
back into its socket, and begged pardon. This lady seemed to him
quite beautiful, with a sort of autumnal sweetness in her face. He
thought she must be rather old, certainly a good deal older than
either Aunt Caroline or his mother. She was dressed in black, with
black lace mittens on her wrists. Her thin hair, not so much white
as colourless, was parted in the middle and smoothed closely down
on either side of her forehead. She wore a cap of soft white lace
with a lilac ribbon in it.

Grif stammered out an explanation of his intrusion and hastily
pulled up his stocking; but the lady only laughed and waved a pair
of scissors at him.

"I won't allow you to catch butterflies here:—if they were cater-
pillars, that would be another matter. How would you like to hunt
for ripe gooseberries instead? Those are the earliest bushes near
the wall."

A tabby cat, with a tail standing up straight and stiff as a poker, stepped down the mossy path and rubbed itself against Grif's legs. Then, jumping on to a bench and from that on to his shoulder, it pushed its face against his cheek, purring loudly, and pulling at his jacket with affectionate claws, as it passed from one shoulder to the other, pressing its warm body caressingly against the back of his head and neck.

Thus accompanied, Grif began his search among the gooseberry-bushes. He had been busy for five minutes or so, and—being not so very particular as to ripeness—quite successfully, when he heard a heavy step on the cinder path, and a deep voice asking, "Who may our young friend be?"

He thought at first the question was addressed to himself, and looked up quickly; but it was the lady who replied.

"I'm afraid I haven't been properly introduced. He is lunching with us, however, and I dare say he will tell us then."

Grif did not know whether he ought to join in this conversation. The mention of lunch recalled to him the fact that dinner was at two o'clock, and that he ought to be getting home. The old gentleman with the deep voice had evidently been gardening, for he held a basket in one hand and a pruning-knife in the other. Like Grif, he was bareheaded. His hair was white and fluffy, his face very red, and his eyes very blue. Also he was dressed in the oddest of clothes. When Grif, stepping out from the gooseberry-bushes, asked him politely what time it was, he produced a huge silver watch, hauling it out of the depths of an immense pocket, like an anchor at the end of a chain. "Lunch-time—lunch-time—half-past-one. You'd better come in and wash your paws. I can see you've travelled far and by difficult ways this morning."

"I've really only travelled from grandpapa's," said Grif.

"Ah! from grandpapa's."

"Grandpapa is Canon Annesley. I am Grif Weston, and we only arrived yesterday. We are going to stay all summer though."

"I'm glad to hear it. We have very few visitors, and I take your paying us so early a call as uncommonly civil."

Grif hesitated. He had an idea that this old gentleman might be indulging in one of those dreary and inexplicable pleasantries to which grown-up people are often addicted. But perhaps he *really* thought grandpapa had sent him. At any rate he would give him the benefit of the doubt. "I'm afraid you are mistaken," he said courteously. "I mean, I didn't exactly call. I didn't know about you. It was an accident. I came through the wood and I wasn't sure of my way home, and that is how I got here."

"Well, the chance guest should be the most welcome, for is he not sent us by the gods? And you aren't far from home—only a mile or so. I am Captain Narcissus Batt, and this is my sister, Miss Nancy Batt."

Grif bowed politely, and they all walked towards the house together. It was built of red brick and stood upon a grassy terrace, below which were other terraces, leading down to the garden. Grif thought he had never seen so beautiful a place. Beside the house, at a little distance, was a stone-lipped pond almost flush with the sward. Water-lilies spread their broad green leaves on the motionless surface, and cedars stretched dark flat branches above it. In the garden, flowers and fruit-trees and vegetables grew in luxuriant profusion. Some of the roses were already in bloom; and there were stocks and carnations, pinks and peonies, while the sweet-pea was everywhere in bud. Against the brick wall beside which they walked trailed a green wistaria, and as they climbed the terraces he had a view of meadow-lands beyond, and in the distance of a river, grey and quiet, winding on into the unknown. The murmur of bees mingled with the heavy scent of pinks and the fresh green scent of newly-mown grass; the birds were silent; while all over there hung the hot, drowsy, June sun.

But, quite apart from its beauty, Grif was aware of something in this place which appealed to him. He had a curious, yet very real sense of being welcomed, not alone by the people who lived here, but by the place itself. There was in its atmosphere something which made him happy, something oddly familiar even in its strangeness. He did not feel as if he were visiting it for the first time, but as if it were a dream-place to which he was coming back. And the impression was redoubled when he entered the house. Then it occurred to him in a flash that the garden—the garden, and still more the house—was haunted.

But not by ghosts. Anything less ghostly could scarce be imagined. There was no shadow of melancholy or regret: all was happy and peaceful. Only he knew there were many voices here, far more than at his grandfather's or even in the wood; and that they were closer and clearer than any he had heard before; and that, though now in the hot windless noon they were sighing and whispering so faintly, some day they would sing aloud and he should be able to make out the words.

He had taken it quite for granted that he would come again, come frequently. These people were his friends, they were *his* kind of people, and he recognized them at once, though he had never met anyone like them elsewhere. At the same time, he knew that he should not bring Jim or Edward or Barbara when he came: he would always come alone—or perhaps now and then he might bring Ann:—which was very strange, for Grif was the least selfish boy in the world. Of course if the others *wanted* to come it would be different, but he didn't think they would want to—unless—they heard about the gooseberries.

The house was cool and the light rather dim. When Grif had washed himself and brushed his hair the captain took him downstairs and introduced him to his other sister, Miss Jane. Miss Jane sat in a deep, high chair, with her thin pale hands folded. She was old, very old, older it seemed to Grif than anything he had ever seen. Beside her Miss Nancy looked almost a girl. And she was so frail, so quiet, so extraordinarily quiet, that he would never have imagined her to be alive if every now and again a word or two had not dropped from her lips, showing that she listened to all that was said. But her voice was so low and toneless that it seemed to come from far back out of a remote past—faint, lingering, like a whisper from a star.

Grif made a much better lunch than he usually did, and drank three glasses of raspberry wine. Afterwards he examined the curiosities which the captain had brought back from all corners of the world. And as he wandered about the room, looking at this and that, on one of the shelves of a cabinet he came upon a flute. He took it up and examined it, he even ventured to ask the captain if he played on it: but the captain shook his head. "It belongs to Billy—Billy Tremaine, my grandson." He paused a moment. "Would you like to take him up to Billy's room, Nancy?" he asked, with a certain hesitation, almost a diffidence.

"No, not to-day, I think. Possibly—some other time. I expect he would rather go for a little stroll with you to-day."

Grif would have liked immensely to have been taken to Billy Tremaine's room, but he showed nothing of his disappointment as he followed Captain Narcissus Batt out into the garden. There the captain smoked pipe after pipe, and as he took his young friend round, stooping every now and again to pull up a weed, he told him curious, involved tales, that perhaps could hardly have been more than "founded upon fact." The captain's ships appeared to have put in at every port in the world, to have weathered countless storms, and to have come through infinitely perilous adventures; but they must certainly have sailed up the rivers of Wonderland too. To Grif the time passed lightly as a dream.

Presently Miss Nancy called them to tea, which was laid under one of the cedars near the pond. And, as he sat talking with them, Grif was more and more conscious of how much he liked his new friends. He himself was transformed. Nobody at home would have recognized him if they had heard his chatter—he who was supposed to live in the clouds. The great thing was that his present companions lived in the clouds also. At any rate they all got on uncommonly well together, and, when he rose to say good-bye, it seemed quite natural that Miss Nancy should kiss him instead of shaking hands.

The captain put him on the road for home, pointing out the steeple of the church. When he reached that he must turn to his left and five minutes' walk would bring him to the Glebe.

CHAPTER VI

MUSIC

'And storied windows richly dight
Casting a dim religious light:
There let the pealing organ blow
In service high and anthems clear,
As may with sweetness, through mine ear,
Dissolve me into ecstasies.'

—*Milton.*

WHILE Grif walked on towards home his impression of the past few hours seemed to dim as rapidly as the house itself receded behind him. The colours altered and sank in, like the colour of a dream in the brightness of morning. The whole adventure lost its wonder and became just a memory of a pleasant visit paid to people who had been kind to him and whom he liked. At the time it had been more than that: it had, indeed, been something quite different, something he could no longer even understand. The change which had taken place was like that which came when after looking through the coloured glass of the landing-window at home on a richer, more enchanted world, he saw it, by a mere movement of his head, in the cold tints of ordinary daylight. Captain Narcissus Batt, Miss Nancy and Miss Jane, were now pleasant, old people who lived in a big red house with a lovely garden: but a little while ago that house had been a wondrous sleeping palace, which his presence had almost, though not quite, awakened into a radiant, dreamlike life. He felt a curious alteration in the atmosphere about him, as if it had grown colder. The murmuring sounds had ceased; they could not reach him here.

Yet his thoughts still ran on what he had seen, what he had heard, though they moved at present along the mere beaten channels of an ordinary curiosity. He would have liked to have asked about Billy Tremaine, for instance, though at the time he had felt

43

that he must not. No further allusions had been made to the captain's grandson, nor to the room which Miss Nancy had not taken
Grif to see. Perhaps Billy Tremaine, too, was a sailor, and only
came home at rare intervals:—perhaps he had just gone out for a
walk. And yet—— They had not appeared to expect him to return,
they had not said that Grif might see him another day:—only that
he might see his room. . . .

He was still pondering these and similar things when he reached
the church, and the sound of the organ playing inside switched his
thoughts on to quite another line.

He remembered Mr. Bradley. That must be Mr. Bradley practis-
ing; and though Grif would naturally have preferred to hear him at
a more interesting hour, such as midnight or thereabouts, he could
not resist the temptation to take a peep in.

The gate was unlocked, and he walked up a straight steep path,
bordered by two lines of yew-trees. The church door was unlocked
also, it was even slightly ajar. Grif pushed it open and slipped
inside. It was not a large building, and very simple in design; but it
was old and cool, and the late afternoon sun, streaming through
the rose window, made it beautiful.

In spite of the sun there was a light burning near the organ.
Grif could see Mr. Bradley as he sat there playing, his head a little
bent; and on tip-toe he glided up to the choir to listen. He loved
listening to music, though he very seldom had an opportunity to
do so. Now, in a corner of one of the choir-stalls, he was quiet as
a mouse, or as a little ghost who had glided in from the grey and
green churchyard outside. He did not know what it was Mr. Bradley had begun to play, but it was sad and quiet, and a kind of heavy
dream seem to float from it, like a coil of smoke, so that Grif forgot
where he was, forgot everything about him, and the walls of the
church drifted away, while another picture took form before him,
and he knew that he was in an old, old city, and that it was night.

The streets of this city were narrow, the houses, with sharp
gables and slanting roofs, stood out clearly in a faint light that was
neither moonlight nor twilight. And each of the streets converged
towards a single point, a kind of open square, at one end of which
an immense church rose against the sky. Above the great central

door was a crucifix, and high up on one of the towers a monstrous bird, black, with curved beak and red, glowing eyes, sat motionless, while from its folded wings darkness and silence poured down.

At first the square seemed empty, but presently he became conscious of a procession of grey, cloaked figures moving across it. They passed beneath the crucifix, and the last figure of all stood still, lifting his head and throwing back his hood. Grif had a glimpse of a white face, but before he had time to recognize it it was blotted out. The streets were once more deserted; the dark bird had disappeared; a pale silvery light flooded everything. Then the whole scene whirled away from him as if blown by a sudden wind, and he was back in his choir-stall.

Had he fallen asleep? He did not feel sleepy. But Mr. Bradley had stopped playing and Grif got up to go. Just then the organist turned round and caught sight of him. There was a jarring scream from the treble notes where his hand crashed down, and Mr. Bradley sprang to his feet, overturning a pile of music-books and the stool on which they stood.

"It's only me," said Grif lamely, perceiving that for some reason he had startled the organist.

Mr. Bradley apparently still failed to recognize him, for he gazed at him as if at an apparition from the grave.

"Who are you?" he asked, paying no heed to his scattered music.

"The boy you met in the lane. Grif Weston."

Mr. Bradley flushed. He seemed relieved, but with his relief he suddenly grew angry. "What do you mean by coming in like that? How did you get in, to begin with? Didn't I lock the door?"

"The door wasn't locked," explained Grif apologetically. "It was even a little open; and I thought you wouldn't mind."

"Wouldn't mind! As if anybody wouldn't mind. You ought to have more sense! . . . . Well, well," he added, his manner growing gentler, "I suppose my nerves must be a little out of order."

"I'm very sorry," said Grif penitently. "I won't come again."

The organist shook his head impatiently. "I don't object to your coming: it's not that. You don't seem to understand. You can come as often as you like so long as I know you're there. Make a noise— rattle at the door—stamp your feet—don't creep up behind me like a ghost." His voice altered again, became almost confidential. "The fact is, something very strange occurred in this church—to me—only last night."

"Were you here last night?" asked Grif, a sudden curiosity overcoming his natural reserve. "It's awfully queer, because I wondered if you were?"

Mr. Bradley regarded him with reawakened suspicion. "Wondered if I was here! What did you know about it?" he asked sharply.

"Aunt Caroline told me that you sometimes came at night to play, and just before I got into bed—very late—I began to think that perhaps you were there."

"Well I was. And what's more, I saw a ghost."

"A real ghost?" Grif whispered, awestruck.

Mr. Bradley was offended. "Yes," he snapped. "Of course a real ghost. There aren't any others—except when *you* come stealing in. I was playing an air I had taught him. I don't know what put it into my mind, but at any rate I began to play it—an old Italian thing—a Spring Song. And in the middle of it I heard him. Perhaps I'm wrong in that: perhaps I didn't hear him: but in any case something made me look round and—there he was, standing behind me, just where you are now. He only stayed while you could count twenty: then he was gone. . . . That's why I lit these candles this afternoon. I thought it might get dark while I was playing, and I didn't want to be caught napping. But we won't talk about him. Now you *are* here, tell me if you have a voice? Have you ever tried to sing? I haven't heard a voice for months. . . . Cats, peacocks, corncrakes—that's what I've got to make a choir of—a farmyard. A man like me—ridiculous—wasted in a God-forsaken hole like this. . . ." His words sank into a mutter and Grif could no longer distinguish what he was saying.

There was a silence while Mr. Bradley wagged his head. Then he looked up. "Well!" he went on querulously. "I'm waiting to try your voice. Sing the scale as I play it."

Grif would not have dreamed of disobeying him, and he began at once to sing, following each note of the organ. When he had finished Mr. Bradley seemed to be in better humour.

"Good boy! And you mean to tell me they never had you taught!

Extraordinary! I expect they muddle your head with all kinds of nonsense—teach you everything except what you ought to learn. They do. You needn't deny it. They always do—idiots! You must sing for me. There's a solo in an old anthem of mine that I will teach you, and you'll sing it in church one Sunday. . . . Mezzo—you mustn't try to sing too high. All you need is a little training. I've heard more powerful voices, but none much sweeter. . . . Do you know this?" He played the first bars of Spohr's *Rose Softly Blooming*. "Don't you know it? Well, we'll have our first lesson now. Sing something you *do* know—anything—I just want to see if you have an ear. We'll try a hymn—you must know lots of hymns. *A Few More Years Shall Roll*? You must know *that*?"

"Yes, I think so," said Grif diffidently.

"Well, sing it. It doesn't matter about the words, if you don't remember them. Any words will do—or none at all. I'm glad you're not shy. There's a boy in the village who has quite a fair soprano. Grocer's boy. I offered to teach him, but the little idiot was frightened to open his mouth."

Thus encouraged, Grif decided not to be a little idiot also, and sang to the best of his ability.

"That's a good boy."

"Did I keep in tune?" he asked softly.

"Perfectly. Now we'll go back to Spohr."

It was much later than he had intended it to be when Grif said good-bye to Mr. Bradley and scudded down the road in the direction of his grandfather's. It must be very late indeed, he thought, for the sun had set, and the sky in the west was ablaze with a soft radiance of yellow and orange. Against this the landscape, rising in a gentle curve, took on a sombre hue, in which green was hardly visible, while the rich brown soil of arable land looked black as black velvet. Some white gulls, passing with their strange lonely cry overhead, were dark as a flock of rooks, and the flies, dancing in fantastic reels against the glowing light, were like little spots of darkness shaken into animation.

For the first time it occurred to Grif that his prolonged absence might have caused some uneasiness at home. . . . And he no longer had Palmer's butterfly-net. Dear knows where he had left it!

CHAPTER VII

QUESTIONS AND ANSWERS

'I met a traveller from an antique land.'
—*Shelley.*

THE sight of the croquet-hoops, looking lonely and deserted on the grey lawn, where they were now scarcely distinguishable, reminded him of the tournament, and when, very shamefacedly, he pushed open the dining-room door, he understood the anxiety his behaviour had created. He stood still upon the threshold, a little dazzled by the bright light and the noise of uplifted voices. Supper was finished, but they were all sitting up for him. The clock on the chimney-piece pointed to a quarter past nine.

"Where *have* you been?" demanded Aunt Caroline. "Do you know that Mr. Drummond and Robert" (the coachman) "are at this very moment scouring the country in search of you?"

Grif remained with hanging head, still not far from the doorway. "I'm very sorry. I didn't know it was so late till it began to get dark."

"But aren't you starving? Have you had anything to eat?"

"Oh yes. I had lunch and tea at the Batts'. Then I met Mr. Bradley and listened to him playing, and he gave me a music-lesson, and then it got dark."

Aunt Caroline seemed relieved. "Well, you're a nice boy! And a nice partner, too," she suddenly recollected. "Here was I waiting for you all afternoon."

"I—I'm afraid I forgot about the tournament."

"Balmer and I beat Edward and Barbara—oh, easily!" Ann patronized. "So did grandpapa and Jim. And Balmer and I beat Miss Johnson and Mr. Drummond."

"We're going to play Drumsticks to-morrow," cried Jim irreverently.

"And now you're going to bed," interrupted Aunt Caroline.

48

"Run away at once, and Ann too. You can hear the prodigal's adventures in the morning."

This was not in the least what Jim had bargained for, and he attempted to divert Aunt Caroline's thoughts by proposing that they should light a bonfire on the drive as a signal to Mr. Drummond and Robert. Meanwhile Bridget appeared with a bowl of soup, and other delicacies. These she set before Grif, who was conscious of being much more in the limelight than seemed at all necessary.

"You must eat an enormous supper," Aunt Caroline warned him. "Otherwise I shall think your outing has made you ill, and be really angry."

"There's a circus coming, and we're going to it," Jim called from the door, where he still hovered, in spite of the failure of the bonfire scheme.

"You certainly won't go unless you're in bed in five minutes," Aunt Caroline replied.

Jim scuttled away, and presently he and Ann could be heard engaged in a struggle on the stairs.

"I'm afraid I didn't bring you back your net, Palmer," said Grif. "I think I must have left it at the Batts'."

"Ah, the searchers have returned!" cried grandpapa, as the sound of a closing door, and then of footsteps in the hall, reached them.

"Come in, Drummond," he called out, and next moment a youthful, smooth-faced parson entered.

"Behold him!" The canon waved a hand at his grandson. "The cause of all your trouble! It was really very good of you. You ought to have a whisky and soda to counteract the effects of your exertions. Next time we'll leave him to look after himself."

Mr. Drummond refused the whisky and soda, but accepted, at the hands of Miss Johnson, a glass of Eiffel Tower lemonade.

"Where was he?" he murmured.

"Oh, just paying a round of visits. First of all he called on the Batts—Captain Narcissus and his sisters:—natural enough that he should seek companions of his own years. What did you think of the captain, Grif?"

"I thought him very nice."

"So he is. Wonderful man in his way. Makes all his own clothes, Drummond—boots too, I believe."

Mr. Drummond was unimpressed.

"I think they might have sent him home a little earlier. They must have known you would be anxious about him."

"Oh, he didn't stay *there* all the time. He also called on Mr. Clement Bradley, and spent a few hours with him—four or five, I think it was."

The curate did not smile. In his opinion this was not the proper spirit in which to take Grif's escapade. He was inclined to agree with Miss Johnson, who had confided to him, over croquet, that she was afraid the children were going to be spoiled.

"That's more than *you've* ever done," the canon went on gaily.

"Yes. I don't care for him."

"He's harmless enough," the canon laughed. "A little odd, though the oddest thing about him is that he should be here at all. He's an Oxford man, you know—in fact he was at my own college—and there's no doubt he's a capable musician."

"The explanations of such mysteries are not far to seek as a rule," the curate replied uncharitably.

"I don't think they'd fit the present case," said the canon. "He doesn't look like a man who had come to grief through drink or anything of that sort."

"Petit chaudron, grandes oreilles," murmured Aunt Caroline.

"He is going to teach me singing," said Grif quietly. "He gave me a lesson to-night."

Mr. Drummond's thin lips closed more tightly. "I don't think I should encourage that," he persisted.

"Nonsense! You're prejudiced against him. After all, he's a gentleman, even if he *is* peculiar. What do *you* say, Palmer?"

This question was called forth by the remarkable attitude Palmer had just adopted. He leaned back in his chair, his eyes nearly closed, but on his face an expression of Sphinx-like attention. His hands were joined on his knee, the finger tips just lightly touching. Even Miss Johnson should have been aware that this was one of the favourite positions of Mr. Sherlock Holmes when tackling a problem. Yet Palmer's freckled countenance failed so completely to recall that of the master that grandpapa alone had discovered the inner significance of his posture.

"You must first have something definite to go on," Palmer said. "The fact of his coming to live in the country doesn't in itself constitute a clue. The thing is to find out a possible reason for his choosing this particular part of the country."

"Buried treasure wouldn't do? Well, poor Bradley's had a good many years to find it in."

Grif had been on the point of mentioning Mr. Bradley's story of the ghost, but for some reason he now decided to keep silence. "Who is Billy Tremaine, grandpapa?" he asked.

"Did the Batts mention him? That was rather unusual, for they don't talk about him as a rule, even to their oldest friends. . . . He was the captain's grandson, poor little chap."

"Yes, I know. But where is he now?" Then the truth dawned upon him. "He's not——"

"He's dead," said the canon gravely. "Didn't they tell you?"

"No: they only said—something about showing me his room."

"They don't talk of his death. . . . You see, he always lived with them. That was his home: they were all the relations he had. His mother died when he was born, and the father was drowned within the same year—his ship was lost and every one on board her. He was a fine boy; very intelligent; as bright a little fellow as I have ever seen. His death was a tremendous blow to them. In a way their whole existence was centred in that boy. Now, I dare say, they feel they have nothing very much to live for. The place will go to strangers—distant cousins or something like that. It is a pity."

"I must say I haven't found either Captain Batt or his sisters very approachable myself," the curate confessed. "Of course they're perfectly civil, but one doesn't really get to know them. I was quite unaware that the captain had ever been married, let alone that there had been a grandson." His tone was slightly aggrieved, and won a sympathetic glance from Miss Johnson.

"It must be nearly four years since the boy's death," the canon murmured, trying to recall the date. "He was just about Grif's age."

"Grif dear, if you've finished your supper I think you had better say good night."

To Grif the conversation had begun to be intensely interesting, nevertheless, at Aunt Caroline's words, he got up immediately.

"How good he is," she remarked to Miss Johnson when he had gone, and Palmer, Edward, and Barbara with him. "I don't think I ever knew a more docile child."

"Y—es," Miss Johnson agreed unenthusiastically. "It doesn't make him any easier to look after, unfortunately."

"You are thinking about his staying out so long? After all, it wasn't very serious, was it? I don't think we need bother ourselves about him another time: he seems to have the gift of making friends."

But Miss Johnson was not so sanguine. "I'm thinking of lots of things," she replied. "I'd rather be in charge of all the others put together than of Grif. One at least knows where one is with them. And I'm not sure that he's always perfectly truthful."

She regretted these last words as soon as they were spoken, but, even if they were an exaggeration of what she felt, it was perhaps just as well to put Miss Annesley upon her guard.

"How do you mean?" asked Aunt Caroline, in surprise. "I can hardly believe he is *untruthful*. He certainly doesn't look it. He's got as honest a pair of eyes as any little boy I ever saw."

"I don't mean, of course, that he would tell a downright lie," the governess hastened to explain. "But his accounts of where he has been, and of what he has been doing, and—things like that— are sometimes very unsatisfactory. And the friends he makes are *not* always desirable. He once went away for a whole day with an Italian organ-grinder. Fortunately the man turned out to be less disreputable than might have been expected, and brought him back in the evening safe and sound. I gave him a piece of my mind as he stood on the doorstep grinning and bowing like a monkey. I told him he might consider himself lucky that I hadn't called in the police. And after I had done Grif actually shook hands with him, and thanked him for the pleasant day he had had, and apologized for what *I* had said. As for giving an account of what he had been doing or where he had been, he simply produced a farrago of nonsense like some story in the *Arabian Nights*."

"Don't you think it is a mistake to expect children to be perfectly literal. He was probably very much excited, and mixed up some of the things he wanted to see with what he *had* seen."

Miss Johnson did not argue the point, but she had an idea that before the end of her visit she should be able to bring out triumphantly that popular phrase, 'I told you so.'

CHAPTER VIII

GREY WEATHER

'With hey, ho, the wind and the rain.'
—*Shakespeare.*

THE day promised badly from the beginning. During breakfast a slight drizzle began to fall, and it was decided that the croquet tournament, which was now nearing its finish, had better be postponed. Then came the unfortunate affair of Palmer and Miss Johnson.

For towards midday, seeing that the rain had cleared off, and that even a flicker of wan sunshine was trying to pierce through the heavy atmosphere, Miss Johnson, having put on a waterproof and a pair of thick boots, boldly set out to take a walk. She had looked for a companion, but the girls, under Hannah's supervision, were in the kitchen baking, while Jim had disappeared, no one knew whither. Miss Johnson set out alone.

Resolved on fresh woods, and pastures new, she bent her steps in the direction of the river. She walked by dripping trees and drenched hedges, upon which a grey mist hung in silken webs; she passed the churchyard wall; and finally, her path unexpectedly coming to an end, picked her way carefully across a ploughed field. It was at this point that, pushing through a broken fence and finding herself at last upon the river bank, an appalling sight met her eyes. It held her transfixed, but only for a moment—a moment of frozen horror: then a stifled scream came from her parted lips and she withdrew.

For what Miss Johnson had seen was a naked man. To be sure, this particular man was not very old—sixteen years or there-abouts—but to the governess's startled vision he might have been Adam. In a few seconds she was back in the ploughed field, plunging ankle-deep in mud.

Miss Johnson was seriously angry; her morning, she decided, was spoiled; and on her return to the house she dwelt long and bitterly on the disgraceful state of things which made it impossible for her to go out for a walk without the risk of coming on such scenes. She didn't know what the boys were thinking of—particularly Palmer—the others had at any rate been *in* the river. They oughtn't to be allowed to bathe except at stated times, and certainly at *no* time without bathing things. *Anyone* might be passing at such an hour—the very middle of the day. It was in vain that Aunt Caroline assured her that nobody ever *did* pass, except an occasional bargee and his family; Miss Johnson was not to be pacified; and at lunch the whole matter was revived when Jim, on Palmer's entrance, threw up his hands with a scream of dismay. Jim was sent from the table in disgrace, but this, as the governess knew, simply meant that he finished his dinner with Bridget and Hannah, by no means a great hardship, judging by the radiant face with which he returned. Jim was being spoiled; his manners had already deteriorated; and Miss Johnson resolved without further delay to send a letter to his mother.

Bang on the top of this came the matter of Daniel and the Lion's Den. Jim invented the game, and it was played by himself and Pouncer and Johnnie, the boy who cleaned the knives and boots. Johnnie's tearful account of it was that Master Jim had persuaded him to be Daniel, and when he had got into the den—in other words the ashpit—Pouncer had been introduced, a veritable and only too eager lion. Wilfully encouraged according to Johnnie's version, simply in a moment of high spirits according to Jim's, the fact remained that the lion actually had bitten Daniel. There could be no doubt of it. A triangular, flapping rent in Johnnie's trousers was in itself sufficient proof were such required; and this time Aunt Caroline was genuinely cross. Johnnie was—with considerable difficulty and some bribery—pacified; Johnnie's trousers were attended to by Bridget; and Jim was told that if he gave any more trouble he would be sent to bed and kept there.

He rejoined his brothers and sisters, the picture of outraged virtue. "He didn't even bleed!" he said contemptuously. "He only got a pinch; and he yelled like a bull. He's fifteen, too—nearly a man!"

"What else can you expect if you play with a chap like that?" asked Edward contemptuously.

"I'll never play with him again. I offered him a shilling—it's all I've got—but he went howling into the house."

As he spoke he produced from a pocket in his knickerbockers a rather dirty handkerchief rolled up into a ball, from the middle of which he abstracted two unappetizing-looking sweets. One of these he bestowed upon Ann, the other he proceeded to suck himself.

Meanwhile the rain was coming down in torrents, and they looked out at it disconsolately, all save Grif, who, curled up on the sofa, was deep in a tattered volume of the *Arabian Nights*.

"What'll we do? It's not going to clear up; it's getting worse."

"Ann, *please* don't breathe into my ear!" There was a querulousness in Barbara's tone which was perhaps explained by the depressing weather, and by the fact that before dinner she had been set to practise scales, when the others were free to do as they wished.

"A fellow at school once tried to raise the devil," said Palmer, reflectively. "He got how to do it out of some book on magic."

Ann's eyes grew very round. "But wasn't that awfully wicked, Balmer?"

"Oh, he didn't manage it. He couldn't get the proper things."

"What *are* the proper things?" asked Ann, fearfully.

"The fat of corpses, and consecrated hosts, and all that kind of stuff. You have to boil 'em into a sort of broth and smear yourself with it and dance about and say the most frightful curses and blasphemies. He tried to make the broth out of substitutes, but he didn't succeed in raising anything except an unholy smell. There was a big row about it, too, and he was nearly expelled, besides being more or less barred afterwards by every one. You see, he made a couple of kids help him, and one of them got frightened out of his life and blabbed the whole thing:—wrote home about it. *You* remember, Weston?"

Edward grunted. "He *was* expelled. At least, his people had to take him away at the end of term."

"I think it served him right," said Ann gravely. "I didn't know boys *could* be so wicked."

"Oh, he was like that," answered Palmer lightly; "he couldn't help it. My pater, when I told him about it, said he was a morbid degenerate, and ought to be treated by a doctor."

"And supposing the devil *had* come; he might have taken the whole school, and you and Edward too. . . . I expect that was why you all got diphtheria."

"*We* hadn't anything to do with it. It was only him and the two wretched kids he got hold of."

"I think you ought to say your prayers pretty often, Balmer."

"But I tell you I didn't even know about it till it was all over."

"Still, you were near the place where it happened."

Ann's voice had a suspicious break in it, and her mouth took a downward droop as she held Palmer's hand firmly, prepared for an instant tug-of-war with any malign power which might suddenly enter to whisk him away.

"Don't be so silly, Ann," said Barbara, unsympathetically.

But Palmer, who divined that he had, though quite unintentionally and he knew not how, touched a hidden spring of tears, returned, unnoticed, the pressure of her hand. "It's all right," he said. "It's only nonsense."

Ann's devotion, simple and undisguised, secretly pleased him. He thought she was a jolly nice little kid.

"We might make up riddles!" Jim proposed, "and give a prize to the one who guesses most."

"We might get Miss Johnson to finish reading her novel," said Ann, happy once more.

Palmer shrugged his shoulders. He and Miss Johnson were not at present on good terms. "It was pretty rotten, what she *did* read," he said.

"I thought it was lovely," Barbara murmured dreamily. "But

she's lent it to Mr. Drummond. I saw her giving it to him."

"I tell you what would be a good rag." said Palmer. "We'll dramatize the novel and act it."

"You can't dramatize it if you haven't got it," Edward objected.

"That doesn't matter. We know quite enough of it. We can rig up a sort of stage in the back drawing-room, and give a performance this evening."

"I don't know that Miss Johnson would like it," said Barbara, doubtfully.

"Of course she'll like it. Why shouldn't she?"

He sketched out a play-bill, while the others leaned over his shoulder.

This Evening at 8. Original Performance of
BE TRUE FOND HEART
A TRAGEDY IN THREE ACTS
founded on
The Celebrated Novel by Miss Johnson
Admission Free.

"I vote we charge sixpence for admission," said Jim. "There's a shop in the village where you can get fireworks."

"Well, we can fix that later. We'll have to settle who's to take the parts first of all, and then everybody can help to write the play."

"I'll be Reginald," said Barbara, her conscientious scruples yielding to the fascination of that darkly romantic hero.

But a brotherly voice replied: "Oh, rot! you can't be. You and Ann will have to take the girls' parts."

Barbara's smile faded. "I *hate* Angelina; she's so stuck up and idiotic."

"They're all idiotic, but you can be the other girl—what's her name."

"Maud Vivien," said Ann. "I'll be Angelina, Balmer, if you'll be Reginald."

"Edward will be Captain Victor De Lancy," said Palmer, drawing up the cast, "and Grif and Jim can be the old father and mother."

"Oh, I say!" cried Jim.

"I'm afraid there's nothing for you, Pouncer, old chap. Every one has to write his own part, so we'd better get started at once. Do you hear, Grif? Somebody waken him up."

This was immediately accomplished by the simple method of confiscating the *Arabian Nights*, and Grif was told what he had to do.

"But how can we write our parts when we don't know what the others are going to say?"

Such difficulties, for Palmer, did not exist. "You'll have to guess. We'll settle the acts first, and then it will be all serene. . . . The first act will be where Reginald has sprained his ankle, and has to lie about the house and talk to Angelina and Maud Vivien. Angelina gets jealous of Maud, and then, when Captain De Lancy comes along to see how Reginald is, she makes up to him, just to show that she doesn't care. He, of course, falls in love with her, and is jealous of Reginald. . . . In the next act Reginald and Captain De Lancy have their quarrel and Reginald is shot. . . . The last act is where Reginald dies."

"I don't exactly see where Grif and me come in," said Jim, ruefully.

"And there's not much for Maud Vivien," added Barbara.

"Of course there is. There's just as much as you like to stick in. At all events we won't have time to do it any other way if we're going to act it to-night."

"May we dress up, Balmer?" asked Ann softly, to whom this part of the performance was the main thing.

"Rather. I need black bags. Reginald's always in faultless evening dress. I wonder if I could get an old pair of your grandfather's?"

"I need them too, if I'm going to be Angelina's father," cried Jim. "And so will Edward for Captain De Lancy."

"Oh, nonsense!" said Barbara. "You can't *all* wear grandpapa's trousers."

"Not if he's to attend the show himself," Palmer admitted. "All the same, the father can't come on in knickerbockers. I'll lend Jim my Sunday things."

"But they're grey, and quite a light grey."

"That doesn't matter: all you want is longs."

Ann, who was nothing if not practical, said, "I think we'd better go at once and ask Aunt Caroline; because if we can't get the things to dress up in there's no use bothering about words."

"Right-o. But don't say what piece we're going to do. That's to be a surprise. Just tell her it's a play we're composing ourselves."

Ann and Barbara were dispatched on this important mission, while the four boys went down to the back drawing-room to see what could be arranged in the way of stage effects.

There were at all events curtains which could be drawn, and the first and last scenes presented little difficulty. The trouble was to prepare a wood for Reginald and Captain De Lancy to quarrel in.

"We'll just have to put down a few plants and things here and there; and we can have a notice saying Trespassers Prosecuted. It won't be a long act anyway. You can have Jim's pistol."

"I've used up all the caps," said Jim.

"That's a nuisance: we want something to make a bit of a noise."

The scenic arrangements, though simple, occupied a considerable time, and still more was taken up by the sorting and allocation of the various garments Ann and Barbara had managed to collect. Moreover, Barbara now wished to take the part of Angelina, seeing how much more this lady was to be in the picture than the fascinating Maud Vivien. She tried persuasions first, and then more forcible methods, but Ann stoutly refused to make an exchange. In this she was backed up by her brothers, whose masculine sense of fair play was not to be overruled even by Barbara's threat that she would withdraw altogether.

"If you don't want to act," said Edward, "you needn't. Jim can do Maud Vivien, and we can cut out the father."

All this caused delay, and when the actual composition of the drama began it was already nearly teatime; nor did it then, save in Palmer's case perhaps, get much beyond the stage of pencil sharpening and mutual observation.

Jim, to whom all forms of literary composition were a matter of considerable physical effort, lay flat on his stomach on the carpet, a sheet of foolscap before him, upon which he traced laboriously, and with much deep breathing, certain cryptic sentences. Ann's muse had not yet descended. With one hand toying with her pigtail, she sat sucking a pencil, while her eyes rolled from collaborator to collaborator, in helpless perplexity. Then the point of Jim's pencil broke and he scrambled to his feet.

"How much have you done?" asked Palmer.

"Duck all. I'm going to *think* my part."

As an aid to reflection he immediately enfolded Ann in the brilliant dressing-gown Reginald had elected to die in, and there was a violent struggle, accompanied by stifled screams from the entrapped heroine. Ann was rescued, and Jim was again placed on the floor, and this time sat upon. But his example proved infectious, and one by one the other authors of the piece decided to 'think' also.

"I'll not show the play-bill till just before we begin," said Palmer, who secretly shared Barbara's idea that Miss Johnson might raise objections. This idea was strengthened at teatime, when he learned that Mr. Drummond, who had dropped in to arrange about croquet, was to be among the spectators.

It was while the spectators were at dinner that the dressing up began, but, owing to a great deal of experimentation, it was not till an imperative summons had been received from Aunt Caroline that it ended. Then the players filed downstairs to the hall, and gathered in a whispering, giggling group by the back drawing-room door.

The audience, which included Bridget, Hannah, and Pouncer, meanwhile waited patiently in the front drawing-room, and Aunt Caroline was on the point of dispatching a second and still more urgent message when a hand, unexpected as that which appeared at Belshazzar's feast, suddenly appeared between the drawn curtains, and a programme was hurled into her face. There was a scuffling sound, as of a startled rabbit, and immediately afterwards the curtains were pulled back.

Clad in a rich ball-dress, and with a black lace mantilla draped about her shoulders, the lovely Angelina reclined gracefully upon a couch, while not far away, in equally brilliant costume, sat her bosom friend Maud Vivien. Nevertheless, these ladies did not appear to be on speaking terms, and a profound silence reigned, a silence broken at last by an angry whisper from behind the scenes: "Buck up! Say something, can't you!"

A stifled gurgle from Angelina, whose countenance had gradually grown purple, was the only immediate response to this appeal, but presently Maud Vivien remarked, "I thought I heard some one coming in. It sounds as if he was lame. I hope there hasn't been an accident."

ANGELINA: I hope so too.

(*A silence.*)

MAUD (*sotto voce*): Why don't you come in? What are you waiting for? (*Aloud, and showing great surprise:*) Ah! Here they are—two strangers—gentlemen—and one of them is lame! He can hardly walk.

MAUD *has barely finished speaking when the two gentlemen enter. Indeed there is nothing else for them to do, though it had been understood that the introductory scene was to run to something further than three brief remarks. One of the gentlemen has red hair, the other is flaxen-polled, but in two points they closely resemble each other; both have remarkably thick black eyebrows and fierce black moustaches. Also both wear hats of clerical shape—probably the latest thing, since they are obviously not parsons, but men-about-town, and dressed with extreme fastidiousness. The red-haired gentleman limps painfully and leans upon an umbrella. Mr. Drummond, who seems to recognize this particular property, follows his progress with ill-concealed anxiety. He displays still further uneasiness as one of the hats is dropped carelessly on a chair—suggesting that it may be sat upon later, in a passage of comic relief.*

FIRST GENTLEMAN (*with winning affability*): You must excuse us coming in like this, but my friend has sprained his ankle, and as we were nearer your house than any other, we just dropped in here. I am Captain Victor De Lancy, and this is my great friend Reginald Ashley. Played together on the village green and all that sort of thing—what? Allow me to introduce you, Reginald, to Miss Angelina Ravenshawe, the heiress, and Miss Maud Vivien, her friend—cousin, I mean—no, friend.

ANGELINA (*shyly*): I'm glad to see you, Balm—Reginald.

REGINALD (*fingering his moustache*): Charmed, I'm sure! One meets so few heiresses! (*He staggers and catches hold of the back of a chair; then gradually sinks down upon the curate's hat, only to recover himself when Mr. Drummond, no longer able to restrain his emotion, utters a cry of anguish. The hat is revealed, still unharmed, as in a conjuring trick, and the curate, recognizing too late that all this is intentional and performed for his especial benefit, endeavours to look as amused as the rest of the audience.*)

CAPTAIN DE LANCY (*under his breath, to* ANGELINA): Ask him to sit down on the couch, stupid!

ANGELINA: Won't you sit down on the couch, Balm—Reg—Mr. Ashley. I see you've sprained your ankle very badly indeed.

REGINALD (*gallantly*): I don't regret it, Miss Ravenshawe, since it has given me the pleasure of making your acquaintance.

MAUD (*dubiously*): I'm afraid Mr. Ashley won't be well enough to go away for a long time.

ANGELINA: I think so too. Will you, Mr. Ashley?

REGINALD (*shortly*): Certainly not.

MAUD: Angelina dear, you'd better call your father and mother. I know they want to meet Captain De Lancy and Mr. Ashley. They've seen them in church.

REGINALD (*seizing his chance, and addressing the audience*): Not me. I never go to church—except to interrupt the service. I lead an awful life, you know—a life of cynical laughter and smouldering passion. Men have always feared, and a few women have worshipped me. Even in the cradle I was dangerous, and the nurse gave notice. I was expelled from five public schools, and ran away from my last—an industrial one. I was sent down from Oxford—permanently—in my second term. I gambled away a fortune before I was twenty. And there is that ugly story of Lady Paston, who pawned the drawing-room clock and followed me to Monte Carlo. It is only one scandal among many, and yet—and yet—(*with a pathetic catch in his voice*)—in a locket which I wear under my clothes, there is twisted a strand of a dead woman's hair—my mother's. (*Bursts into tears.*)

(*Giggles from* ANGELINA, *and murmured commendations from* CAPTAIN DE LANCY:—Keep it up, old cock. Just have a squint at Miss Johnson's face!)

ANGELINA (*inspired*): I'll tell father and mother to bring some wine.

(*Enter* MR. *and* MRS. RAVENSHAWE. MR. RAVENSHAWE *wears a light grey suit, very loosely fitting, and has a couple of reefs in the hems of his trousers.* MRS. RAVENSHAWE *apparently finds considerable difficulty in managing her skirt. There are further introductions, enlivened by* MRS. RAVENSHAWE's *curious movements, which suggest that she has already been sampling the wine. Finally, as she steps forward to greet the recumbent* REGINALD, *there is a sharp continuous crepitating sound, as of many Chinese crackers going off, and she drops upon her knees.* "Now you've done it!" *remarks* CAPTAIN DE LANCY *brutally. He assists her to rise by tugging at the scruff of her neck: and a voice from the audience questions anxiously,* "Grif, dear, I hope you haven't torn my dress? Hold it up when you walk." MRS. RAVENSHAWE *follows this advice, but a portion of her clothing, semi-detached, trails ominously at her heels. Everybody sits down. The accident to* MRS. RAVENSHAWE *appears to have checked the flow of dialogue, so that* MAUD VIVIEN's *next remark is singularly apt.*)

MAUD: Nobody seems to be talking very much.

REGINALD (*to* MRS. RAVENSHAWE): Your daughter has kindly asked me to stay until my ankle is well again. I hope it won't put you to much inconvenience?

MR. RAVENSHAWE (*hastily replying for his wife*): Rather not! We were just going to ask you ourselves, weren't we, dear?

MRS. RAVENSHAWE: Yes, Aubrey.

CAPTAIN DE LANCY (*glancing at his watch*): It's getting late. I must be going. I'll roll round and see you now and then Reggie.

(*Exit.*)

MR. *and* MRS. RAVENSHAWE (*with remarkable unanimity*): I think we must be going too.

MAUD: So do I.

(*Exeunt, leaving* REGINALD *and* ANGELINA *alone.*)

REGINALD (*sentimentally*): Time won't lie heavy on my hands while I have you to nurse me, Miss Ravenshawe.

ANGELINA (*giggling*): Neither will it on mine.

REGINALD: I feel as if I had known you for ages. So I have. I have seen you passing in your car. How lovely you looked! Unfortunately, I am a poor man, Angelina. May I call you Angelina?

ANGELINA: If you'll let me call you Reginald.

REGINALD: It has been the dream of my life to hear those lovely lips pronounce that name. (*With deep feeling*): No woman has called me Reginald since—since the last scandal. (*He breaks down once more.*)

ANGELINA (*simply*): Well, you'll hear it a good deal from this on.

REGINALD: I once heard it in a dream . . .

ANGELINA (*wisely changing the subject*): What do you think of Maud?

REGINALD (*unguardedly*): I think she's very beautiful.

ANGELINA (*exhibiting unmistakable signs of jealousy*): Well, I don't, so there.

REGINALD: Don't you?

ANGELINA: No: and she's not an heiress.

REGINALD (*significantly*): Would that some one else were not.

ANGELINA (*fluttered*): Balmer, do you mean——?

REGINALD (*hastily*): No, no: I mean nothing. I am going to sleep, I think. (*Closes his eyes.*)

ANGELINA (*rising in distraction*): Oh, he loves her. I see it all now. The way he looked at her. And he said he thought she was beautiful. What shall I do? I will call mamma and tell her everything. No, I won't, though. That isn't the way. I will never return an unrequited affection. I'll show Reginald I don't care. I'll be nice to Captain De Lancy. That will show him.

(*Re-enter* CAPTAIN DE LANCY.)

ANGELINA: So you've rolled round already! You *are* quick!

CAPTAIN DE LANCY: I've forgotten my umbrella—what? Ah, here it is.

ANGELINA: He's asleep. Don't make such a row.

CAPTAIN DE LANCY (*amorously*): I don't want to wake him. I'd let him sleep there all day, if it gave me a chance of talking to you.

ANGELINA (*coyly*): Oh, Victor! May I call you Victor?

CAPTAIN DE LANCY: Certainly. You may call me Vic, if you like. (*Consults watch again.*) Well, I must be going. Good-bye.

ANGELINA: I'll come to the door with you.

(Exeunt together.)

REGINALD *(opening his eyes, and fixing the audience gloomily)*: They thought I was asleep, but I heard all. And better a thousand times that it should be so. Who am I to claim that pure, unstained flower of maidenhood? I who behaved disreputably at Monte Carlo, and was kicked out of the hotel for getting drunk before lunch. . . . Never—never. . . . I may be poor, but I am proud. I may have behaved like an ass, but my honour has never been tarnished.

The curtain falls amid tumultuous applause, at the end of which a clear treble voice, extremely like MR. RAVENSHAWE'S, *announces peremptorily,* "Act two will be left out, because they won't do it." *So the curtain rising on the third Act reveals* REGINALD *lying in much the same position as before, except that now his couch is furnished with a pillow and an eiderdown quilt, and he himself is sick unto death, mortally wounded in that fatal quarrel.* ANGELINA *has apparently been giving, or is about to give, him his medicine. She stands beside him, a bottle and spoon in her hand.*

REGINALD *(sitting up and clutching at his breast in agony)*: Hell and damnation! This pain again! *(Swoons.)*

ANGELINA: How he must suffer!

REGINALD *(once more reviving)*: Take that stuff away. I am past all first aids now. Angelina! *(Deliriously, and with a frantic gesture.)* Take it away!

*(*ANGELINA, *alarmed, drops the bottle, which strikes the leg of the couch and breaks.)*

ANGELINA: Oh!

(A Voice from the audience:—"What was in it, dear? I hope it won't leave a stain on the carpet. Bridget, you'd better go and wipe it up at once.")

ANGELINA *(reassuringly)*: It's not ink: it's only liquorice wine.

MR. RAVENSHAWE *(from the hall)*: I knew you'd break it, and you said you wouldn't. You can just make me some more.

ANGELINA: Don't be so greedy. It wasn't more than half full, and you'd watered it twice.

(Enter BRIDGET, *with a cloth and a bucket of hot water.)*

BRIDGET: You'll have to get up, Master Palmer. It's all run under the sofa.

REGINALD (*rising from his death-bed*): Oh, dash it all, you know. That spoils the whole thing.

The other members of the company enter, and Maud Vivien says rather
*   spitefully, "It's Ann's fault. She would insist on being Angelina."*

"Are we to take it that the performance is concluded?" asked the canon, getting up out of his arm-chair, "because, if so, I fancy you'd better wash before supper. We all enjoyed the play immensely."

"Look at Edward," giggled Ann. "His moustache has spread all over his face."

"Oh, can't we have supper the way we are?" cried Jim. "What's the use of fagging about washing when we'll have to do it over again in the morning?"

But Aunt Caroline was firm. "There must be washing. And proper washing with soap," she added. "I've got my pillow-cases to consider."

"Were we good?" asked Ann, modestly.

"Yes dear, very good. I don't know how you made it up so well."

"I don't think Miss Johnson liked it," Ann whispered. "Her face got awfully red."

"It's rotten that bottle breaking!" said Palmer, as, in the seclusion of the gentlemen's dressing-room, he divested himself of Reginald's attire. "It was in the last act that I was going to have the best rag of all—when Reginald's dying. . . . Look here, Jim, you might fold up those clothes instead of chucking them all over the place!"

"I'm going to fold them if you give me time."

"I think it's just as well we stopped when we did," Edward remarked. "Your language, Reginald, was beginning to get fairly sultry."

"It was only dramatic—to express suffering."

"It did that all right:—sounded as if you'd just taken a full-pitcher on the knee."

"I noticed old Drumsticks looking a bit fidgety," cried Jim, fluttering about in his shirt, pursued by Pouncer, who was bent on licking his bare legs. "Lend me that dressing-gown, Palmer. It's not worth while putting on proper clothes just to have to take them off again in about ten minutes. Ouu!" he squealed. "Go away, Pouncer, you old rascal. Grif, call him away. He's frightfully tickly!"

"Miss Johnson didn't like it," said Grif. "Perhaps we should have done something else."

He appeared to be the only one, however, who felt pangs of uneasiness, and indeed, with the exceptions of Palmer and Edward, all had acted their parts in perfect good faith, and without the least desire to travesty Miss Johnson's work.

"I wouldn't have done it if she hadn't kicked up such a row this morning," Palmer defended himself, "and everybody knows it was only a joke."

"Oh, she'll get over it," said Edward, more callously. "Serves her jolly well right too!"

"I think it was rather rotten," said Grif, "though of course we didn't intend it to be. I never thought she'd mind, till I saw she did. I'm going to tell her I'm sorry."

"Well, run away and tell her now," cried Edward, angrily. "Nobody will stop you. You didn't do much anyway, except tear Aunt Caroline's skirt."

CHAPTER IX

POUNCER

'Wherefore hast thou left me now?'
—Shelley.

THE circus was but a sorry affair—a poor travelling show, with a few lean horses, a troup of performing dogs, a sick monkey in a cage, and several dubious specimens of humanity decked out in tinsel and colour,—yet the news that after all they were not to go to see it was received in a dead silence of disappointment. Later on, in the shrubbery, it was discussed freely enough, Jim inveighing noisily against the evil of not fulfilling promises that had been definitely made. He preached open defiance and gained nothing thereby save a gloomy threat from Edward that if he didn't shut up his head would be smacked. Grif alone accepted the new decree with equanimity.

He had been in the town with grandpapa when the miserable procession had gone by to a hollow merriment of drums and cymbals, and had listened to grandpapa's angry condemnation of a civilization that permitted such barbarities to exist. The sight of those scared, half-starved, professional brothers of Pouncer had in fact quite extinguished Grif's own enthusiasm for the circus, and he had suggested, as an immediate remedy, that grandpapa should buy up all the quadrupedal members of it, and establish them in comfort at the Glebe for the rest of their lives.

"It's all very well for you not to want to go," Jim pointed out indignantly. "You've seen it already—at least, you've seen some of it."

Grif admitted that he had, while Edward and Palmer conversed in undertones.

"Perhaps they'll stay over the week-end," suggested the optimistic Ann, "and then we'll be able to see them in church."

This remark was received with derision, and poor Ann retired from the council feeling hurt, for, after all, she wanted to go to the circus quite as much as any of the boys.

Thus it came and passed, Johnnie's mixed and meagre description of them being the only glimpse they were vouchsafed of its mysterious glories. There had been songs and riding and the performing dogs and a kind of Wild West play with a lot of firing off of guns, but it hadn't been much good, and the sick monkey had failed to get through its tricks even when stimulated by a whip. Some of the spectators had expressed their dissatisfaction openly at the second performance, and the show was moving on that day, Johnnie said, probably to the next town.

This was Johnnie's report, and Grif had forgotten all about it when, on coming out on to the croquet-lawn after dinner, he found Ann there alone and in tears.

"What's up?" he asked, putting his hands on her shoulders. "Where is everybody?"

"They've gone to see the circus off," said Ann, wiping her eyes.

"And they promised before dinner I might come, and then they said I mightn't, because they would maybe have to run to catch up with it."

Ann could pour out her troubles to Grif, though she would never have dreamed of doing so to her other brothers or to Barbara. But Grif was different from them; he was somehow always nicest when other people weren't nice at all. Every one knew that—even Jim, who had rarely any troubles that could not be cured by a few minutes' passionate brawling with the Fates.

"Is Barbara with them?" Grif asked consolingly.

"No; she says circuses are vulgar: she's going to pay visits with Aunt Caroline."

"Well, let's play a game of something."

"It's too hot," said Ann, whose heart was with Palmer and Edward and Jim, racing along a dusty road in pursuit of fugitive mountebanks.

"We'll play jacks, if you like; it's not too hot for that. Or I'll read you the *Arabian Nights*. I'm in the middle of a story, but I can tell you the beginning."

Ann tugged at her pig-tail. All traces of grief had vanished from her plump and ruddy countenance. "I saw a man with earrings round at the back of the house just before dinner. I'm sure he was a circus man."

"What was he doing?"

"Nothing. I told Edward and Jim about him, and they said he couldn't be a circus man, because the circus was leaving. If he wasn't, then he was a birate. He looked just like one."

"What would a pirate be doing here? Besides, there aren't any pirates now—at least there are only a few. He may have been a Lascar."

"What's a Lascar?" inquired Ann, with sudden interest.

"He's a kind of sailor—one that wears earrings and gets up mutinies. No captain will take a Lascar on his ship unless he's short-handed and has to."

"I'd rather like to be in a mutiny," Ann said.

"You mightn't like it if you got marooned—put on a desert island and left there."

"I *would* like it. When I grow up I'm going to live on an island anyway."

"You're on an island now," Grif reminded her.

"I mean a quite small island," pursued Ann, reflectively. "One that you can see all round."

"If it's so small as that there'll be nobody there."

"There'll be a coast-guard station there. I like coast-guards. And I'll ask Balmer to come and stay with me: and maybe you—now and then. But I won't have any ladies: I'll have nothing but boys and men: and I'll be their queen and send them to berform tasks; and then when they come back they'll kneel down and kiss my hand, and I'll think of something else for them to do."

"I'm afraid I'll not be able to come to your island even if you *do* ask me," said Grif apologetically. "I'll probably be in Arabia."

Ann felt her island growing very small indeed. She wished she had thought of Arabia.

"Arabia's far better than an island," Grif went on. "You can't go out to take a walk there without something happening—some queer kind of thing. And there are deserts that nobody has ever crossed since the beginning of the world, except Solomon. That's where the demons and the efrits live. After riding on a camel through the desert for days and days you come to a bronze statue of a knight on horseback. Then you get down and push him round on his pedestal and he points with his lance to show you what way you're to go. And you come at last to a city where everything is silent and asleep, and you walk through the streets, but you see no one, and you go into a palace and across marble courts with fountains playing, but still there is no one. At last you reach a door that is just a little open, and through the door you hear the sound of a boy reading out of the *Koran*. He is kept there a prisoner by a female efrit, and you help him to escape, because that is your destiny and nobody else could do it. Both of you get on an ebony horse, and it flies up into the air, and very soon you see a black cloud, like a thunder cloud, coming after you. But the boy knows that this is really the female efrit, and she comes frightfully fast, and just when she is over your head she lets a big stone drop on the horse and breaks it, and you are falling down into the sea when a roc catches you and brings you to its nest. When the roc flies away next morning you climb down a cliff and find a door leading underground, and you come to beautiful gardens where the plants talk, and there are big dogs like Pouncer, only far bigger, with eyes like mill-wheels. . . . Where *is* Pouncer? Did Edward and Palmer take him?"

"No. . . . There they go!"

This last remark was called forth by the resplendent apparition of Aunt Caroline and Barbara, who had come out of the house and were walking down the drive.

"She told me she *loved* paying visits," Ann said, despondently, as she gazed after her sister. "How can anybody love sitting on a chair and not talking except when they're asked a question?"

Grif stretched himself on his back, with all his limbs outspread. "I expect she likes the cakes and things."

"She says it isn't for that. And when I asked her what it *was* for, she said I was too young to understand. I think she's awful when she gets into a grown-up mood."

"Girls are always like that—at least, they get that way sooner or later."

"I won't ever. I hate wearing my best dress, and I hate wearing gloves, and I hate sitting in drawing-rooms."

"You'll get to like it some day. That's the difference between girls and boys. All girls go the same way. It's a kind of disease. Edward's nearly as bad, though he isn't a girl. I mean, he likes dressing himself up and putting grease on his hair and going out to parties where there's dancing."

"I *hate* dancing," said Ann. "So does Balmer. I *love* Balmer. He's the nicest boy I ever saw."

After a minute she added, "You're nice too."

"Master Grif, have you seen Pouncer? Other days he does be looking for his dinner long before it's ready, and to-day he hasn't come for it at all."

The speaker was Hannah, and her words had an electrical effect on Grif. Instantly there flashed upon his mind a vision of the man with the earrings. What had he wanted? Why should he have come prowling about the house?

He turned to Ann. "Where was the man you saw this morning? Where was he going to?"

"He was in the wood, and he wasn't going anywhere. I was under the ash-tree, playing Jonah in his bower, and I saw him through the branches. But when I came out to have a better look he wasn't there."

The search that followed was rapid and thorough—a search in which Bridget and Hannah and Ann all joined—but no Pouncer was to be found. Then, without saying a word to anyone, bare-headed and in his slippers, and with his breath rising painfully in his throat, Grif rushed down the drive and out on to the road.

As he ran towards the town he *knew* Pouncer had been stolen. His face had lost its colour, and was strained and woebegone, but he had no time for lamentations, he must catch the circus and get Pouncer back. Just outside the town he passed the field where the booth had been pitched. It was bare now, littered with torn papers and rubbish, and the grass was trampled down. Only two or three children were playing near it; there was no sign of his brothers; and Grif ran on to the town.

He stopped at the first shop he reached—a butcher's—to ask which way the circus had gone. The big red-faced butcher was standing at his door taking the air, and Grif was so breathless and incoherent that his question had to be repeated several times before the butcher was able to grasp it. Even then his answer, being mingled with hostile criticisms of the show and of the perform-ers, came with provoking slowness. "They'll likely be stopping at Rathcarragh," he at length surmised, "if they get that far without being jailed." He was dwelling on the improbability of this when he became aware that Grif was no longer with him, and, in aston-ishment, watched him scudding on down the street. He entered his shop to communicate the tidings to his wife, and Grif tore on at full speed.

For he had heard the whistle of an engine, and now saw a white trail of smoke thinly outspread against the sky.

Could he do it? His legs were giving under him, and once he fell and cut his stocking and his knee. But he did not stop. Though his heart seemed bursting, and everything swam before his eyes, he ran on; while the white road seem to tilt up steeply in front of him in an impossible hill.

He could hear the shrill, rending noise of escaping steam now, and the slamming of doors. Another second or two and he staggered into the station. The train had not yet started, but the guard was waving his flag. Grif sprang at the door of the nearest carriage, which happened to be empty, tugged the handle round, and scrambled in.

He was safe; the train was already moving out from the platform: then everything grew suddenly dark, and his head dropped back against the cushion.

When he recovered they were rushing through a sun-scorched landscape of meadows and farmlands. He wet his handkerchief and wiped the dirt out of his cut knee. Fortunately it was not bleeding much; and he turned down his stockings, and brushed the dust off his knickerbockers.

He looked eagerly out of the windows on both sides, but could see no sign of a road. The time went by with almost unendurable slowness. They tore through a small station, and he began to fear that the train might not stop at Rathcarragh after all, or that perhaps they had already passed it, for he had not been able to read the name of the place they had left behind. They seemed to have been travelling for miles and miles, for hours and hours, when the engine whistled, and he felt that they were slowing down.

The train drew in at a platform, and before it stopped Grif jumped out. He had no ticket, but luckily he had enough money to pay for one, though it left him destitute. As he made his way through the streets of the town he looked out for a poster of the circus, but saw none. It was market day, and there were a good many people about. Nobody, however, took any notice of a rather forlorn-looking little boy in slippers, who eagerly scanned every wall where there was a bill pasted up. A few minutes' walking brought him to the edge of the town. Beyond this there were only detached houses and gardens; and then the open country. Grif did not know what to do.

There was a public-house near, and he went in to make inquiries, but nobody had heard anything about a circus. The man in charge was quite friendly, however, so friendly indeed that Grif told him his whole story, and became, in an atmosphere heavy with the fumes of stout and whisky, the centre of a small group of solemn listeners, whose fishy eyes and thickened utterance suggested that a considerable amount of refreshment had already been given and taken. When Grif's tale was finished, and the rather fuddled sympathy of the audience had been expressed, the potman produced some biscuits and cheese, and insisted that he should fill his pockets. He was also able to point out the road by which the circus would arrive if it were coming, and where Grif might watch for it. He began to give his own version of the affair to three or four new customers who had drifted in, and in the midst of it Grif made his escape.

He followed the road the man had pointed out, though no longer very hopefully. He felt now that it would have been wiser to have waited at home, trusting to grandpapa and the police. Unfortunately he had come too far to turn back, nor had he any money to pay for a second railway-ticket. He walked on and on, under a blazing sun, which lay upon the wide expanse of fields and meadows like the heavy breath of a furnace. There seemed to be no air, and the white road, with its thick carpet of dust, dazzled his eyes. The heat of the sun upon his bare head, the strong glare reflected from the earth, seemed to enter into his brain in a burning blinding light. His feet began to drag a little, his slippers were filled with dust, but he trudged on bravely, though his weariness added to his depression, and he would have liked to have lain down by the roadside and cried.

With his thin leather slippers he was but poorly shod for a tramp like this, and his feet began to ache, till at last each step he took caused him pain. Only the thought that every moment of delay might increase Pouncer's danger kept him up, lent him a kind of nervous strength to continue plodding on. The town he had left behind him had long since dropped out of sight. Whichever way he turned now the landscape presented the same monotonous, dazzling aspect. The tall green corn and barley stood motionless in the fields; the cows were lying down in such shade as they could find; the birds were silent and hidden: only an insect life hummed and thridded and buzzed in the hedgerows. He felt very thirsty, but he had not passed a cottage for some time, nor passed a stream. And the glittering light seemed to bend and quiver before his tired eyes, weaving strange patterns, casting reflected, shimmering flames, as if from the burnished roofs of a city of mirage.

Two hours must have gone by; he had climbed hills and descended valleys; yet no sign of the travelling circus appeared. The heat was no longer so intense; the glare had decreased; the sun was sinking—casting longer and longer shadows. He reached at last a little copse of beech-trees, and heard the sound of running water. He scrambled through the hedge. He could rest for a while here, and still watch the road; nothing could pass without his hearing it and seeing it. He bent down to the stream and drank from his cupped hands, and splashed the cold water over his aching head. It brought him instant refreshment, but, more even than the water, the shadow was delicious as some healing balm. Leaning against the bank he closed his eyes for a moment the better to enjoy it, and a delicious darkness, like a cool, sweet-scented oil, caressed his sun-scorched nerves.

When he awoke it was quite dark and he knew he must have slept for many hours. It took him but an instant to realize his situation, and with its hopelessness he broke down and cried. He had slept through those hours when he should have been watching. What use to look for the circus now?

He would never find it:—never, never. And Pouncer must have passed with it! He would not understand; he would know only that he had been deserted—left to these cruel men who would certainly ill-treat him. Perhaps he had felt that Grif was near, and had barked, while his master had slept on in brutal unconsciousness. A passion of grief and remorse shook his slight frame as he lay sobbing, his face buried in his arms. Above him the night wind whispered in the dim trees—remote, yet strangely gentle. Moonlight chequered the dark grass with pools of milky pallor. A dead silence, save for this rustling leafy murmur, was over everything.

CHAPTER X

THROUGH THE DARKNESS

'But who that beauteous Boy beguil'd,
That beauteous Boy to linger here?
Alone, by night, a little child,
In place so silent and so wild—
Has he no friend, no loving mother near?'
                                        —*Coleridge*.

'Let not the dark thee cumber:
What though the moon does slumber?
The stars of the night
Will lend thee their light
Like tapers clear without number.'
                                        —*Herrick*.

SUDDENLY Grif sat up, for he had heard a bark. Was it only in his imagination, that low, deep wow-ow-ow-ow, coming to him through the darkness? He sat listening intently, afraid almost to draw his breath. Then it came again:—it was Pouncer.

Grif started to his feet. The barking came from the other side of the copse, and though in the stillness of the night in this solitary place such a sound might travel far, he felt that it was not really very distant. Perhaps two hundred yards away, possibly less; at all events it would be there to guide him, for now he heard it once more.

He had not the faintest idea what time it was, but judging from the darkness it was probably close upon midnight. It might be later, but he did not think so. In any case the circus must have encamped for the night, and be at this moment within a short distance of the very spot where he had fallen asleep.

The first thing to do was to get out of the copse, for here, at every step he took, he seemed to tread on a dry stick which snapped with a noise like a pistol shot, and silence was essential to the carrying out of his plan. In a few minutes he had reached the fields beyond the trees, and with that he paused to consider what he should do next. Pouncer's bark sounded from somewhere on the left of the road, and, keeping well in the shadow, he moved along the rising ground with all the stealth of an Indian. He wished he could be a little more certain as to the time, for he felt that much depended on this—depended on whether the camp were fixed up for the night and its occupants asleep. On the other hand, he could not afford to wait too long, since it might already be nearer morning than he imagined. No doubt the circus people would be up and abroad quite early, and, though he knew pretty well where he was, a long journey still stretched between Grif and home.

Now that he was out of the plantation there was plenty of light; there was indeed too much; the fields and open ground being flooded by the moon. There was another outburst of barking, this time quite close at hand: then, as he reached the brow of the hill he had been climbing, he saw the caravan straight in front of him, not fifty yards away, its dark heavy outline black against the sky. Immediately beyond it he saw the gate by which it had entered. So they had not come by the road after all, or, if they had, they must have branched off on reaching a lane or side-track.

Grif stood still and gazed. There were no lights in the caravan— at least he could see none—but he wished he had some means of telling when they had been put out. Gradually he crept nearer. The caravan was drawn up beside the copse, from which it jutted at a right angle, the door being turned outward to the field. The animals probably were tethered close by. As he took another step forward a huge dark shape rose up heavily almost at his feet, sending Grif's heart into his mouth, till he recognized that it was only one of the horses. He advanced nearer and nearer, taking each step with the utmost precaution. Then his foot caught in a bramble and he stumbled. There instantly arose a furious and united barking in which the individual note of Pouncer was lost, and Grif hastily drew back among the trees.

But the noise went on, and presently, as he peeped out, he saw a woman step down the ladder into the moonlight, a thick stick in her hand. She called to the dogs angrily, but as the tumult did not cease proceeded to take more forcible measures, and Grif could hear the hollow thuds of her stick, followed by shrill yelps, as she scattered blows indiscriminately. His blood boiled to think of Pouncer being beaten. Probably he would have sprung out of his hiding-place there and then had not the woman suddenly stopped. After a few more threatening words she retraced her steps, and disappeared again inside the caravan.

Grif waited for perhaps ten minutes, during which time the only noise he heard was an occasional whine, and the deep note of Pouncer: then he walked straight to where the dogs were tied up. There followed a fresh outburst of barking, but it ceased almost immediately, for he was perfectly fearless with animals, and, as he stood among them, patting their heads and talking to them in a soft whisper, the circus dogs recognized a friend and fawned upon him, while Pouncer struggled and tore at his chain, next moment covering Grif, who squatted on the ground beside him, with a thousand licks and caresses. So excited was Pouncer by this sudden appearance of his master that Grif found it difficult to set him free. With the other dogs it was an easier matter, however, and in a few minutes all were at liberty—the bulldog, a great Dane, three terriers, and a spaniel.

In his eagerness Grif did not notice that the woman had reappeared, till a sudden shrill cry awakened him to his danger. She was followed this time by a half-dressed hobbledehoy, who, as Grif took to his heels, started in pursuit. With Pouncer racing on ahead, Grif tore down the lunary field towards the point he had come from, but, as he ran, he could hear the thudding steps and panting breath of his enemy growing rapidly nearer. He was racing downhill like the wind, the circus dogs scattered in all directions and the air full of their noise; already the road was in sight, when he slipped and fell headlong. With a gruff shout of triumph the circus boy darted upon him, and at the same moment Grif saw a compact whitish form rise in the air and strike against the body of his pursuer with a heavy thud. There was a scream of terror and pain, a rending, worrying sound, followed by another and another scream. Then something seemed to be torn away, and Grif was conscious of a dark flying figure which leaped madly for an overhanging branch, caught it, and, with a display of acrobatic energy and skill that probably surpassed anything ever seen in the circus ring, swung itself into safety.

"It serves you jolly well right for stealing dogs, and I hope he bit you well," Grif panted.

His remark was greeted by a flood of filthy language, oddly mingled with threats legal and bellicose, and wails of impotent suffering.

Pouncer meanwhile stood motionless and watchful, a deep, vibrating rumble, like the bass note of an organ, coming from his throat and chest. Then a shrill cry was raised behind them, and Grif, wheeling round, saw the woman with the stick. The boy in the tree saw her also, and redoubled his shouts and wails. Followed by Pouncer, Grif trotted on, while the voices of his enemies, who nevertheless made no further attempt to molest him, sent a stream of abuse after them through the night.

He was surprised, now that he had time to think of it, that no one else had joined in the chase, but he had not the slightest inclination to await further developments. He hurried along the road till the silence behind him told him that all immediate danger was passed; then he began to wonder where the other dogs had gone to, and to hope they would be wise enough to seek more comfortable homes. If he only had been able to bring the monkey with him, his expedition would have been really successful!

They had been walking for a considerable time, Grif with the cheerful sense that each step must be bringing them nearer home, when they reached another wood, though this one, surrounded by a stone wall, seemed to be a portion of a private estate. Surely, Grif thought, they would be quite safe here, and could sleep the rest of the night away! The wall of rough stone would be easy to climb, and the circus men, even if they discovered their hiding-place, would never dare to follow them.

So he helped Pouncer over and then climbed up himself. Once inside, they came immediately on a broad path, and presently caught sight of a big square house, looking very white and silent. But Grif walked past it, and on over moss and bracken, till, in a little hollow, he dropped down, and cuddling up close to Pouncer lay staring at the stars. The air was warm and filled with a delicate

aromatic fragrance; the stars were very near and twinkled kindly;
the old moon seemed to laugh down on a good boy. He had a
sense of being quite close to human beings, for the house was but
a hundred yards away, and, after he had shared the remnants of
his biscuits and cheese with Pouncer, he said his prayers and fell
quietly asleep.

CHAPTER XI

INSPECTOR DORSET

> 'Hark, hark!
> Bow-wow.
> The watch-dogs bark:
> Bow-wow.'
> —*Shakespeare.*

ANN had followed Grif a little way down the road, but she
soon turned aside to hunt for Pouncer on her own account.
Not that she had much hope of finding him: it was indeed more
from a sense of duty than anything else that she now and then
called aloud, "Bouncer! Bouncer!"

But no Bouncer replied, and Ann presently returned to the
house.

She did not think of telling grandpapa, principally because they
had all received strict injunctions from Aunt Caroline that grandpapa's study was never to be entered except by special invitation:
and then, she did not really feel anxious herself; Bouncer would be
sure to turn up; for Grif had not told her of his suspicion, and Ann
never for a moment connected the missing dog with her Lascar of
the morning.

So when, towards teatime, the boys returned, she was in the
midst of giving a Sunday School lesson to a class of inattentive
dolls and a stuffed elephant. She broke off a sensational and cir-
cumstantial account of Joseph's adventures to ask if they had seen
Grif.

"No; and we didn't see the circus either, though we went ever so
far. They must have taken some other road."

It was Jim who replied, while he gazed down at his sister's dolls with a sneaking desire to join in the game.

"Grif went out to look for Bouncer. He's been lost since dinner-time."

"Who has? . . . That's my elephant, you know."

"Oh, Jim! it isn't; you gave it to me your very self!"

"Who's lost?" Edward took up.

"Bouncer. We all looked for him—Bridget and Hannah and me and Grif. And then Grif ran away down the drive, and I don't know where he's gone."

"He's probably having a singing-lesson. . . . What are you going to sleep for, Dorset?"

Palmer, seated with his back against the tree under which Ann's Sunday School class also reposed, made no reply. An idea had just occurred to him, and his finger-tips were joined. He knew that from this sign Edward ought to be able to see that he was thinking deeply, therefore there was no need for words. As a matter of fact, the same suspicion that had flashed on Grif had occurred to Palmer, though their methods of following it up were characteristically different, and Palmer's deductions went a good deal further. He did not mention to Edward what these deductions were; he made no attempt to contradict the singing-lesson fallacy; his chum, like Doctor Watson or Bunny, would be informed when a plan of action had been properly matured, but in the meantime Palmer must have a free field.

Presently he dropped his attitude of passive dreamer for that of man of action. He sprang to his feet. "I want you to lend me fifteen shillings and your bicycle."

Edward stared.

To be quite truthful, the first portion of Palmer's request had been thrown in purely for the sake of dramatic effect. He knew just as well as Ann and Jim and everybody else did that Edward had not got fifteen shillings, nor five shillings, nor, probably, even one shilling. Grif was the only one who ever had any money, and that was simply because he usually forgot to spend it till he was thoughtfully reminded by his brothers and sisters that a suitable occasion had arisen. Therefore Palmer did not repeat his demand, but retired, leaving his audience duly impressed, and raised the necessary sum in the kitchen.

"It's only for three days," he assured the good-natured Hannah, who would have been quite content to wait for repayment till the day of judgment. But it eased Palmer's conscience to set himself this strict time limit. He knew that to borrow money from an obliging cook was not at all the proper thing for a gentleman to do, and only the direst necessity, and the fact that he must be in possession of it before six o'clock, would have caused him to take such a step. A minute or two later the little group on the lawn saw him scorching down the avenue at full speed on Edward's bicycle, and Ann and Jim began to speculate wildly as to what he could be going to do. Edward, on the other hand, felt sulky and ill-used. Even prolonged experience of it could never reconcile him to Palmer's love of secrecy.

The problem was interrupted by the return of Aunt Caroline and Barbara. Ann and Jim raced to meet them, screaming out the news about Pouncer and Grif, and adding a rapid account of the bewildering behaviour of Palmer.

"They weren't at the Batts'," said Aunt Caroline, who, like Edward and the others, appeared to take it for granted that Pouncer and his master were together. "We've just come from there. I do wish that child had some rudimentary sense of time. There's not a bit of use waiting tea for him. He's just as likely to come back at eight as within the next half hour."

This was perfectly true, but to-night Palmer also was late for tea, and when he entered the room it was with an air of reserve which a lively cross-examination carried on by Ann and Jim quite failed to break down.

When eight o'clock came, and still Grif had not appeared, Aunt Caroline began to grow uneasy. Miss Johnson, who considered that she had been most unjustly snubbed for certain remarks made on the last occasion of his absence, carefully refrained from commenting on the matter, but Aunt Caroline decided that she had better tell grandpapa.

"He really must stop this kind of thing," said the canon, mildly. "I'll just stroll over to the church and see if he's there, and if he's not I'll go on to Bradley's lodgings. I'll have to tell Bradley that he's not to keep him so late, though I'm afraid he's hardly more reliable than Grif himself."

"And if he isn't there," said Aunt Caroline, "what will you do?"

"I suppose I'll come home without him. I know, dear, it doesn't sound brilliant, but what else is there for it? We can hardly send poor Drummond out again to scour the country. After all, nothing very much can happen to him; and surely when it begins to get dark he'll be reminded that tea is at six."

"But perhaps he didn't find Pouncer, and it may be that that's keeping him."

"Well, I'll go to the church in any case."

At a quarter to nine, however, the canon returned alone. "Has he come back?" were his first words, and Aunt Caroline's disappointed face was sufficient answer to them. "Bradley says he hasn't seen him since the day before yesterday. It's rather provoking!"

Aunt Caroline looked worried. "We can't allow this sort of thing to go on," she declared. "If I only could be sure that he had just not bothered to come home I should be very angry."

"Well, as you're evidently not sure, I suppose you aren't," said the canon, lightly. "I don't see how he could lose himself even if he wanted to. He must have discovered some new friends. I think I'll go into the town and make inquiries."

Aunt Caroline laid down her work. "If you wait a minute I'll put on my hat and go with you." Then, becoming aware of the presence of Palmer and Edward and Barbara, she added peremptorily, "And you children run off to bed at once!"

"It's not Dorset's and my time yet," replied Edward, resenting the injustice that would deprive him of ten legitimate minutes.

"It's always time to do what you're told," returned Aunt Caroline sharply, and Edward felt he had better say no more.

Meanwhile Palmer was 'torn by conflicting emotions'—the desire to bring a carefully arranged plan to its brilliant conclusion and show all his cards in one dazzling surprise, and the guilty consciousness that he was withholding information which would certainly throw light on the matter in hand. The struggle was a brief one, and before Aunt Caroline had time to go upstairs for her hat he said, "I think Grif has gone after the circus."

"The circus!" Aunt Caroline almost screamed. "What circus? You don't mean to tell me that you knew all along he had run off with those horrible men?"

"I don't know anything," Palmer answered quietly.

But Aunt Caroline's suspicions were now thoroughly aroused. "What made you think of it then?"

"Because he went out to look for Pouncer, and I think Pouncer was stolen by one of the circus men. Ann saw a strange man with earrings prowling about just before dinner."

"Really, Palmer! you might have said all this at first, when you *knew* how anxious we were! I think it's too bad of you! Goodness only knows what may have happened to the child! I can't imagine how you could be so stupid as to sit there dumb all the time, while we were racking our brains to think what had become of him! And you too, Edward! I'll never be able to put the least confidence in either of you again."

"*I* knew nothing about it," cried Edward, indignantly. "And Dorset's only guessing, because Grif wasn't at Mr. Bradley's."

"You both of you knew about that horrid man being here."

"I knew what Ann told us, but I'd forgotten all about it."

"Well, well," the canon interrupted, "we're only wasting time. If you're coming, Caroline, you'd better get ready at once."

"What did you keep so dark about it all for?" Edward asked his friend, when they were safe in the privacy of their own room. Jim, though he had determined to lie awake and listen for Grif's return, was already sound asleep.

"Because I had a good reason for doing so," Palmer answered dreamily.

"I don't know what it was, then!" growled Edward. "Did you find out anything when you went off that time on the bike?"

Palmer shook his head. "I found out everything that I *have* found out when I was sitting under the tree—sleeping, as you called it."

But Edward was feeling rather sore at Palmer's reticence, and, when he thought of the unfortunate Grif, other emotions, too, seemed to clamour for expression. "Well, I think it's pretty rotten not saying something. You knew Grif was only a kid, and not even a kid who's much good at looking after himself. Anything may happen to him if he gets in among those toughs, especially if they have stolen Pouncer."

Palmer looked troubled. He wished himself, now, that he had spoken sooner.

"I'm sorry," he muttered, gazing out of the window. "I didn't tell you, because they none of them ever do till the whole thing's fixed up."

"Who's 'they'?" asked Edward impatiently. "I don't know what you're talking about."

"I mean Sherlock Holmes never told Watson, and Raffles never told Bunny."

Edward laughed unpleasantly.

"I suppose you think you're like them, don't you? Well, you aren't, and never will be. And even if you were, I'm certainly not your Watson or your Bunny."

These words, and still more the laugh which accompanied them, touched Palmer where he was most sensitive, and his cheeks flushed. "I *have* a plan," he said, "although you may talk. And I always intended you to be in it. I was going to tell you not to undress."

"You needn't bother: I'm not likely to till I know what's happened. If they go out to look for Grif I'm going with them."

"It won't be necessary," said Palmer, gloomily.

He went to a chest of drawers, and opening the lowest drawer pulled out a package hidden under sundry articles of clothing. He stripped off the paper.

"Where did you get that from?" Edward asked.

"I got it this afternoon. I saw it in the saddler's shop last week. It's a second-hand one, but it's all right, and I know how to use it." He eyed the revolver with a sort of melancholy joy.

"What are you going to do with it?"

"Perhaps nothing:—it all depends."

"Depends on what?"

Palmer was silent: he hated having to reveal his plans in this way. Then he said slowly: "In a little more than two hours from now I'll introduce you to the man with the earrings."

Edward's jaw dropped. "Where?"

"Here. I am expecting him to-night."

"But how——"

"The man with the earrings is the man who stole Pouncer."

"But how do you know he will come?" asked Edward, quickly growing sceptical as he recovered from his surprise.

"I can't tell you any more at present: you will learn everything in good time. Only, I promise you he will be here. What's more, I'm going to make things easy for him. As soon as the servants have gone to bed, and the house is locked up, I'm going to unlatch the pantry window. It would be rather a lark to see him cut out a pane of glass, but on the whole it's better to make things as simple as possible. . . . And I've got this for *you*." He dived again into the drawer, and brought out a life-preserver.

"But that's grandpapa's!"

"I know. I got it from his room when he was out at Mr. Bradley's."

Edward gripped it, and described two or three flourishes before bringing it down remorselessly upon the head of an imaginary burglar.

"You'll be a great man, Dorset," he whispered, "if this comes off. And I'll take back what I said about Raffles. . . . Only—you don't think anything will happen to Grif?"

"Nothing will happen to him, because, for one thing, he won't find the circus. *We* couldn't find it, and he didn't start till long after-wards. He may have got lost, but somebody will bring him home either to-night or to-morrow morning; and when he does come we'll have Pouncer for him."

Edward had suddenly grown thoughtful. "But suppose the other chap—the man with the earrings—has a revolver too?"

"He won't get a chance to use it. That's why I'm leaving a window open for him—a rather small window, at a fair height from the ground. When he's half way through I'll bag him."

"I see. It sounds all right, but wouldn't it be better to have Robert here—just in case of accidents."

"We don't require Robert. If we can't do a simple job like this on our own, we'd better go to bed and lock the door and latch the windows. .... While I keep him covered you'll tie his hands. Then we'll shut him into a room till the police turn up: or we can take him ourselves to the station. .... In the meantime, while we're waiting, we may as well read or something. We might have a game of bézique." All this dialogue had been carried on in an undertone, so as not to awaken Jim; and Edward, who had gone to the window, now whispered over his shoulder, "I believe I hear grandpapa and Aunt Caroline coming back." They both peeped out.

"Yes; here they are! I think I'll slip down and see if there's any news."

"Don't say a word about what we're going to do," Palmer warned him.

"Of course not. All the same, I think it's a bit risky—supposing the fellow *should* happen to turn up. I mean, if it came to the point, you couldn't really fire at him."

"I'm going to fire if it's necessary," said Palmer quietly, and his tone was so convincing that Edward felt uneasy.

"You're a queer chap, Dorset," he muttered. And it suddenly struck him that his whole relation with Palmer was queer; he who was a swell at games, and therefore, from any sensible and natural point of view, immensely Palmer's superior. Their mutual positions should have been exactly reversed. There seemed indeed no reason whatever why Palmer's will should always prevail, for he never blustered and very seldom got angry. Nor had Edward ever been particularly conscious that it *did* prevail until this moment. He had a transitory sense of discouragement. Things were not as they ought to be, and he somehow felt that in his dealings with Palmer they never would be altered.

All this flitted through his mind as he glided quietly downstairs to make inquiries about Grif. When he returned Palmer was lying on his back on the bed, staring up at the ceiling. He did not even look round as Edward came in.

"They've found out where he went to," Edward began excitedly. "He took a train, and they've telephoned to the police to look for him. Robert and another man have gone to search along the road. The circus hasn't turned up at Rathcarragh, and the police think they must be camping out, though they don't know where. They've promised to send word as soon as they hear anything. Grandpapa and Aunt Caroline aren't going to bed at present. I shouldn't be surprised if they sat up most of the night."

These last words alone appeared to interest Palmer. "Dash it all! that will mess up *our* plan!" he muttered, frowning. "It's nearly eleven now. In about half an hour we'll have to begin our watch, for there's no good leaving anything to chance."

"They'll hear us if we go downstairs," Edward said. "They'll be listening for every sound." He cast a tentative, sidelong glance at the recumbent Palmer, and, as that hero took no notice, went on more boldly, "I don't know that there's much in this plan of yours, Dorset. I dare say if we were to tell grandpapa he'd let us keep watch downstairs. If anybody *did* come he'd go away when he saw we were ready for him."

"We don't want him to go away," said Palmer, without altering his position, or even turning his head. "*I'm* going out. You needn't come if you don't want to. But if you spoil the thing now by blabbing either to your grandfather or to Miss Annesley I'll never tell you anything again as long as I live."

"I don't want to blab," answered Edward angrily.

"I'm going out by the window," Palmer continued. "I'll use a rope. I could get down by the spout if it was necessary, but the other will be less trouble."

"Where will you get a rope from?"

"There's one under your bed. I thought we might want it."

Edward peered under his bed and saw that there was indeed a coil of rope there. The whole thing seemed suddenly to grow more serious—too serious in fact—and in a state of not altogether pleasurable excitement he sat down to wait. As for Palmer, he appeared to have fallen asleep, and Edward's incredulity was once more gaining the upper hand when he heard him say, "If you're coming, put on your tennis-shoes. I'll fix the rope."

Edward obeyed, for he was not going to drop out, even if it meant a hand to hand tussle with the sinister person of the ear-rings, whose visage now, unaccountably, sprang up before his imagination, scowling, malevolent, the glare of murder in his eyes.

"If he has a knife," he whispered, "I'll not be able to do anything. I don't mind being shot, but the very thought of a knife makes me sick;—I can't help it."

"You won't have to tackle him at all. You can stay in your hiding-place till I call you. If he has a knife I'll very soon make him drop it. Put that cord in your pocket: it's to tie his wrists with."

Edward stuffed away the cord, and Palmer, noiselessly pushing up the window as far as it would go, climbed out on to the sill.

Edward watched him doubtfully. He wished he knew what was really passing in Dorset's mind, but he had not the slightest idea. He would have felt very much more comfortable if he could have been sure that the whole thing was only bluff, but he was growing less and less certain of this every moment.

"Shut the window after you," Palmer said. He knelt on the sill, and, catching the rope, lowered himself very quietly to the ground.

He stood there waiting while Edward, after closing the window as he had been told to do, followed him.

"Round by the back," Palmer whispered, and they stole along, keeping in the shadow of the house.

They crossed the moonlit yard and passed the stables. "I'll give you the tool-shed," Palmer whispered. "You can't possibly be seen if you're inside it, and there's a hole in the door you can look out through."

"But it's locked," Edward objected feebly.

"I have the key," Palmer replied, producing it as he spoke.

The tool-shed was merely a rough lean-to built against the wall, beyond which lay the wood; and it was through the wood that Palmer expected the burglar to come.

"Can't we both be together?" Edward asked.

"If you like, though I don't think it's so good."

This, nevertheless, was the plan they adopted, and Palmer closed the door, leaving it, as Edward noticed, unlatched. "We can sit on the roller and be perfectly comfortable. Better put this matting over it: it will make it softer and also warmer."

He tried the door, pushing it gently backward and forward, but it made no sound. "I've oiled the hinges," he explained, "so that it won't squeak. . . . I don't want you to move until I call you. Remember that—whatever you may see me doing. Probably I will shadow him when he is looking round. Of course he won't try to get in once he spots the light, and it's when he's coming back that I'll cop him. If they're two of them I dare say I'll have to let one go. . . . You needn't be afraid. If I have to shoot I won't miss. I know how to use these things, and I've had plenty of practice."

Edward made no reply, and the vigil began.

But the idea that there might be two burglars—which was a new one so far as Edward was concerned, and horribly plausible— was anything but reassuring. He wondered when Dorset would consider they had done their duty. He could not help believing now that his chum was acting on some positive information, and he wished the whole thing were well over, or that they had Robert and a policeman with them. Through everything he felt a strong admiration for his fellow-watcher. He recognized quite clearly that he was not so brave as Palmer was: all illusions on that score had dissolved like smoke. The only thing left for him to do was to pre- vent Dorset himself from guessing this, and Edward felt he would die in that attempt. Where his friend led he would follow, even should the very marrow be frozen in his bones. . . .

Surely it must be nearly morning! Surely Palmer must have fallen asleep! He hoped that grandpapa had not gone to bed, for somehow there was comfort in the thought of a friendly light burning not so far away. Then a horrible idea occurred to him. Suppose the burglars had been watching all the time and knew they were hidden in the shed: suppose, instead of passing the door, they suddenly crept in upon them in the dark, and with a knife. That wretched knife! Edward shivered and began mournfully to consider which part of his body he should prefer to be stabbed in. Not in the back:—anywhere, he thought, rather than in the back. But presently, like a pendulum, his reflections swung again towards hopefulness. If a burglar had been coming he would have arrived before this. He heard a cock crow in the distance, and the sound was infinitely welcome. He could have blessed that bird. Doubtless, like the Ancient Mariner, he *did* bless it unawares. The cock crowed three or four times, and then, as no other cock replied, relapsed into silence. Edward decided that he would count up to five hundred slowly, and then suggest that they should return to their room.

He had got as far as a hundred and seventy-nine when he felt a hand pressed down on his knee, and started violently. It was far too dark to see anything, but he felt Palmer's lips brush against his ear, and he heard the whispered words, "Somebody is coming through the wood."

Edward's heart began to thump so vigorously that he was afraid Palmer would hear it. That queer, hissing noise, too, must be his breathing! He stopped it at once. Somebody *was* coming; somebody was quite close to the wall. It was dreadful! A faint scuffling sound told him the wall was being climbed. And all the time he felt Palmer's hand gripping his leg firmly, as if to keep him still.

But the sounds at the wall had ceased. There was a longish pause, and then he became aware of voices whispering—of one voice at any rate. There followed another silence.

Edward felt that Palmer's hand had been withdrawn, and the next thing he noticed was the door of the shed slowly and noiselessly opening. He could see the thin streak of moonshine widening, he could make out Palmer's form as he stood peering out. Next moment he was alone in the shed.

Edward stood up. He seemed for the first time to realize that Palmer was running into great danger, and with that consciousness a new feeling dawned, a feeling that somehow passed through his blood like a warming, reviving cordial. He too rose and slipped out into the doorway, keeping in the blackness of the shadow. There was nothing to be seen. The man, if there was a man, had disappeared, and Palmer had disappeared also. Edward waited and watched and listened, his life-preserver stoutly gripped and ready for instant application.

And then, all at once, the thing happened. The two figures were clearly before him in the moonlight. There was an oath from the man, followed by Palmer's voice: "Put up your hands and stand still, or I'll let you have it."

The man obeyed, and Edward was about to rush out to tie him

up when he saw him make a sudden bound, striking at Palmer with a sidelong sweep of his arm. Palmer leaped back and the man ran for the wall, over which a head now appeared, shouting hoarsely, "Come on, George! It's only a kid!"

"No you don't," sang out Palmer, rushing in pursuit. "I'm damned if you do!"

There was a flash and a report, and George yelled: then he slipped on the damp grass and went down. Palmer *had* fired! Edward's brain blazed with excitement, as if a thousand rockets had shot up within it. He rushed out of his hiding-place just as George scrambled to his feet. "He's got me," George muttered plaintively, taking another step forward.

But Palmer was close behind him. "If you don't stop, I'll give it to you again, and this time through the body."

A dull crashing of breaking branches announced a hasty retreat on the other side of the wall, and George, forsaken, stood still, whining out a rapid string of entreaties: "Lemme go an' I'll say nothin' about what you've done. I could get you five years for this, young fella. You've no call to go shootin' a man that's not done any harm—only a bit of trespassin'.' "

"Tie his wrists, Weston. Hold your hands out, my man, we're going to jolly well tie you up, and then take you to the house. There are some questions we want to ask you, and we can talk more comfortably inside."

The captive redoubled his entreaties, for, like the others, he had heard the sound of a door opening, and of approaching footsteps. "Lemme go: I'm bleedin' to death," he begged. "An' I'll bring back the dog in the mornin'. It wasn't me took him, but I'll bring him back, misther. I haven't done nothin', an' you've had your plug at me."

"Are his hands tied, Weston?"

"Yes," answered Edward.

"Who's there?" called out the canon nervously. "What's all this? Edward—Palmer—what are you doing here, and who is this man?"

"They're after shootin' me, your riverence, that's what they've done," George began to whimper. "Just all along a' me havin' a dhrop a' drink in me, an' comin' over the wall. This young fella, he whips out a revolver, an' he has me desthroyed. I've a boot full a' blood already. But I don't want to make trouble. Just tell them to let me go quiet an' you'll hear no more from *me*."

"It's the man who stole Pouncer," said Palmer. "His name is George. He stole Pouncer to get him out of the way, so that he might break into the house. He came over the wall from the wood and I followed him; but as soon as he saw the light he thought better of it, and tried to get away."

"Come into the house," said the canon. "If you have been shot the wound will have to be seen to."

"No, yer riverence. I'll do that myself. Just you let me go quiet."

"Come on," said the canon. "I suppose you can walk?"

George muttered something, but he began to limp across the yard, Palmer, still keeping him covered, following in the rear. In this order they entered the house, where Aunt Caroline stood waiting for them in some alarm.

"You'd better get warm water and bandages, Caroline," her father said. "Our friend here has been winged, I'm afraid."

In the kitchen the patient was examined. There was only a flesh wound, and that not a very serious one, the bullet having passed clean through his leg, fortunately without cutting an artery. Palmer himself bathed it and tied it up with great neatness.

"And now," said the canon, "you'd better give an account of yourself. It was you who stole the dog, was it?"

"You'll not give me in charge, yer riverence? The dog's safe, an' I've bin punished enough. You'll get him back in the mornin'."

"And with the dog out of the way you were going to rob the house?"

"No, yer riverence," cried George indignantly. "I never thought of it. I'll own up about the dog. But I'm tellin' you the God's truth, that was all we——"

"What brought you back then?"

"We come back because of the dhrink, and thinkin' there might be somethin' to pick up about the yard. It was the dhrink done it. If you'll not set the police on me, I'll bring back the dog an' never throuble you again."

"Come now, tell the truth; and remember if I catch you lying I will give you in charge."

"That's the thruth, yer riverence. It was only afther the dog was away we thought a' comin' back, and then just along a' the dhrink. Sure, if we'd wanted to break into the house we wouldn't a' kept the dog as evidence; we'd a' poisoned him the night we come."

"That would certainly have been more intelligent, but I don't know that I've any reason to think you *are* intelligent, George. And perhaps you knew the dog slept in the house, which would have made poisoning impossible."

"Well, that's the God's thruth, yer riverence. God——"

"Answer my questions," the canon interrupted, "and stop blaspheming. You belong to the travelling circus that was here, don't you?"

"Yes, yer riverence. If you saw the show, I'm Prairie Dick that does the riding act. An' now with this leg——"

"Where is the circus?"

"About five mile away, yer riverence."

"When were you with it last?"

"About three o'clock, yer riverence."

"And do you know that a little boy out of this house is missing, and that I have reason to believe he followed the circus to try to get his dog back again? One of you was seen prowling about here shortly before the dog disappeared."

"I haven't seen the boy, yer riverence. But if he did get to the circus he'll have come to no harm. They wouldn't touch a hair of him, so they wouldn't."

"I hope not. The police are out looking for him now; I'm expecting word every minute. Do you see all the trouble you've brought about?"

"I'm very sorry, yer riverence; an' if you'll only let me go quiet I'll have the dog brought back first thing."

"Well, I'm going to keep you, George, for the present. Whether I give you in charge or not depends entirely on whether I find you have been telling me the truth."

"Thank you, yer riverence: you'll never regret it."

There was a sentimental ring in George's voice, but the canon, being hard-hearted, was unimpressed. "Possibly not, though I shouldn't be surprised if somebody else did. I suppose your friend has decamped?"

"I don't know, yer riverence."

The canon gave him a long look, which George, who objected to being stared at, did not meet. "I'm going to send now for the doctor. I'll ask him to come round and have a look at your leg. Then I shall want you to act as guide—to take the car to where your camp is. . . . You'd better look after this, Palmer. You can explain the situation to Doctor O'Neill."

Palmer nodded. He still held his revolver, but he now offered it to Canon Annesley. "You may as well have it, sir, in case he gives trouble. I'll go on the bike."

He departed, and the others sat down to wait. A policeman was the first to arrive, and the canon interviewed him in the dining-room. The circus had been found, he learned, but Grif was not with it; and the policeman related the story of Pouncer's rescue, which was all the information they had been able to extract from the circus folk. "We're looking after them," he added.

The canon did not mention George, who at that moment sat quaking in the kitchen, expecting every moment to be delivered into the hands of his natural enemies. But George had really become a kind of drug on the market; he could not be given up, and as a guide he was no longer required; so when Palmer, in triumph, returned with the doctor, all the latter had to do was to attend a patient.

It was daylight when they gathered in the dining-room to discuss the situation, and the hero of it felt that the adventure was fizzling out far too undramatically. It became still less dramatic when both he and Edward were summarily ordered to bed.

Doctor O'Neill watched them go out, an expression of mingled amusement and interest on his face.

"That's an extraordinary youngster!" he said, after the door had closed. "I'd rather like to have a boy like that." The doctor was a bachelor between thirty and thirty-five, and still young enough to appreciate Palmer's escapade.

The canon shook his head. "I don't know that he did much good by shooting the unfortunate George. By the way, I wonder where the revolver came from! I'm afraid there are a number of things that will have to be inquired into to-morrow."

"I wonder where poor Grif is?" said Aunt Caroline. "It's really dreadful——this uncertainty."

"I somehow feel as if they should all be severely punished," the canon went on. "And yet, on the face of it, there doesn't seem to be anything to punish them for!"

"It's their doing things on their own account that makes all the trouble. None of this would have happened if Grif hadn't rushed off by himself, and if Palmer had told us he expected a burglar."

The doctor shrugged his broad shoulders. "Would you have believed him if he had?" he asked sceptically.

"Of course the burglar was a pure and unadulterated fluke," declared the canon. "He hadn't really any intention of breaking into the house."

"I'm not so sure of that."

"But it would have been madness. The first thing the police would have thought of would have been this circus."

Aunt Caroline sighed. "Well, if poor Grif is none the worse, I shan't complain. But we really must talk to them seriously."

"You're going to have them with you all the rest of the summer, aren't you?" asked the doctor. "You must find it quite exciting!"

The canon agreed. "We are certainly seeing life."

Doctor O'Neill took up his hat, and then suddenly laughed. "Well, as I began by saying, I'd quite like to have a boy like that. I wonder if it would bore him very much to come round some evening to see me."

"Oh, they'll all come if you want them," Aunt Caroline assured him.

"He doesn't," said her father. "It is only the reckless Palmer who has fascinated him."

The doctor nodded. "I admit it. After all, it was rather a big thing, you know, to bring off at his age. It's quite interesting. I've often wondered if coolness and courage of that sort spring from insensibility, or if they can exist along with more domestic qualities. This Palmer, for instance, may really have in him the makings of a first-class criminal—not one like the poor devil he collared, but the real genuine superior article."

"Don't, doctor; you oughtn't to say such things," murmured Aunt Caroline, a little shocked.

"Oh, I'm only joking: any one can see he's a decent little chap. . . . However, I'll not keep you out of bed any longer."

"You're not keeping me," Aunt Caroline assured him. "I shan't get a wink till Grif comes home."

"Well, I'll look in during the day and hear the news."

CHAPTER XII

THE SPRING SONG

'I heard among the solitary hills
Low breathings coming after me, and sounds
Of undistinguishable motion, steps
Almost as silent as the turf they trod.
                              —*Wordsworth.*

'Piping down the valleys wild,
Piping songs of pleasant glee,
On a cloud I saw a child.'
                              —*Blake.*

GRIF was awakened by a din of many voices. He opened his eyes in the sweet colourless light of dawn, and his ears to the loud choristers who sang above him, pouring out a stream of joyous, careless notes, and exulting each one in his own music. He could see some of the singers as they flitted between the branches, he could hear the brushing of their wings:—the light grew stronger and more silvery.

Pouncer slept on through all the clamour, but Grif rose and stretched himself and climbed out of the hollow. Though his bed had been soft and warm enough, he felt rather stiff and uncomfortable. Below him, about a hundred yards away, lay the river—grey, with a whitish mist above it:—and beyond the river were fields, looking strangely solitary in the new daylight. Close to him a large grey hare squatted on his haunches, gazing at him more in surprise than alarm; a squirrel gambolled in the branches of a fir-tree; and the birds fluttered about him, darting over the grass, as if quite heedless of his presence.

He somehow felt that it was not yet the human hour. All the creatures seemed to know this and to ignore him. Above the fields a delicate scarlet flush was rising, staining the sky, spreading rapidly, and always growing brighter. The scarlet faded into a green cloud of light, and streaks of gold fire shot up, like the streaming banners of the approaching sun. To Grif, standing there on the bank above the river, the sound of the tremendous chariot wheels was clearly audible, and the beating hoofs of the great flaming horses, rushing upward, an immense wind and fire in their manes. Before their headlong course the white mist broke and fled in a host of shadowy phantoms, with waving arms and pale tossing hair. He saw them as a white army retreating in disorder: and the light, dazzling, glorious, flowed on and on, spread abroad, resistless, effortless, as an incoming tide.

The fields reflected it; the dew on the grass blazed like a carpet of precious gems; it beat downward and upward; the last lingering remnant of the misty host vanished; and Grif stood, a solitary witness of their rout, on the golden threshold of the summer morning. His eyes were filled with a flickering, unearthly beauty; his whole being was possessed by it as by a soundless, smokeless flame. The birds had ceased to sing: it was the hour of breakfast and all were busy. But Grif's own voice arose and he sang the song of the river. The hare had disappeared, and Grif returned to Pouncer.

Curiously enough he had no feeling of loneliness or anxiety. It was a sign perhaps of that independence, or detachment, of which Miss Johnson had warned Aunt Caroline, when she had alluded to his habit of picking up with strangers. It is true he knew more or less where he was, and had no doubt but that an hour or two's walking would bring him safely to the Glebe; but he was conscious of no particular eagerness to start; the adventure had come to him, and he felt perfectly content to see it out.

When he awoke for the second time it was in the full heat of day. Above him a dark horse-chestnut spread its broad branches like a gigantic umbrella, through which the sun streamed in green bands of fire. The brown soil showed between thin blades of tender green grass. From somewhere behind him came the monotonous crooning of a ring-dove. He called to Pouncer and ran down to the river.

Morning lay in splendour over the world. The sun was high in the heavens, and the trees threw dark shadows on the mossy ground. On the other side of the river was a sea of waving corn-fields. The smoke from a cottage, dark-blue, almost purple, drifted lazily against the sky, and in the river itself the sky and the clouds were reflected, and the green banks that stood high above the sur-face. A waterfowl swam into a leafy clump of willows; the scent of meadow-sweet hung drowsily on the air; a wagtail pruned his feathers as he stood perched on an old stump; and a rat, sitting up on his hind legs, nibbled delicately at the stems of the grasses. The banks were gay with flowers and creepers, blue forget-me-nots, white hemlock, the small pink blossom of the gypsy wort, the ruddy heads of docks and sorrels. Grif undressed and bathed, while Pouncer plunged in after him; and boy and dog splashed in the sweet cold water, and let it wash away the dust of their jour-ney, and all the weariness and trouble of yesterday.

They sat on the bank to dry. A sleepy barge passed, gliding through the summer, while the water lapped faintly against its broad bow, and the old brown horse plodded on with lowered head.

Then, as he stooped above the river, like a little river god, hug-ging his knees, Grif saw a dragonfly floating on the surface. Its green and yellow body flashed in the sunlight, but its gauzy wings had become wet and useless, so that it could not rise. He knew it would float there till a fish or a bird got it, or till it was drowned. He tried to reach it, but it was too far from the bank. There was nothing for it but to go in again.

When he had rescued the dragon-fly he put it on a dock-leaf in the sun, where its wings would dry quickly. He lay watching it, for it was indeed an extraordinary beast, with great eyes and mouth, and splendid, mailed coat, green and yellow, barred with black lines. It lay still for a while as if exhausted, but presently its silvery transparent wings unfolded, and next moment it had sprung into the air. Grif, watching its brilliant flight, felt inclined to clap his hands. He wondered if it could think, if it knew that it had come safely through a desperate adventure. It would be pleasant to understand the thoughts and language of all these creatures who shared his world, and were really so close to him:—in many ways, he felt, almost closer than human beings. . . .

A little lower down, the bank had fallen in, leaving a shallow sandy beach, now dry, for the channel had shrunk after a long spell of rainless weather. Grif, on his hands and knees, began to build a city in the clean yellow sand. He built houses and a church, and set a wall all round; but Pouncer, growing weary of inactivity, rushed upon the church and demolished it, sending the glittering sand flying in all directions as he scratched and burrowed. Then Grif lay down on the bank and wet Pouncer lay beside him, with his big head between his paws, and his round dark eyes full of gentleness and innocence. The activities of the night had been nothing to Pouncer, but they had left his master not very energetic, and he wanted to lie still for a little before starting on his homeward journey. He was hungry, but the biscuits and cheese had been finished long ago, and there was nothing for it now but to wait in patience.

He grew drowsy. Overhead a lark was singing, singing; and the clear notes floated down in a kind of dreamy rapture. Of all music, Grif felt sure, a lark's song must be the most beautiful. He turned on his side, and the bulldog snuffed at him and licked his forehead once or twice. He was getting sleepier and sleepier, but it was so delicious lying here in this half-dreaming, half-waking state, that he could not resist the temptation to remain a little longer. His eyes were nearly closed, like a cat's eyes when it sits in the sun. He seemed to see, through the green dimness of the trees, a whiteness as of some one moving, some bather like himself perhaps, but more probably a faun or a wood-boy. And he knew that it was not really either one or the other, but, like many little boys, he could continue knowing and not knowing at the same time, while the idle dreams that flitted through his mind seemed to be pictures he could watch, pictures he did not try to create, but which came on the wings of the wind, like floating thistle-down.

Somewhere among the tall rushes by the water a flute was being played. It played a strange tune,—sad, yet with a certain gaiety singing through it, and with an odd little twirl at the end. The tune was repeated three times, the second time quite close to him, but the third time it seemed to drift farther and farther over the fields, till he had to complete the final trill in his imagination.

Grif was very happy. Now that the music was ended he had the clearest sense of its reality. This feeling came upon him in a flash of astonishment, for while he had actually been listening it had all seemed a part of a dream. Now it was as if a warm physical touch on his cheek had awakened him. Where had the music gone to? He only knew that it had crossed the river and floated over the fields. Yet, if he had had wings or an aeroplane, he was sure he could have followed it. And he was sure it would have led him to some definite place, which he would have recognized at once as *the* place, the end of his journey, the home of his hidden friend.

But nature reminded him that he was getting extremely hungry, and he thought of the house so near, and of all the good things houses contain. He would go and ask for something to eat, and ask them to drive him home, for, more than he felt hungry, he felt suddenly and strangely tired. Once he had hit on this plan he did not hesitate. His view of the world was socialistic, though perhaps not one which most socialists would have recognized. Where there were houses there was food, and both food and houses were for every one. Also, when the houses were large, there were usually motor-cars, and motor-cars, too, were for every one. His simple philosophy was based on these premises, and he lived according to his philosophy, nor had it ever yet failed him. Therefore it was without the least sense of doing anything unusual that he rang at the hall-door and went in to lunch.

CHAPTER XIII

THE PERFUMES OF ARABIA

'Beware! Beware!
His flashing eyes, his floating hair!
Weave a circle round him thrice,
And close your eyes with holy dread,
For he on honey-dew hath fed,
And drunk the milk of Paradise.'

—*Coleridge.*

LOOKING rather tired, with a large hole in the knee of his stocking, and a very dirty collar, but in the glory of a motor-car, Grif arrived home when the others were finishing dinner. The car had departed again before any one had time to reach the door, but Grif and Pouncer were there, upon the step, and in her relief at seeing him safe and sound Aunt Caroline forgot all about the scolding she had prepared.

He was dragged into the dining-room by excited young Westons, though in the general hubbub nothing could be made out very clearly, except that he was home once more and had had his dinner. Ann, finding it difficult to get near her brother, devoted herself to Pouncer.

For a minute or two the noise was deafening, because everybody tried to talk at once. Then Grif's adventures were drawn from him in jerks, and the tale of Palmer's burglar, who that morning had been discharged and sent back to his comrades, was told by Edward.

In the first lull Aunt Caroline pounced upon Grif. She wanted him to go to bed, or at least to lie down on the sofa. Only through repeated assurances that he could not possibly sleep was he absolved from this, and, even then, promises were extracted from him that he would keep quiet, and not run about in the sun. She accompanied him to his room and watched him change his stockings and his collar.

"If Doctor O'Neill comes round before you go to bed this evening you're to see him," she suddenly declared.

"I'm all right," Grif protested. "I know I am, and I hate doctors."

"But *I* don't know it," said Aunt Caroline. She looked at the
sallow face, at the dusky lines under the dark eyes, and felt dissatisfied. "Where are you going to now? Why can't you stay quietly in
the house?"

"I'm going to be quiet. I want to read about Tobias. Grandpapa
told me it was in the old Bible in church."

"The church is locked up."

"He told me I could have the key," said Grif. "He left it for
me in the drawer of the hat-stand, so that I could get it when I
wanted."

"Come and let me brush you; your jacket's covered with dust.
Grandpapa spoils you all. If you *do* go, remember you're not to be
late for tea. I'll be very angry if you are, and not allow you to go
out by yourself again."

"How can I help forgetting, if I do forget?" Grif argued gently,
as Aunt Caroline turned him round to brush the back of his coat.
"I mean I can't *remember* not to forget."

"You can remember to come straight home at any rate," said
Aunt Caroline. "You must have *known*, Grif, that you shouldn't
have run off the way you did yesterday, without telling anybody
where you were going to!"

Grif listened patiently, and as she dropped the brush stooped
and picked it up for her. "I didn't know: I hadn't time to think: it
was hearing the engine whistle that put it into my head. And at all
events I got Pouncer."

"If you had stayed at home, if you had told grandpapa, you
would have got Pouncer; and you wouldn't have needed to wander
about out of doors all night."

She let him depart, reluctantly, for after the events of yesterday
nothing seemed safe, though it was difficult, unless an aeronaut
descended and carried him off, to imagine what harm could come
to him now. She herself was going into Ballinreagh to return
Palmer's revolver. She had insisted on grandpapa's confiscating
that immediately after breakfast, and she felt that she shouldn't be

happy till it was safely back in the shop, and till she had said a word
or two to the man who had sold it.

She had kept Grif so long, however, giving him various injunctions, and examining him minutely as to the state of his health,
that when he at last escaped from her clutches the others had disappeared. He went round to the back of the house and whistled
two or three times; then, getting no answer, trotted on down the
drive by himself, and out on to the road.

He took a short-cut across the fields, but, characteristically,
stopped to scratch the face of a cow, and to brush away the flies
that kept buzzing round her eyes and settling at the corners of
them. The cow lowered her head till it was well within Grif's
reach, and then stood perfectly still, breathing her sweet breath
into his face, while he rubbed all round her eyes where the flies
tormented her. Solemn, motionless as one of those extraordinary
wooden beasts of Noah's Arks, she probably would have been
pleased to pass a good portion of the afternoon in the enjoyment
of this novel and delightful sensation, but Grif, having scratched
for several minutes, moved on. The cow followed him as far as the
next stile, where she stood, her head stretched over the bars. A low
moo brought the tender-hearted Grif back again, but he couldn't
scratch the cow forever, and, giving her a last pat on her wet soft
nose, he turned and ran across the field and on to the church.

He opened the door with his big iron key, and went up to the
reading-desk for the Bible. It was a large book, and a brown powder
from its calf back came off on his jacket as he carried it under
his arm. He brought it out into the sunlit churchyard and looked
about for a comfortable corner. He wandered among the graves,
most of them marked by head-stones stained green by time and
weather, some with their lettering almost indecipherable, and
some lying prone on the grass. He read the names and the dates,
now and then having to kneel down and pull away a creeper that
had half hidden an inscription:—

> Our Life a Vapour
> Our days do quickly pafs
> Fade as a flower
> And wither as the grafs.

It seemed odd to Grif to think that many of these people who lay here had lived more than a hundred years ago—some of them a great deal more. It made the world appear very old, and gave him a curious impression of dabbling in past times.

> Here lieth the Body of
> Henry Tisdale
> Who was present at
> the Action off Cape Trafalgar
> October 1805.

In the midst of it all he remembered Billy Tremaine, and began to search for *his* grave, looking among the newer stones. Yet, when he found it, it was rather an old one, and there were several names on it, the one he sought for being the last:—William Batt Tremaine, aged fourteen years. There was no text, merely at the top of the stone an engraved crest, with a Latin motto which he could not make out. All the other people buried in this grave had been old, and it seemed to Grif rather sad that a boy should have to lie here among men and women, not one of whom but had attained his allotted span of three score years and ten.

The grave was close to the wall, and just beside it Grif sat down, with his book on the grass near him. The hot sun made him sleepy and comfortable and not inclined to begin reading, so he remained for a while thinking of the Batts, and of Billy's room, which he had not yet been taken to see, though he had gone to the house a good many times; and presently he heard the thin, creaking, rather battered voice of the wall:—

> In the old grey stone wall grow daisies,
>   White and gold,
> With green trembling leaves like feathers
>   And roots that hold
> Firmly between the grey crumbling stones.
>
> In the old grey stone wall grow thistles,
>   Purple and strong,
> And the ivy clings there and dark mosses
>   Creep along
> The battered ancient stones.

Here out of the wind and in the sunshine
   I find a nook;
Pleasant to lie here in simple idleness,
   Or with a book
Sit, leaning my back against the stones.

While overhead the sky is blue,
   And at my feet the grass is green,
And a bee crawls on the thistle,
   And a lark sings, unseen.

And quietly the spider spins his web
   Between the stones, and waits for foolish flies;
And a cock crows in the distance, and a dog barks,
And when the wind passes, when the wind shakes it and awakens it,
   The old elm-tree sighs.

Grif opened his Bible and after some trouble found the Book of Tobit. He read it carefully, but with a good deal of disappointment, for, though it was like them, it did not seem to him nearly so interesting as the stories in the *Arabian Nights*. The genii that fled from Tobias into "the utmost parts of Egypt" was evidently not so powerful as those which King Solomon had sealed up in brazen jars and thrown into the ocean; nor was the magic which Tobias used very exciting. He only burned the heart and liver of a fish, and it was just the smell that the genii didn't like. Perhaps it was a herring, Grif thought, for he himself detested the smell of herrings. Moreover, Tobias's dog, which he had imagined as playing a principal part in the adventure, was just mentioned and no more. Grif believed he could make up a better story out of his own head, and one more like the picture.

He shut the Bible and placed it on the grass beside him. Through sleepy, narrowed lids he looked at the square tower of the church. He wondered if it could be getting late already, for the sun seemed to be setting; and he thought dimly of teatime and then forgot it. Across the dusky flush of the sky he saw a bridge of golden light, and he knew that if he could walk up this bridge it would lead him to fairy-land. Above his head he heard a heavy flapping of wings, a flapping growing louder and louder, till at last it made quite a wind in the trees. An immense shadow suddenly darkened the churchyard, and Grif, lifting his face, saw an enormous lizard-shaped creature, with great green protuberant eyes, eyes brighter than the brightest motor-lamps, circling over him and dropping closer and closer to the ground. Its flaming green and yellow body shone as if it were coated with precious stones; it had huge claws, and its legs were in a kind of bunch in the front: all the rest of it seemed to stretch out in an enormous tail. From its open jaws came a glow like the glow of a smith's fire, brightening and dulling as it breathed. Suddenly, with a startled little scream, he saw it drop on to the church tower and swing there, its tail reaching nearly to the ground. For a moment he felt afraid, and then, as it slid to the earth and sprawled over the graves, his fear vanished, for he saw it was only the dragon-fly he had saved that morning. . . .

He sat up and rubbed his eyes. The dragon had vanished; the dragon-fly too; but the sound that had awakened him persisted. It was the sound of some one running, running quickly, down the cinder path. He sprang to his feet and was just in time to see Palmer disappear through the gate, which he slammed behind him in Mr. Bradley's face.

CHAPTER XIV

THE RECOGNITION

'Like a vapour wan and mute,
Like a flame, so let it pass.'
—*Rossetti.*

GRIF, clutching his Bible under one arm, ran across the grave-yard, but Palmer was already speeding down the road like a hunted deer, while Mr. Bradley leaned over the gate waving his ebony stick, his white hair loose, his face flushed with anger. He presented at that moment a formidable enough appearance, and Grif could perfectly understand young Dorset's having taken to flight: what perplexed him was how Palmer had got there at all. He waited, a little awe-struck, till Mr. Bradley turned round.

"What was he doing?" Grif asked wonderingly.

"Doing! He was spying—watching me. And when I caught him at it he had the impudence to tell me he had come to listen to the organ! A lot he cares about the organ! I don't think he'll want to listen to it again!"

"But what was there for him to spy?" Grif ventured gently. "What harm could he do?"

"He came to ask questions—to find out things. I didn't see what he was up to till I had been talking to him for five minutes or more. But when I did——" He broke off abruptly to throw a threatening look over his shoulder at the fugitive, who, some fifty yards or so down the road, had come to a standstill, and was watching them with irritating composure.

Grif did his best to pacify the organist, but so long as Palmer remained in sight this was not easy. "I'm annoyed," Mr. Bradley said, with a curious mixture of malignity and childishness, "very seriously annoyed:—so much annoyed that I won't be able to give you a lesson—if you came for a lesson." Then he suddenly remembered that Grif had been lost, and asked: "What happened to you? Your grandfather came to me last night, looking for you, saying you had disappeared."

"I came back to-day," Grif told him.

"And where have you come from now? You weren't hiding in the church, were you? *You* had nothing to do with this?"

"No," Grif hastened to reply, seeing him ready to flare out again. "I was asleep till I heard the noise. . . . I was reading, and I fell asleep—over there, under the wall."

The organist looked in the direction he pointed to. "Oh," he said more mildly. "Well, well: and now, I suppose you want to have a singing-lesson?"

"I don't think so," Grif answered. "I'm—I feel rather lazy to-day. Of course if you'd like me to——"

"No, no. Tell me where you've been to. We'll go and sit down where you were sitting."

Grif left the Bible back in the church and rejoined Mr. Bradley under the wall. There they sat side by side, while the little boy related his adventure, and his companion nodded his head and said "hum—hum" at various places. Grif could talk to him easily, because he somehow felt that there was not really very much difference between them in point of age. That is to say, Mr. Bradley gave him the impression of looking at the world from much the same angle as he himself looked at it. He was serious over the same kind of things, and he had none of that wisdom which freezes up the flow of confidences, and makes one feel that they are rather silly and that one ought to have grown out of them. What Grif felt was that Mr. Bradley himself had *not* grown out of them, and even if he had had a great deal of experience, it was for the most part experience of a similar kind. He was not, for instance, nearly so grown-up as Edward or Palmer. If he had told Edward or Palmer about hearing the flute they would have made him feel he was babyish, made him feel ashamed, whereas Mr. Bradley never for a moment doubted the truth of his story, merely grew interested and began to ask questions.

"What was the tune you heard?—can you remember it?"

Grif hesitated. "I think so."

"Sing it—sing it," the organist urged him with a curious eagerness, and Grif sang the tune in an undertone.

The effect upon Mr. Bradley was remarkable. His eyes seemed to light up with that strange, cat-like, amber-coloured light which now and then came into them, and the expression of mysterious expectation upon his face changed to one of certainty. "You had never heard it before? You are quite sure you had never heard it before?"

"No, I don't think so," answered Grif, in surprise. "What is it? Is it a real tune?"

"It is the tune I taught him," Mr. Bradley whispered, laying his hand on the little boy's arm. "It is the last tune I taught him. He was to have played it at the village concert."

"Who?" asked round-eyed Grif.

Mr. Bradley pointed with his ebony stick to the grave beside them, and somehow Grif did not need to be told any more.

Yet the knowledge came to him with a kind of shock, and a little shiver passed through his body. He felt suddenly that he was alone here with Mr. Bradley, and that he wanted to go home.

"It is the tune I was playing when I saw him—when he came

back that night in the church," the organist went on in a low confidential voice, his long thin fingers still clutching Grif tightly by the arm. "An old Italian tune that I don't suppose half a dozen people, apart from a few musicians, have ever heard. It was written by an Italian organist called Gian Peruzzi, nearly two hundred years ago. I got it along with a heap of old church music. . . . You had better not talk about it."

"Talk about it!"

"Don't tell anybody about it;—even about hearing the flute at all. Captain Batt would be very angry if he got to know. He would be angry with me, and perhaps with you too, even though he wouldn't believe you. *I* believe you, because I heard it myself, and because I know such things happen." He gave a strange low laugh, and his eyes slid away from Grif to the grave, and back to Grif again.

"And did—he not play it at the concert?" Grif faltered, suddenly feeling a peculiar reluctance to pronounce the player's name.

Mr. Bradley shook his head. His eyes now gazed straight into Grif's, and they seemed to grow larger and brighter, so that the little boy could not look away from them. "He died a week before the concert was to have taken place. . . . But," he added with a quick sly smile, "you must promise me that you won't mention this to anyone."

Grif promised, and Mr. Bradley went on, speaking in the same low stealthy voice which, though it was hardly raised above a whisper, seemed to vibrate in Grif's soul, clear and penetrating as the note of a violin. "I wouldn't have told you about it if it had not been that I think you must be in danger, and that I ought to warn you, to put you on your guard."

"What danger?" Grif breathed nearly inaudibly.

Mr. Bradley's eyes narrowed to two shining slits. "From him: it was you he was playing to. And if he did that, don't you see it can only be because he wants to get at you in some way?"

"But—he is dead!" Grif whispered, trying to draw his arm from the organist's grip.

The long slender fingers held him like a steel trap. "There is no such thing as death. The soul does not die. It goes away from the body, but it does not go far. It comes back."

"Why should he want to get at me?" Grif quavered uncertainly.

The organist cast a quick glance over his shoulder and laughed again. "He wants you. You must have put yourself in touch with him in some way. He wants you to go away and play with him— where he is now. He finds it hard to come to you, and perhaps he can only do so at certain times. For that matter, the dead are always trying to reach the living. Sometimes they make use of dreams, sometimes they find other ways. He is trying to lure you to him by the sound of his flute, and the more you listen to him the closer he will come to you and the more power he will get over you."

"But—what does he want?" poor Grif asked again.

"I have told you what he wants," said Mr. Bradley, impatiently. "He wants you to be his playmate: he wants to take you into his country. It is not anything dreadful. His country is really here, all around us. Probably he feels lonely. . . . If you are frightened to go with him you must be careful. There is danger everywhere. There is danger in mirrors; there is danger in still water; there is danger at this moment in sitting talking about him. Do you see how your shadow is lying just across his grave?" (Grif drew back hastily.) "The soul and the shadow are united very closely—far more closely than most people think. The shadow is not really the image of the body at all. I will tell you some day all about it, for I know—yes, I know."

Grif was silent. He felt all at once quite weak and helpless, and he no longer tried to draw away his arm. He wished now that he had not promised to keep this unwelcome secret, but when he begged the organist to let him off his promise he refused to do so.

"It wouldn't do any good if you *did* tell," he repeated. "I have tried to help you, but nobody can really help you. All depends upon yourself."

"But I don't want to die," said Grif, tremulously.

Mr. Bradley received this remark with surprise. "Death is nothing," he declared. "All music is a preparation for death. It is a foretaste of it. In music you live as you will live then, not as you live now at ordinary times; and you are fond of music. All that you see about you is only the reflection of the other world." He took Grif's hand and patted it gently. "This hand here is nothing," he said. "All it can do is to feel pain. It is not *you*, it is not even a part of you, it is no more a part of you than those old stones are. When you are dreaming and happy do you ever miss your body? You have forgotten about it, though it may be lying there, tossing a poor aching head upon your pillow. Yet when you are dreaming you are alive, and playing in beautiful meadows, and bathing in rivers, or singing music, or doing any of the things you like to do at ordinary times—only far more perfectly, and without any effort or tiredness. When you look at me now I can see your spirit peeping out of your eyes. It is like you, but it is brighter, gayer; it is laughing and merry, while you are frightened and sad. If I called to it, 'Grif! Grif!' it would try to jump out and scamper away over the fields. It would stand there for a moment on your forehead while it shook out its wings: then—pouff!—it would be gone, and I should see it glistening like a rainbow in the sunlight, and dancing over the old graves and over the wall and over the church tower and over the tops of the trees. And I should hear it singing, away—up, up in the air, like a little brown lark."

Grif began to laugh, and Mr. Bradley seeing him laugh laughed too, though his eyes still shone with their strange yellow light.

"What time is it, please?" the little boy asked, and Mr. Bradley looked at his watch.

"Ten minutes to six. Time is another nuisance you would be rid of."

But Grif, finding himself free, had jumped to his feet. "I must go," he said quickly. "Tea is at six and I promised not to be late. I hate promising things, because it makes you break your word when you don't mean to. Good-bye."

He was gone before Mr. Bradley could even take a pinch of snuff.

CHAPTER XV

DANGER

'Light thickens; and the crow
Makes wing to the rooky wood;
Good things of day begin to droop and drowse.'
—*Shakespeare.*

JIM once more dipped his finger into the pot, and then proceeded to suck it luxuriously.

"I say, you might leave just a little," Palmer remonstrated. "Of course if you're very keen on it——"

'It' was a brownish, extremely unattractive-looking preparation, of a treackly nature, which Palmer had compounded with the intention of smearing the trunks of the trees after dark, to entrap moths for his collection. Jim protested virtuously:

"I've hardly touched it: you needn't be so rottenly selfish." He returned to his stamp album, whose leaves presented that richly glossy appearance which is imparted by an over-liberal use of gum. "I wonder if the Batts could give me some stamps? They must have lots in the house: the old captain must have sent letters from all kinds of countries."

"I don't think you'd better ask," said Grif. "I expect his grandson got any there were."

"They might tell me I could have his collection, if I asked," remarked Jim, thoughtfully.

"They wouldn't. They keep all his things. They're all together in the room he used to have."

"But you don't even know that he collected stamps; and at any rate there isn't any harm in trying."

"If I were you I would go up to the church to-morrow afternoon and ask Mr. Bradley for some," said Palmer, ironically. "*He's* sure to have a lot."

"To-morrow's Sunday," Jim objected.

"Oh, that won't matter with such a friendly old chap."

"The reason he got angry with you," said Grif, "was because you frightened him. I did it too, the first time I went."

Palmer nodded. "He's very easily frightened. There's something queer about him altogether."

Grif frowned a little: he did not like his friends to be criticized. "I don't see how it's your business, even if there is," he said.

"There are some things that are everybody's business," returned Palmer, wisely.

"What things?"

"Oh, all kinds of things."

"He thinks Bradley must have done something wrong," Edward interposed.

"He hasn't," said Grif, "and even if he had it wouldn't be any business of Palmer's."

"You don't think Mr. Bradley is a burglar, do you, Balmer?" asked Ann, in thrilled tones; for more than ever now she was willing to take Palmer's opinion upon any subject that happened to crop up.

Palmer seemed annoyed. "I don't know what he is," he answered shortly. "I only said there was something queer about him. What are the letters he's always expecting, and which never come? And why does he want to go at night and play on the organ? It must be because he can't sleep. And if he can't sleep it may be because there is something on his mind to keep him awake."

"I think it's rotten to talk like that," Grif burst out indignantly. "And I think all that sort of prying about and asking questions is rotten too. You may call it being a detective, but I don't like it, and I don't believe any decent boy would do it."

Such an explosion, coming from such a quarter, was so unusual that everybody stared.

Palmer coloured, and Grif instantly became filled with contrition. "I'm sorry, Palmer," he said quickly. "I know you're not like that. Only—why can't you leave him alone?"

"I shouldn't *tell*, even if I did find out," said Palmer, coldly. "That is, unless he was dangerous. And I believe he is," he added with a sudden change of tone. "I don't see why otherwise he should have wanted to hurt me to-day. And he *did* want to—pretty badly. If you'd just seen his eyes! I never saw anyone look like that before."

"Jim and Ann, it's bedtime!" Aunt Caroline stood upon the threshold, surveying the assembly. "Grif, I think you had better go, too. In fact we'll all be going soon, for I'm sure nobody got much sleep last night."

Undressing by candlelight, Grif that evening for the first time regretted that he was not in the room with the other boys. For the first time he remembered what Aunt Caroline had told him about his sleeping quarters being so far away from those of the rest of the household. It was true he had Pouncer with him, but he should have liked somebody else as well, though nothing would have induced him to confess this, or ask to be moved.

He felt a strange depression, a sort of shadow on his mind. The loneliness and the darkness weighed upon him, and the sound of the wind in the trees was unfriendly and forbidding. He was in a mood when everything turns to gloom, and when the sense of proportion is temporarily obliterated. He was sorry he had offended Palmer. Not knowing that that curious boy had already found solace in an envious appreciation of the methods of Doctor John Thorndyke, he magnified the offence till it was driven from his memory by vaguer and more ominous broodings. The physical lassitude which had been with him all day had turned at last to a kind of mental distemper. He had left his candle burning on a table by the bed, but the draught from the window bent and bowed the flame, causing it to throw black shadows on the wallpaper, and in this way bringing back to him, in a distorted and more terrible form, much of what Mr. Bradley had said that afternoon. The vague, fantastic danger Mr. Bradley had spoken of became a real danger. It was curious how much more meaning seemed to have come into the organist's words now that Grif was alone with them in the silence of the sleeping house. He felt very tired. A heaviness of sleep weighed upon his eyes and on his brain, but a superstitious dread of what might happen should he lose consciousness kept him awake and alert. He listened for the sound of the flute, but the idea of hearing it had lost all beauty for him now, and he only listened because he could not help doing so. In his weariness, as he sat up against the propped pillows, his head would begin to nod, and then, just as he was dropping off, his fear would reawaken him. Every now and again his eyes slewed round, like the eyes of a frightened dog, towards the looking-glass, as if it, too, possessed a fatal fascination.

At length he blew out his candle. But when he glanced round again he found he could still see the polished, reflecting surface of the glass, and he buried his face under the bed-clothes.

The night was warm, with an oppressive, sultry stillness, and in a little while he became bathed in perspiration and was obliged once more to put his head out on the pillow. Then he got up and turned the looking-glass towards the wall. At last, through sheer exhaustion, he fell asleep, and his sleep grew deeper and deeper, though, from his tossed limbs and restless movements, it might have been gathered that it brought him little peace. Outside, on the landing, a clock struck;—and Grif stirred uneasily.

It was perhaps some twenty minutes later when he sat up in bed. Noiselessly, yet without hesitation, the slight, pallid figure threw back the sheet and coverlet, and got out on to the floor. He went with wide, yet sightless, eyes straight to the door, and turned the handle. Soundlessly he stole downstairs, though not alone, for Pouncer was following him—Pouncer quite awake, and not understanding in the least the reason for this nocturnal ramble. Grif unlocked and unchained the hall-door, and went out, Pouncer still following closely on his heels. And just in time, for Grif pulled the door behind him and the latch clicked.

He walked across the grass in the moonlight. The troubled look had left his face, and he even smiled a little. The sound of a fitful wind that had arisen washed through his dreams, like the tide of an enchanted sea, and the sound was once more beautiful, and seemed to lead him on and on. He passed the croquet-lawn and moved down the wooded slope towards the road. The long wet grass reached above his ankles, and he seemed to be guided by an invisible hand as he threaded his way between the trees, while he listened to the song of the night:—

Swift, in the light of the stars,
    Comes our darling, our sweet:
White on the dark green grass,
    White are his feet.

Under the wrinkled old moon,
    See, he pauses and stands:
Dew on his dark dim hair,
    Dew on his hands.

Moonlight and starlight fall
    Soft on his lifted face—
Lord of this kingdom of leaves,
    Prince of this place!

Sing to our little prince!
    Our angel, our lovely boy!
Pipe with a silver flute
    A hymn of joy,

To welcome him into his kingdom
    Of fountain and grove and lawn:
Pipe till the stars grow dim
    In the light of dawn.

Prince Grif and his orange Pouncer,
    That truest and dearest friend—
But hush!—the birds are awaking,
    Our song must end.

Suddenly his foot struck against the root of a tree, and he stumbled forward and awoke. He scrambled out of the bushes into which he had fallen, while a cloud of pale moths fluttered about him. For a minute or two the shock drove the blood thundering to his ears, and everything wheeled round and round in a dizzy circle. Then terror gripped him. Where was he? Who had brought him here? He gave a cry, and something tugged at the jacket of his pyjamas, while a warm heavy body leaned against him, and a warm tongue passed over his hands. It was Pouncer; and in his relief Grif dropped down on his knees and hugged him, while the bulldog licked his face and neck.

He knew now that he must have walked in his sleep. He was

living still, and this was the solid old earth beneath him, but for
one brief terrible moment he had imagined he was dead. The dew
penetrated through his light flannel clothing, and he felt it cold
and pleasant on his burning skin. He heard the cry of a bird he had
frightened in falling; he saw the pale moths settling down once
more in the shadow of the bushes.

He hurried back through the trees, till, beyond the croquet-lawn,
he saw the house standing square and white and strange—that
sleeping house out of which he had wandered. The freshness of
dawn was in the air. When he came up to the porch he found the
door shut, and knew that his adventure was not yet over.

He walked round the house, for he thought he might perhaps have come out through a window, but all the windows on
the ground-floor were shuttered and latched. He would have to
ring and awaken somebody. Then another plan occurred to him,
and he gathered a handful of gravel from the drive, and stepping
back from the porch threw in a small stone at the boys' bedroom
window. He threw a second and a third, listening between each,
till at last he heard a movement. Directly afterwards a head and
shoulders leaned over the sill, and Grif whispered eagerly, "Don't
make a noise. It's me—Grif—I've been shut out. Come down and
let me in."

The head was withdrawn, and Grif entered the porch. In a
moment or two the door was softly opened.

Grif slipped inside, followed by Pouncer, while Palmer, a lighted
candle in his hand, asked, "How on earth did you get out there?
What have you been doing? I thought at first it was one of those
chaps from the circus come back."

"I walked in my sleep. Keep very quiet going upstairs; I don't
want anybody to know."

They crept up like mice, Palmer following Grif to his room.
There he put down the lighted candle on the dressing-table, and
he himself sat down on the side of the bed to consider this curious
exploit.

Grif had been rummaging in a drawer in search of a clean sleep-
ing-suit, and he now began to change. "I'm wet through," he said.
"It's the dew. I was in the long grass and it was soaking wet."

"But how did you get there?"

"I walked in my sleep. I've done it often before, though not lately, not for more than a year. Are the others awake?"

"Edward and Jim? No. I was wakened because a stone hit me on the head."

Grif slid between the bed-clothes while Palmer, with wrinkled forehead, still gazed at him, as if uncertain what he should do next.

"Are you all right?" he asked doubtfully. "Are you sure I shouldn't fetch Miss Annesley or Miss Johnson? I mean, oughtn't you to get something to drink—brandy or something? How long were you out?"

"I don't know. Not very long. . . . I'll be all right thanks. . . . I was frightened a little when I first woke up, because I didn't know where I was; but as soon as I saw Pouncer I knew."

There was a silence till Grif added, "I'm awfully sorry, Palmer."

"Sorry! What about? You couldn't help it, could you?"

"Oh, I don't mean about this: but—for being so beastly this evening—what I said to you."

"Oh, that! I'd forgotten what you said," answered Palmer, truthfully. "I don't think it was fair to me, of course. I mean, I really *do* think there's something wrong about Bradley. For one thing, I know he's not here under his own name. Bradley is only a part of his name. I found that out this afternoon. His real name is Tennant. I haven't told anybody else, and *he* doesn't know I know. I'm telling you in confidence."

"All right. And you will keep it a secret about my having walked in my sleep?"

Palmer considered. "No, I won't," he said. "I'm going to tell Miss Annesley in the morning. And I'm going to stay with you myself to-night."

"But!" Grif cried in astonishment and indignation.

Palmer patted him on the shoulder. "Don't get in a bate. It's not that I want to tell but that I must. It's too dangerous. You might just as easily have gone out by the window as by the door, and if you had you wouldn't be talking to me now."

"I wouldn't have been killed," said Grif stubbornly. "It's not very high. Besides, there's grass below."

"You'd have been badly hurt anyway. And you *might* have been killed: you might have fallen on your head."

"But I won't do it again. I told you I hadn't, for more than a year; and the doctor at home said I had outgrown it."

"Well, you see you haven't. I'm not going to risk it, Grif, so there's no use arguing. Of course, if you let me nail up your window tomorrow so that it will only open a few inches, and let me lock your door from the outside every night, I dare say that might do. But if I *do* do that it will be seen at once, so it will all come to the same in the end."

"I hate having my door locked from the outside."

"*Some*thing must be done."

Grif was silent.

"Do you think it would be a dreadful thing to die, Palmer?" he asked suddenly.

The question was not of a kind Palmer was accustomed to, but he was always ready to discuss a problem. "I think it would be dreadful to die in a stupid sort of way like that. I think it's all right running risks for some purpose, and I'd run them myself fast enough; but this has no purpose, it's simply waste."

"But suppose there was something you couldn't avoid; some—some kind of danger hanging over you? Suppose there was somebody who *wanted* you to die?"

"I'd find out who it was, and if I could manage it I'd jolly well see that he died first."

"Suppose it was somebody you couldn't get at—somebody you *couldn't* kill?"

"If he could kill me, I could kill him:—it just depends on who's cleverest. Professor Moriarty was trying for Sherlock Holmes all the time, but he didn't get him: it wasn't Sherlock who went down the precipice."

"But——" Grif paused. Then he said, "Suppose you couldn't kill him, because he was already dead?"

Palmer's lips closed tightly. "I don't like that kind of thing," he said. "And it's all rot, anyway."

"I only said it," Grif protested feebly.

"You didn't only say it. Somebody's been putting notions into your head, and I know pretty well who it is."

He relapsed into silence for a long time, while Grif watched him with varied feelings, and watched the flickering candle that was growing paler and paler in the broadening daylight. One of these feelings was a desire to break the promise he had made yesterday afternoon to Mr. Bradley. He felt extraordinarily weak and helpless, and Palmer, sitting stolidly beside him, seemed, though there was but two years and a few months between them, the embodiment of all that was strong and sane.

At last Palmer turned and looked straight into his eyes. "Will you answer *one* question if I put it?"

"I don't know."

"You've made promises, of course. The boy who tried to raise the devil got the kids to make promises. People of that sort always do. Was it Mr. Bradley who put this idea into your head?"

"What idea?" asked Grif, faintly.

Palmer continued to look at him, his small, clear, brown eyes holding Grif's dark frightened ones. "It doesn't matter," he said with a curious gentleness. "You needn't break your word, for I know it was. And what's more, I know now—I think I know—why he is here, why he came here." Suddenly he flushed. "It's a rotten shame! I'll jolly soon have him fired out of this."

"You—you mustn't do anything," Grif whispered. "It's awfully good of you, Palmer. I mean, you're awfully decent talking to me this way. But—you mustn't——" His voice broke a little and he bit on his lower lip to keep himself from crying.

Palmer again patted him on the shoulder. "Whatever I may do, you won't be in it, so you needn't worry. And I'm not going to make a fuss, or anything like that. Do you know that if I posted a certain letter to-night you would never see your friend again. . . . At least, I believe that—I'm almost convinced of it. But I'm going to get more solid proof before I do anything." His expression changed, and a smile came, first in his eyes, and then spreading to his mouth. "Are you aware that the sun is shining? You're a nice chap keeping me talking here at this hour. I'll go and get my pillow."

He yawned and got up, but Grif put out his hand and still held him. "Don't go for a minute. I don't understand what you mean. You're quite wrong. I like Mr. Bradley very much. He has always been very decent to me, and you mustn't say anything to him, or do anything. Of course I know you're making it up, but——" He relaxed his hold and his hand dropped back on the bed. His face was very white, and Palmer, gazing down at him, saw a sweat break out on his forehead.

"What's the matter?" he asked, beginning to be frightened.

Grif made an effort. "I don't feel very well, Palmer. . . . In the morning—if you would tell—if you would send——"

But the sentence was never finished, for Grif had fainted.

CHAPTER XVI

GRIF RECEIVES A VISITOR

'This hour is mine—
Though thou his guardian spirit be.'
—*Coleridge.*

NEXT morning Grif declared himself better, but Aunt Caroline drew her own conclusions from the fact that he showed no great eagerness to get up. She had sent Edward for Doctor O'Neill, who had not yet arrived. Like an old-time king Grif received an audience at his bedside—an audience composed not only of his brothers and sisters, but which at one time or another included grandpapa and Miss Johnson, Bridget and Hannah. When the others were going he made a sign to Jim to remain behind.

"You're only missing Sunday," Jim consoled him, "and it's never much good anyway. What d'you want?"

"I want you to take a note to Mr. Bradley, but you mustn't let Palmer or anybody else see you giving it to him. You'll have to invent an excuse for staying behind after church. Then, when the coast is clear, you can either go up to the choir and give it to him there, or if you would rather you can wait near the door and catch him as he is coming out. But it must be done secretly, and you mustn't breathe a word about it to anybody."

"That'll be all right," said Jim. "D'you want an answer?"

"No. As soon as he has the note you can come away. Get me a piece of paper and a pencil, and something to write on."

These materials were supplied, and while Grif wrote his letter Jim laid plans for its safe delivery. Morning church, he felt, even with Drumsticks preaching, was not going to be so dull as usual.

Thus it came about that at four o'clock Aunt Caroline was surprised to learn that a gentleman had called to see Master Grif, and she was still more surprised when she discovered the gentleman to be Mr. Bradley, for the organist, as far as she could recollect, had only been in their house once before. Mr. Bradley was shown upstairs, and Aunt Caroline, closing the book she was reading aloud, left them alone together.

But now that his opportunity had come Grif found it difficult to take advantage of it. Mr. Bradley asked him how he was, and they talked a little about the solo he was to sing in church next Sunday. Then Grif said abruptly, "You remember the boy you saw yesterday afternoon?"

"That rascal! Yes, I remember him. I met him again as I was coming over here, and he took off his cap to me. Impudence I expect."

Grif saw that Mr. Bradley's annoyance had passed. It was a pity that he himself should be about to revive it, but he knew there was no other way. "I want to tell you something about him. He—— If he talks to you or writes to you or anything, don't take any notice. He's awfully decent really, but he likes—likes playing tricks." This, after all, was as much as he found it possible to say.

The warning produced no effect whatever upon Mr. Bradley, who appeared to have lost interest in Palmer, and who began at once to speak of something else. Then Grif told him about having walked in his sleep.

Immediately he had done so he regretted it, for he felt, rather than saw, that it had rekindled in the organist a train of thought which Grif did not want to be rekindled. He was powerless to prevent it, however, and as he listened and watched, that strange fascination he had before experienced dropped again about him, like the floating threads of a web. In his weakness it was stronger than ever. He became conscious of it now as an almost physical atmosphere, which had crept into the room, darkening the air about him. Shut in here between four walls, he seemed even less able to escape from it than he had been outside. Through his open window he could see the sunlight, the green waving trees, a warm strip of blue sky; but slowly they receded from him, while something misty and intangible, something cold, baffling, and obscure, crept in between, like a vapour or a cloud. He was drifting back, he knew, into the haunted, tormented, visionary world of last night; and Mr. Bradley, with his soft silver hair, his thin mouth and bright eyes, terrified him. Behind the softness of his voice there seemed to lurk something greedy and inhuman, an immense vitality, a kind of feverish flame that lapped against Grif's spirit and withdrew, and advanced again, a resistless, devouring force. . . . He shrank into himself and wished that somebody would come.

Yet this feeling of dread was mingled with a sense of fascination: his tortured mind was like a singed moth which returns again and again to the burning lamp. As Mr. Bradley spoke he became conscious that he was describing all that had taken place last night as accurately as if he had been present in the room. He seemed to have divined that Grif had been afraid, that the looking-glass had glittered, that the shadows had grown alive, that his room had been invaded by a ghostly activity, which had permitted him to drop asleep only that it might draw him more certainly out into the darkness. And when he spoke now, it was no longer of a secret playmate, of a happy boy and of the open sky, but of an enemy, a beast hungry for its prey, a crouching cruel antagonist.

Grif had ceased altogether to reply to him. He lay perfectly still, his dark eyes wide and troubled, while Mr. Bradley told him dismal tales whose very craziness seemed to make them more real. And as his low voice vibrated with a curious, passionate gluttony, the churchyard, no longer green and pleasant, but a place of grisly horrors, seemed to creep closer and closer to them, till at last its white tombs lay just beneath the window.

"I will tell you how I first came to be certain of these things," the organist whispered, drawing nearer and bending down, while his long thin fingers curved and straightened themselves on the bright counterpane, and his eyes glittered into Grif's. "I must go back a good many years, to an autumn night long ago, when a young man, walking home through the streets, began to watch his shadow gliding over the ground in the light of the gas lamps. It was not till he was half way home that he noticed how unfamiliar it looked, and then something about it attracted his attention and he stood still. A strange, a horrible thought had entered his mind. He struggled against it as people struggle against a bad dream. Then he hurried on, and looked at his shadow again as seldom as possible.

"When he reached home he felt a little ashamed, and yet he still had a lingering sense of uneasiness and depression. He went straight to bed, and it was later than usual when, next day, he woke out of a heavy stupid sleep. Immediately he knew that something had happened, that he had learned some secret—a secret he did not want to think of, but which he could not forget. He went out after breakfast. The sun was shining; the streets were full of people. 'I won't look,' he said; but a moment later he cast a hurried glance at a whitewashed wall he was passing, and on the wall he saw the shadow.

"The thing was true then! It was worse even than he had imagined! For in the night, while he had slept, it seemed to have altered, and what had been vague was now clear. His forehead grew damp, and he felt a kind of sickness, as he glanced furtively from side to side to see if anyone were watching. He crossed over to the shady side of the street, and hurried home, but from that hour he began to be haunted by the dread of discovery. Day by day this fear increased, till at last it became almost impossible for him to stir out of his room when the sun shone or when the lamps were lit. And if he did go out he slunk along back streets, and where there was darkness he chose the darkness.

"And yet he had done nothing evil in the past. This curse had dropped upon him as if out of the clouds; had struck him down like some hideous secret disease. In the night he would wake up in agony and pray, but he knew, he always knew, that it was hopeless. He dreaded going to bed and to sleep, for when he slept it was to become at once what his shadow proclaimed him. Again and again in dreams he committed horrible crimes, and again and again, with his victim's shrieks still ringing in his ears, he awoke. Then a subtle temptation entered his mind. It seemed to him that if he could gratify his shadow once it might leave him in peace. He saw it, like a crouching beast, drinking its fill of blood, and then lying down, satiated and quiet. If he did not gratify it detection was certain, sooner or later. He no longer left his room.

"But every evening, when he was alone and unlikely to be disturbed, he would lock his door and spend hours gazing at his shadow. He loathed it, it filled him with horror, but he could not resist the desire to watch it, to watch its growth, which was like that of some unclean fungus. In the brilliant light he would stand staring at it, putting it through its ugly pantomime, for he now began to see it at work; and there were times when he could feel it, clammy and cold,—when he felt its threatening fingers clutching at his own throat.

"He became pale and haggard-looking. Even his features, it seemed to him, were altering, growing from day to day more like the shadow. But as yet, owing to the precautions he took, nobody had guessed the truth. At last he consented to consult a specialist in nervous troubles. An appointment was made, and he went out with his younger brother. At first he felt safe enough, for it was dull and cloudy, and their shadows were invisible: but as they approached a railway-bridge the sun slid from behind the clouds, and, simultaneously, the two shadows sprang into life on the white asphalt, and on the walls of the houses. Never had his own shadow been so active and strong. It seemed to leer and grimace at him, and he began to talk and laugh so loudly that people turned to stare after them. He gripped his brother's arm and pointed out things to right and left, trying to distract his attention; and in his efforts he could hear himself that his voice was growing shriller, his laughter wilder. His brother in his turn seemed to grow uneasy. Then suddenly they both became silent.

"But he now suspected his brother of deliberate treachery. Why else should he have enticed him out here? Why else should he walk with his head lowered, his eyes on the ground? Where were they going to? Into what trap was he being drawn? And then, just as they reached the middle of the bridge, his brother gave a little laugh and said, 'How funny our shadows look!'

"The miserable wretch must have discovered his secret long before! He had been gloating over it; it was for this he had lured him out;—to gain this last positive proof. He saw it all now;—saw how this soft persuasive manner was only a mockery; understood the stealthy, sidelong glances. His brother *knew*! But if he knew, it should not be for long. An immense, rapturous strength seemed to shout within him for freedom, for action. He gripped the spy by the throat: he laughed aloud as he gripped him, and squeezed and tore and forced him back against the low parapet of the bridge. He pressed him against it, he bent him across the wall till he could feel the body limp and broken and utterly helpless, before he flung it over. Then he seemed to be fighting with a whole crowd of people who wanted to kill him, and who kept crying out in answer to his cries. The air was full of noise and laughter and screams. Joy! joy! and a tearing of flesh, and horrible pain!

"He remembered nothing more till he found himself shut up in a place where the walls were padded, and where he stayed for long years, till he got better. And he still stayed there, on and on, but at last one day he was brought out into the world again, for a new shadow had been given to him—the other, that misty, murderous vampire was gone. . . ."

Grif said nothing, but his mouth felt dry and hot, and a mortal oppression weighed upon him. He wanted to get up, to go away, to get away from Mr. Bradley, but he could not move. And then, as he hid his face in the pillow, he heard the door open, and knew that Aunt Caroline had come back.

He looked up. In spite of the evidence of his senses it almost seemed as if he must have awakened from a nightmare. For Mr. Bradley was not bending over his bed, but standing by the window, smiling and talking pleasantly to Aunt Caroline; and he was telling her that he, Grif, had been asleep.

"Good-bye," he said gaily, stepping jauntily to the bedside and wagging a playful finger. "I'm afraid we didn't have much of a talk after all. The next time I pay you a visit I'll wake you up at the first snore."

He was gone, and Aunt Caroline with him. Grif stared with miserable, clouded eyes at the opposite wall.

CHAPTER XVII

FANTASY

'Then thy sick taper will begin to wink.'
—*Donne.*

DOCTOR O'NEILL called again that evening, simply, he said, because he happened to be passing. Yet he stayed some little time, and when he came downstairs with Aunt Caroline he did not go away immediately, but followed her into the dining-room, where they were alone.

"How do you think Grif is?" she asked him.

"That's just it: I want to put a few questions. . . . I don't find him at all so well as he was this morning."

Aunt Caroline sat down, but the doctor remained standing, looking, as she thought, rather put out, as if something had happened to annoy or perplex him.

"Isn't it only that he's tired?" she said. "I'm afraid he had too many visitors to-day."

"I see." He nevertheless added almost immediately, "I can't help feeling that there must be something else. And while I think of it, I fancy you would be better to let him have his dog back again."

"I thought it wiser—— I mean, when he has been cooped up in the one room all day long——"

"I know: I quite understand. In this case, however, we must stretch a point. It is worrying him, and the less he is worried the better."

"Then I'm to put Pouncer back again?"

"Yes." He hesitated, his hands in his pockets, a slight frown drawing a line down his forehead. "I really don't know why he *should* be worse to-night, but he is—a good deal. It's very much as if something had happened—as if he had had a shock." He turned to her abruptly, with one eyebrow raised, a trick that always irritated her. For that matter they never talked very long together without treading on each other's toes.

"But what shock *can* he have had?" she asked.

"I don't know. And whatever it may be, I'm afraid we'll learn nothing from Grif himself. . . . You can't think of anything that might have occurred?"

Aunt Caroline shook her head. "He hasn't left his room all day."

The doctor nodded, but he seemed still to cling to his idea. "It is as if there were something weighing on his mind, some secret trouble. He's not as he ought to be;—as I expected to find him," he added almost angrily. "His pulse is absurd; he's feverish; and I don't like the look in his eyes. I'd very nearly swear he has been frightened, that there's something he's afraid of at this moment. His nerves are strung up. He's all wrong. . . . And he wasn't that way when I saw him this morning."

"Then you think there's more in it than these last two nights can account for?" she questioned, with just the faintest shade of scepticism in her voice. "He didn't have much sleep, you know."

"If it comes to that, last night itself hasn't been accounted for," said the doctor. "Why did he walk in his sleep? He tells me he hasn't done so for more than a year."

"I'm sure I don't know what it can be. . . . He's so very reserved," she added rather lamely.

Doctor O'Neill smiled. "Yes; I discovered that. He's also immensely polite. He did everything to help me except tell me what I wanted to know. . . . By the way, where's this Palmer boy? I'd like to have a chat with him."

"Oh, Palmer hadn't anything to do with it," said Aunt Caroline, hastily.

"No; I didn't suppose he had."

"Do you really want him? I'm afraid he is out."

"Oh, it doesn't matter. I have an unbounded respect for that boy's perspicacity, that is all." He took a turn up and down the room, while Aunt Caroline followed him with her eyes, wishing she could order him to sit down and behave properly.

He stopped again before her, and this time the frown had disappeared from his rather ugly yet rather fine face. "I'm afraid I

must be alarming you by so much mystery. There's no need to
be alarmed. All that's necessary is to be careful—very careful.
What makes it more serious than it ought to be is that he has no
stamina—nothing physical to fall back upon: which means that we
never know where we are. I'd almost be inclined not to leave him
alone to-night. I suppose that could be managed?"

"Oh yes; I'll sit up with him myself."

"No need to keep awake, you understand. As long as you're
there, that is all that is required. But he must have some sleep. I'll
send up a sedative when I get back, though I don't want you to give
it to him unless it is necessary. If he can do without it it will be all
the better."

He departed, leaving Aunt Caroline in a state of extreme
dissatisfaction.

Her anxiety diminished considerably as she watched Grif sleeping, and without the aid of any drug. She sat in an armchair, with a
lamp burning on a table close by her elbow, while Pouncer, restored
to his former position of guardian, lay on the floor, lost in noisy
slumbers. No sedatives were required to lure Pouncer to the Land
of Nod. His regular snores were in themselves a kind of narcotic,
and under their influence Aunt Caroline dropped into a doze.

But Grif, though he lay so still, was acutely conscious. That is,
he became conscious from hour to hour; and sometimes when he
opened his eyes it seemed to be daylight, and again it seemed to
be night. For he had slid into a queer kind of world where time
no longer existed, a world in which he heard voices and saw faces
that he knew; but those faces were so oddly mixed up with others
he did *not* know, that he at last let them drift by him without question, merely watching in patience the endless procession, now
bright, now dim. More than anybody else Mr. Bradley was with
him, and often when he went away his shadow remained behind.
It crouched in a corner near the door: it was waiting, Grif knew,
for him to fall asleep.

He opened his eyes in the dark. A great peacefulness had

descended upon everything, and the quiet wrapped him round like the stillness of a pond. A thin ray of light shone across the room and lit up the two white china dogs that stood upon the chimney-piece. Pouncer got up once to bark at them, but as they took no notice he went back to his bed. In the silence Grif could hear very distinctly the ticking of the tall clock in the landing. He began to count the ticks, and had reached fifty-three, when he was surprised by a quick little bark that certainly wasn't Pouncer's. This bark had a stealthy sound; it was really a whispered bark; and Grif couldn't imagine where it had come from. Then it sounded again, and this time he saw distinctly the tail of the right-hand china dog wag. Grif had never even noticed that it *had* a tail before, so closely did it keep it tucked into its body. At the same moment the other china dog got up, stretched out its paws, lowered its back, and yawned.

"Are you sure he's asleep?"

"Yes, can't you see he is? He's been asleep for hours—for days—for months."

"I suppose we can talk, then? It's very difficult to get saying a word with him always in the room. I wonder why they put him here?"

"I wonder how long he's going to stay?"

Just then the deep voice of Pouncer joined in. "What have you got to talk about anyway—stuck up there on a spare bedroom chimney-piece from one year's end to another?"

"We've plenty to talk about; but you wouldn't understand; you oughtn't to be here at all. We know more than anybody except Pan and Syrinx."

"The question is what *do* you know?" growled Pouncer.

Grif was never to learn, for, as he moved, the room suddenly became silent once more. He got out of bed, but somehow found it curiously difficult to walk. Pouncer looked up at him with dark eyes liquid with sleep, as he staggered to the chimney-piece and lifted down one of the dogs. It was perfectly stiff and solid, yet he fancied he could detect a faint, rapidly fading warmth in it. There was a crash, and everything turned to darkness. . . .

He felt very tired, and yet he must walk on. He could not

remember where it was he had come from, but he knew that when he reached his journey's end he would be safe, and that now he was in danger. Something was pursuing him. He could not see it; he could not hear it; it was still a long way off; but he knew that it was coming.

This high wall beside which he had been walking for hours seemed endless. Then, with a thrill of dismay, he discovered that though he was walking he was not moving. This gate straight before him was the same gate he had seen an hour ago. He broke into a run, but when he stopped the gate was still there. . . .

Perhaps if he went through it he might reach the house sooner! He felt that he must get home early or something dreadful would happen. Early!—but it was already dark as pitch! the roads were deserted; he was walking in the night! Where had he been then? Why had he taken so long? And that gate, with its tall spiked bars!—how could he open it or climb it? Even as he wondered, it swung slowly back, and Grif hastily stepped inside. Then the gate closed behind him with a heavy metallic clang, that struck upon his ears, cold and sinister, like a note of doom.

At the same moment the moon swam out and he saw that he was in a graveyard. He had made a mistake; he must get out again quickly; it was madness to linger in such places, and so far from home. He wrenched at the gate, in terror, but it would not open. The moon shone full upon a white tomb just at his feet, and he read the name on it, and, in a flash, remembered everything. Mr. Bradley was buried here. He must get out quickly. He beat and hammered at the bars in an agony of fear, but his blows fell soft as summer rain upon them, though the effort he made brought the sweat out on his body. Oh joy! the lock was yielding a little. If the gate would only open at once he might still escape! Then, down below him, down under the tomb at his feet, he heard a long low chuckling laugh that froze the blood in his veins. . . .

He staggered and fell back. It seemed to him that he was lying on his own bed in his own room, and that the shadow was once more lurking in the corner. He watched it draw nearer and at last lean over him, but he could not move hand or foot to fight against it, nor could he utter a sound. He felt it creeping over the bed now, settling down upon him like a cold heavy mist. He could make out a dim crouching form, he could see through the misty coil two white blazing eyes. The long cold fingers were at his throat; they tightened; they choked him; but when he tried to tear them away he could clutch nothing; there was nothing there.

Yet those fingers were strangling him! His struggles grew weaker, and he was losing consciousness, when he heard a growl and a bark, and felt some heavy body leap upon the bed. The battle now began in earnest, and as Pouncer tore at the hideous creature who was murdering him, as they strained and fought together, the grip at Grif's throat relaxed, and he opened his eyes.

CHAPTER XVIII

GRIF AWAKENS

'Care-charming Sleep, thou easer of all woes,
Brother to Death, sweetly thyself dispose
On this afflicted prince; fall like a cloud,
In gentle showers; give nothing that is loud,
Or painful to his slumbers; easy, light,
And as a purling stream, thou son of Night,
Pass by his troubled senses; sing his pain,
Like hollow murmuring wind or silver rain;
Into this prince gently, oh, gently slide,
And kiss him into slumbers like a bride.'

—*Fletcher.*

"GET down Pouncer, naughty dog!"

It was Aunt Caroline who spoke, and Pouncer jumped off the bed, though he still continued to growl with a deep threatening note. Grif gazed around him. The room was lit by a shaded lamp, and a fire was burning in the grate.

"What's the matter?" he asked. "What has happened?"

"Nothing, dear. It was only Pouncer who jumped on to your bed. I was asleep, I think, or half asleep, when I heard him growling; and then before I could move he had sprung right up beside you. I expect he had been dreaming, for he seemed very angry and excited, just as if he were going to attack some one."

"So he was," said Grif. "There was something there—a shadow. Hasn't there been a shadow over there, near the door, for a long time? It is gone now, but it was there all evening. Didn't you see it? It was there for hours before it got on the bed. Pouncer must have killed it, or frightened it away."

Aunt Caroline appeared to take his words for the lingering echoes of the delirium through which he had passed, for she did not answer, but only tried to soothe him. "How are you feeling, dear?" she asked softly. "Do you think you are a little better?"

"Yes, thanks." He tried to lift his hand, but it was strangely heavy.

"You must go to sleep again. Would you like a drink?"

"Yes, please. Haven't I been asleep? Won't it soon be morning?"

"No; it is just half-past twelve."

"Then I've only been asleep a little while. I thought it must be Monday morning. I'd like something to eat."

"Monday morning is passed. This is Wednesday night. You've been ill for three days."

"Three days?" His mind was too languid to grapple with the idea, and he let it go.

"And now you must get well quickly."

Grif lay and listened to her as she moved quietly about the room, preparing some food for him. He felt very weak, and yet, somehow, happy, and he allowed Aunt Caroline to feed him just as if he were a baby.

"Will you read to me a little?" he asked.

"What shall I read?"

"An animal story."

"But I'm afraid I haven't got one here."

"Well, it doesn't matter. Pouncer!"

"Oh, you don't want Pouncer, dear; he's too heavy, he will only tire you."

"I just want him for a minute."

Pouncer sprang on to the bed and began to snuff and snuggle his nose into Grif's neck. The little boy laughed and kissed a silky ear; but Aunt Caroline would only let Pouncer stay for the prescribed minute; then she put him down again.

"Do you really want me to read to you, Grif?"

"No, it doesn't matter. I think I can go to sleep."

He lay drowsily watching Aunt Caroline, while the firelight was reflected in his dark eyes. Then the lids drooped lower and lower, and Aunt Caroline, listening to his soft regular breathing, knew that he was going to get better.

CHAPTER XIX

DOCTOR O'NEILL CALLS IN A SPECIALIST

'Some that do plot great treasons.'
—*Webster.*

DOCTOR O'NEILL, by what he considered great good luck, found young Dorset alone on the croquet-ground. He at once seized his opportunity.

"Put away your mallet," he said abruptly, "I want to talk to you. Shall we be disturbed if we stay here?"

"Very likely."

The doctor had expected him to betray some surprise, but judging from his manner Palmer might have been granting mysterious interviews all his life. His unruffled serenity, indeed, slightly took the wind out of the doctor's sails.

"Well, where will we not be disturbed? I want to speak to you in private."

"There's Jonah's Bower," the boy remarked, pointing to the ash-tree. "Nobody will interrupt us there, unless Ann routs us out, and if she does we can send her away."

"All right."

They retired to the bower, and the doctor found it contained a seat which had been put up for Ann by Palmer himself, who included carpentry among his many accomplishments. He took the seat, and the red-haired boy, facing him, sat upon the ground cross-legged, like a Turk.

"I want to talk to you about Grif."

"Yes."

Doctor O'Neill looked gravely into Palmer's pleasant countenance, while he tried to think of a way to induce him to commit
himself. "Or rather I want you to talk to me. I want you to tell me
everything you know."

Palmer's expression did not alter. "So far, I only know that there
is some particular thing you are uneasy about."

"Don't be cheeky."

"No, sir."

The doctor frowned. "Well then, fire ahead, and tell me what
you think."

Palmer only gazed at him with wrinkled forehead, as if slightly
at a loss. "I don't see how I'm to fire ahead, when you won't even
tell me what you would like me to fire at."

The doctor hesitated. "You aren't surprised that I should ask
you about Grif?"

"No, sir."

"Then you *do* know something. . . . Now, I'm going to take you
into my confidence."

He paused as if to allow Palmer time to acknowledge this
favour, but the boy retained his attitude of silent imperturbability,
and his faint smile struck the doctor as being even slightly cynical.
It was at all events quite apparent that he believed he had very few
confidences to bestow.

"I'm not satisfied about Grif's illness. I believe there's something more in it than we are aware of; something behind it; some
reason for it of which I know nothing."

Palmer nodded slowly: he quite understood.

"Now I want you to tell me *your* ideas on the subject, if you
have any."

There was a perceptible silence, during which Palmer appeared
to be turning the matter very carefully over in his mind.

"If I had been allowed to listen to what Grif said when he was
ill, I think I could have helped you," he at last produced cautiously.

"How do you know he said anything?"

"Don't people always talk when they are delirious?"

"They usually talk a great deal of nonsense."

"Based on something else?"

"Possibly."

"It's the nonsense, isn't it, that you want to find out about?"

The doctor eyed him sharply. "I want to find out if there has been any influence at work upon his mind—any unhealthy influence."

"And you suspect somebody, sir?"

"I don't say that. . . . At any rate I haven't mentioned my suspicion to anyone but you."

Palmer received this compliment somewhat coolly. "If I speak, I suppose there is no danger of what I say going any further?"

"My dear boy, the greatest danger you run at present is that of developing into a prig," said the doctor, a little ruffled.

"It's a very remote one, isn't it?"

"Not nearly so remote as you appear to imagine. But I agree to your terms: I'll not give you away, if that's what you mean. Don't you see that I have only given myself away, by taking it for granted that you have thought of the matter at all?"

"Well, you weren't mistaken," the boy admitted. "In fact, if you hadn't spoken to me I should probably have spoken to *you*—in a few days."

"Why in a few days?"

"Because I might have had more to say then."

"You are investigating the case?"

Palmer's small brown eyes regarded him with quiet amusement. "I have given it a few hours, sir," he said.

"I'm glad to hear it. You haven't, I suppose, reached a definite conclusion?"

"No. But I know where to look for one."

"The deuce, you do!" the doctor murmured.

"Also I dare say I can tell you one or two things even now that may interest you:—always, of course, speaking in confidence."

The doctor eyed him somewhat grimly, but Palmer went on, quite undisturbed:

"First, however, I want to *ask* a question. How long have you known Mr. Bradley, sir?"

"For several years—ever since I've been here."

"But you don't know him very well, perhaps?"

"No, I can't say I do. I called on him once, but he didn't seem anxious that there should be any intimacy. . . . Why do you ask? What has Mr. Bradley to do with——"

"Has it never struck you that nobody *does* know him?" Palmer interrupted. "Nobody knows, for instance, except me and Grif whom I told, that his name isn't Bradley."

"*Isn't* Bradley! What is it then?"

"His name is Tennant."

Doctor O'Neill stared. "You aren't——? This isn't a game, is it?"

Palmer shook his head. "Not so far as I am concerned."

"Then why on earth——?"

"For the same reason that brought him here—among strangers. He doesn't want to be recognized. Have you ever heard of his having had a friend to stay with him—I mean anyone who knew him before he came here?"

"I don't remember. I was never particularly interested in the matter."

"Canon Annesley says he has never had a visitor."

The doctor considered. "But what has all this to do with Grif?"

"I think it has something to do with what you want to know," said Palmer.

"And is that all you have to tell me?"

"It is all I have a definite proof for. I have only a theory of what the rest may be."

The doctor waited.

"Would you like to hear my theory?" asked Palmer sweetly.

"I would like to pull your ear," answered the doctor.

Palmer smiled. "Mr. Bradley is peculiar," he said slowly, "and peculiar in a very unpleasant way. I had an interview with him in the church, and found him a good deal too handy with that stick of his. In fact I don't mind admitting that at one time, when he got me cornered, I was pretty badly scared. . . . I thought over it afterwards and added it to one or two other things I had picked up about him, and I tried to find an explanation which would cover everything."

"I see. . . . Well?"

"It mayn't be the right explanation of course, but it does cover a good deal."

"And what is it?"

"Perhaps you will only think it silly," said Palmer, "but it seemed to me that a man who had been put under restraint for something he had done in a fit of insanity might, on coming out, want to live in a place where nobody would know anything about him, and might even want to drop his surname. Also, after a time, he might begin to drift back again towards the condition he had been in before, and under such circumstances he might want to talk to somebody—to talk about things more or less bordering on the subjects that interested him."

The doctor nodded, and Palmer, encouraged by the attention with which his theory was received, developed it still further.

"There would be no use talking to you, or even to me. He would have to find a listener with whom he would be safe; a listener whom he might possibly bring round to look at things in his own way. You'll get chaps like that at school, as of course you know. . . . And he naturally would be delighted when he found such a person—even if he was only a kid."

"Grif?"

Palmer's small eyes narrowed craftily. "Grif, perhaps. Almost any quiet, thoughtful kind of kid would do, so long as he wasn't the kind that blabs."

"And Grif doesn't blab?"

"He hasn't blabbed to you," Palmer smiled. "Mr. Bradley was with Grif most of the afternoon last Saturday, and on Saturday night Grif walked in his sleep. I came down and let him in, and he spoke to me afterwards, up in his own room, in a very peculiar way about some danger."

"What sort of danger?"

"I didn't quite understand; but not a very nice sort:—a danger that would come from a dead person."

The doctor drew in his lips, but he said nothing.

"Mr. Bradley was also with him on Sunday afternoon, and on Sunday night Grif was taken ill. I have an idea that on Sunday afternoon they talked pretty freely—about the interesting subjects—because Mr. Bradley told Miss Annesley they hadn't talked at all, that Grif had been asleep most of the time:—which was a lie."

"How do you know? Did Grif say so?"

"No; he didn't give his pal away. He was even anxious to believe he *had* been asleep;—which probably means that the subjects were a little *too* interesting."

"And what were they?"

"I don't know: I can only guess. He may have told him what he had done, and what made him do it. If I had been allowed to sit up with Grif, as I wanted to, I believe I should know at this moment what he *had* done. I believe Grif knows, but he will never tell."

Doctor O'Neill had watched Palmer, as he produced these explanations, with an ever increasing curiosity. He now grunted, "I wonder!"

"He's been here since then," Palmer went on, "but he hasn't seen Grif. I saw him instead."

"And—you have kept all this to yourself?"

"Yes."

The doctor was silent. Then he said simply, "You're a wonderful boy, Palmer! I shall give myself the pleasure of calling again upon Mr. Bradley."

"Hadn't we better find out first what it was he did before they shut him up? It seems to me very likely that he gets dangerous."

"And how do you propose to find out?"

"I'm going to try your way: but I'll call when he's not at home. There's always a chance of picking up something on the spot."

"And if he comes back and finds you?"

"That will be exciting, won't it? You see, he knows already that I'm watching him, and he hates me like poison."

"And you're willing to undertake this—to try to carry it through by yourself?"

"I haven't anybody to help me."

"And you won't be afraid?"

"Not too much—when the time comes. I'd rather have had my revolver, of course, but it was sent back to the shop and the man was told not to let me get it again. I'll just have to make sure Bradley doesn't catch me."

"But suppose, for a moment, everything you say to be true. The man may be homicidal!"

"I think that's what he is."

The doctor pondered. He rejoiced in this Palmer, though he might not perhaps have been able to give a very good reason for doing so. Still, the fact remained, that he rejoiced in him exceedingly. "I tell you what," he said, "we'll take on this job together. I'm not sure that I shall be free to-night, but if I can't manage to-night I'll arrange for to-morrow. I'll let you know. What's more, I'll have your revolver for you:—though for heaven's sake don't use it," he added hastily. "We'll call on Mr. Bradley when he is out, and wait for him. For one thing, I'm extremely curious to watch your methods of work. I'll promise not to interfere, and you must promise me on your side not to do anything without my knowledge."

"All right."

Doctor O'Neill still gazed earnestly at the boy seated like a Buddha on the ground before him. Then a smile passed across his face, to which Palmer instantly responded. "I don't suppose we can do anything more at present," he said, getting up.

Palmer also rose, and peeped through the green drooping branches of the ash-tree.

"Don't go out that way," he cautioned his companion. "The others are on the lawn, and they might see us and begin to ask questions. If we go out at the other side they'll imagine we've just been for a bit of a stroll."

"You think of everything, Palmer," the doctor murmured, as he profited by this advice.

CHAPTER XX

MISS JOHNSON'S BIRTHDAY

'Accept at our hands, we pray you,
These mean presents, to express
Greater love than we profess.

Gifts these are, such as were wrought
By their hands that them have brought,
Home-bred things.'

—*Campion.*

DOCTOR O'NEILL did not join the young people on the lawn, but merely waved a hand to them before getting into his car.

Edward lay on his back on the grass, a tin of toffee by his elbow; Grif, now convalescent, Barbara, Ann, and Jim, were playing croquet. They gave up the game, however, when they caught sight of Palmer, and Edward pushed the tin of toffee towards his chum. They had all, in fact, been waiting for him, for this was Miss Johnson's birthday, and preparations for its proper celebration had been in progress ever since breakfast.

"We ought to build the bonfire before tea," Jim cried.

"So we will; there's plenty of time," returned Palmer, lazily. He dropped down on the grass beside Edward as he spoke, while the sound of the doctor's car died in the distance.

"But the fireworks have to be got ready, too."

"I thought you said they *were* ready."

"The set-piece is, but the others will have to be pinned up."

"That won't take a jiff."

Palmer lay watching the sunlit lawn, his thoughts far enough away from both Miss Johnson and fireworks. Sometimes he stole a glance at Grif, who sat very quiet. The chequered shadows on the grass, the green branches of the trees, the dark summer sky—to Palmer Grif was as remote from him as all these. Now that he had more or less constituted himself his protector he had begun to observe him closely, and he found him very easy to understand. He looked at Edward; he looked at Jim, at Barbara; and he wondered if he and Grif could become friends. Edward, of course, had always been his friend, and he still liked him fairly well:—it was only that he liked Grif better. He was quite aware that he was not Grif's sort; (that sort, he imagined, would be rather difficult to find). The little boy made him feel rough and coarse and—something else he could not altogether understand. But his way of speaking pleased Palmer, his manners, which were so gentle and gracious; and he wondered how he would get on at school, for he was to come back with Edward and him after the holidays. He decided that he should have to look after him, and he also decided that it was fortunate he should be there to do so. Even with all the looking after in the world it seemed to him that Grif would have a pretty thin time.

"There aren't really enough," said Edward. "The whole show will be over in about two ticks."

"What show?" asked Palmer absently, leaning his head back on the grass, and gazing up through green leaves at the sky.

"The bonfire won't," said Jim.

"How old do you think Miss Johnson is, Balmer?" Ann inquired, nestling up to him.

"Oh, I don't know. About seventy."

"No; but really. I want to put candles round the cake I've baked for her."

"You'll jolly well spoil that cake if you go messing about with it," said Edward. "Why can't you leave it alone!"

"But I want to have the candles," Ann persisted, "and I don't like to ask Miss Johnson her age—she's so particular about questions."

At that moment Miss Johnson herself appeared, in search of Barbara, whom she was taking into the town. "Are you ready, Barbara?" she called out, straightening her glasses, and surveying her pupil through them to see if she were quite tidy.

Barbara dropped her mallet and declared that she was.

"Miss Johnson, just a sec," said Palmer, shaking off his reverie, and springing to his feet. "I want to try a puzzle: it won't take half a jiff." He produced a pencil and a rather dirty-looking letter from home, which had evidently been in his pocket for many days. These he handed to Miss Johnson.

"Another time, Palmer," the governess said, for, ever since the evening of the dramatic performance, she had regarded all the red-haired boy's overtures with mistrust.

"It won't take a minute," Palmer coaxed, and Miss Johnson, after some further hesitation, yielded so far as to accept the paper and pencil.

"What am I to do?" she asked.

"Just think of a number—any number—and write it down on the envelope and multiply it by three."

Miss Johnson, conscious that all eyes were fixed upon her, did the necessary sum. "Well?" she said.

"Add one to it, and then multiply the result by three again."

"I hope this is all," said Miss Johnson severely, while at the same time she cast a penetrating glance round the assembled company. She noted in particular the solemn gaze of Ann and Jim, and immediately her suspicions in regard to a trap were confirmed.

"Very nearly. Now add the original number you chose."

"No, Palmer: this will go on for ever! I haven't time. Besides, you can get one of the others to do it;"—and she gave the paper and pencil to Ann. "Come, Barbara, we must hurry. The shops close early to-day."

Palmer submitted politely, while Miss Johnson, satisfied that, if any foolish joke had been intended, it had failed, withdrew, taking Barbara with her.

"What am I to do, Balmer?" Ann asked.

"Oh, just add the original number to what you have there. The original number will be the first one of all."

"But what do I add it to?"

"Here, show it to me," said Edward brusquely, taking the paper out of her hand. "Right you are, Dorset. This is a very ancient trick."

"I didn't say it was new," replied Palmer, yawning, "but if you read out the result it may have answered its purpose."

"What purpose? Three-forty-three."

"The purpose of finding out that Miss Johnson's age is thirty-four. Ann wanted to know."

"Oh, Balmer, how frightfully clever of you!" cried Ann, in ecstasies.

"It's all swank!" exclaimed Edward, incredulously. "You can't get a person's age that way. It just gives you whatever number they happen to choose. It's an old thing out of the *Boy's Own Paper*."

"That's all that is wanted," said Palmer. "What is the first number that is most likely to come into Miss Johnson's head to-day? Her age. I don't say that it's sure to be right; but I'll bet three to one in tins of toffee that it is. Will you take it on?"

"No," replied Edward simply; "it isn't profitable to bet with you, Dorset: you're too fond of certainties."

"It isn't a certainty. You know as much about it as I do. The only difference is that I'm willing to back my opinion, and you aren't."

"Well, I'm not going to bet anyway."

"I think you ought to apologize for that remark about certainties."

"All right: I take it back."

"But I can't put thirty-four candles on the cake," Ann said sadly. "It isn't nearly big enough."

"I tell you what," cried Jim. "We'll let off thirty-four rockets. . . . Only we haven't enough, unless we take down the set-piece." Then he had a bright idea. "I'll go and tell Aunt Caroline what it's for, and she'll maybe give me the money to buy the extra rockets." He was off before anyone had time to speak, but in a very few minutes he came back, looking rather crest-fallen.

"Aunt Caroline says Miss Johnson wouldn't like it, and that we're not to mention her age at all. She asked me how we knew what it was."

"And what did you tell her?"

"I told her Palmer had worked it out by arithmetic, but she didn't seem to understand."

"I wonder why Miss Johnson wouldn't like thirty-four rockets?" pondered Ann. "*I* would."

"It's because it makes her seem so old."

"Grown-up people never want to be thought old," said Jim. "If you ask them their age they always say eighteen, or twenty-one, or something silly, and then they laugh as if they had been funny, and all the others laugh."

"Thirty-four *isn't* old," said Ann. "Grandpapa read out of the newspaper the other day about a lady who was a hundred-and-two."

"What a ripping lot of rockets they could have had for her!" said Jim, regretfully.

"Oh, but they couldn't very well, because she had just died."

"They needn't have waited till her very last day to have them."

Ann considered this. "Maybe she died suddenly."

"I'm sure it wasn't that:—it was just that they didn't think of it."

"Miss Johnson says more opportunities are wasted by want of thought than by anything else," said Ann, improvingly.

"She doesn't think of many things herself—at least not of things anybody else wants to do."

"She thinks of the things *she* wants to do, I expect. She says the thing she likes best of all is to watch the sun setting over the sea."

Jim was puzzled. "Why; what happens when it sets?"

"I don't think anything happens. She says it's just a sort of feeling you get inside you:—and that it's sad."

"Something *must* happen then—in her inside. I hate feelings like that, and I don't see how anybody could like them." He eyed his stomach dubiously.

They both remained pensive for a minute or two, as if held by a memory of past indispositions; then they dismissed the subject from their thoughts.

Palmer and Edward had remained silent during the discussion, but the latter now got up. "Come on," he said, "and let's build the bonfire."

But neither rockets nor bonfire were to be witnessed by Palmer, for at half-past seven Doctor O'Neill's car drove for the second time up to the door, with a note for Aunt Caroline, requesting that Master Dorset should be allowed to pay the doctor a visit; and Aunt Caroline left it to Palmer himself either to accept or refuse the invitation.

He turned to the others.

"Why can't you put it off?" grumbled Edward, voicing the general opinion.

Even Aunt Caroline felt it rather strange that the doctor shouldn't at least have asked Edward as well. She objected very strongly to such favouritism, more particularly, perhaps, because the favourite was not one of her own nephews. All she said, however, was, "You must remember Doctor O'Neill is very busy, and can't choose his own time."

And Palmer added, "I think I'd better go."

This decided the matter, and it spoke highly for his fellow-pyrotechnists that his conduct was not criticized by them. All seemed to have an idea that a summons coming from such a quarter was more or less compulsory, and that if anyone were to blame it was the doctor himself.

Besides, the joy of fireworks is a great and a solid joy, though unhappily, when capital is limited, far too transitory. Still, while it lasts, it leaves no room for regret. Miss Johnson liked the fireworks very much indeed. The catherine-wheels, attached to the trunks of trees, whirled round, sending golden stars sailing into the darkness; the Chinese crackers hopped along the ground making a terrific noise; and when the set-piece flared out, somewhat reluctantly, with its "Many Happy Returns" in flaming letters, the governess was quite touched, and thanked them in a little speech for their kind thoughts.

Edward replied in a few well-chosen words, which included a graceful allusion to the novel. Then a belated Chinese cracker, going off suddenly and away from its neighbours, produced a scream from Bridget, and the ceremony was finished.

For the bonfire, which was to have been the principal item of the evening, and would have served as a pretext for sitting up till all hours, was cruelly nipped in the bud. Hardly had Jim and Grif and Edward set their matches to it, hardly had the first crepitating sounds rejoiced their hearts, the first tremulous flames flickered up with a delicious cloud of aromatic smoke, when grandpapa intervened and commanded them to put it out.

The 'putting out' was perhaps not performed so expeditiously as it might have been, and there was a good deal of kicking of blaz-

ing sticks about the grass; but grandpapa was firm, and it had to
be done. It was at this trying moment that Miss Johnson revealed
the excellent sportswoman she had secretly been all the time, by
proposing that they should come indoors and play games instead,
and that the hour of bedtime should be postponed, even for Jim
and Ann, till the delirious stroke of ten.

CHAPTER XXI

PALMER AT WORK

'Go and catch a falling star.'
—*Donne.*

IN full view of the Weston family Palmer took his seat in the car,
closed the door, and nodded reply to the chauffeur's "All right,
sir?"—nevertheless, this was not the way he would have managed
things himself. Much better to have done it quietly on the following evening, and without sending the car at all. For Palmer was,
after his own fashion, a true artist, and showiness did not appeal
to him, though there might be a bit of swagger when the work
was done. He felt no admiration, rather a good-natured contempt,
for those who run unnecessary risks, and if he sometimes mod-
elled his manner upon that of certain story-book heroes, he did
so simply to satisfy his dramatic instinct, and only when there
was no danger of its interfering with his plans. The whole thing
was a game, an elaborate and curious game. Those day-dreams in
which Inspector X. of Scotland Yard happily remarked, 'It's well
for us, Mr. Dorset, you're on the side of the law!' were really but
a survival from the period when he had sailed under the skull and
cross-bones, or taken to the road on a coal-black stallion, a true
minion of the moon.

He had been frightfully lucky, he considered, to have chanced
on these two cases—mentally he always referred to the unfortunate George as a case—the only drawback had been their
simplicity. He had been frightfully lucky, even though the cases
were not up to the standard of those he sometimes conducted in

imagination. Of course, for the real thing, he was badly handicapped. He had no electric torch, no disguises, no burglar's kit, no means of taking casts of footprints, no chemicals by which to secure the prints of fingers. The persons he pursued did *not* drop cigarette ashes, and if they had done so, he couldn't see how it would have helped matters. George, if he smoked cigarettes at all, almost certainly smoked Woodbines:—and at any rate establishment of identity was not the question in either case. It was of no importance whether Mr. Bradley left finger-prints on the church music, of no importance that there was a slight twitching in his left eyelid—all such things availed nothing: he had to work at present on the impalpable stuff of intuition and imagination.

It might, for instance, be important that Mr. Bradley appeared, as he walked along the road, now and then to cast a furtive glance at some invisible thing beside him. Palmer had had a little talk with Aunt Caroline that afternoon before tea, and he had tried an experiment with Grif—a very small one, it is true, for he had been mortally afraid of going too far—but the results had left him nothing solid to work upon. How could they? he reflected, since a sane mind cannot possibly put itself into touch with an insane one, cannot follow a reasoning which itself follows no law. It was like trying to catch a will-o'-the-wisp, or build walls round a mirage.

The car stopped at Doctor O'Neill's, and he got out. He rang the bell, and was shown into the consulting-room, where the doctor was busy, seated before a large roll-top desk.

He glanced up as the door opened. "That you, Palmer? I'll have finished directly." He scribbled something in a book, while Palmer looked slowly round him.

Presently the doctor closed the book with a snap and threw it into a drawer. He pushed back his chair a little, and smiled at his visitor. "So you managed to get away? No further news, I suppose?"

Palmer shook his head, and the doctor opened another drawer, from which he took a revolver—not the old one Palmer had been obliged to relinquish, but a new one, smaller and lighter. The boy examined it admiringly before dropping it into his coat pocket.

"That is a present from me," said the doctor, "though I couldn't get you a licence for it, because they won't issue licences to anyone under eighteen. You must keep it a secret,—I mean, until you go back to your own home. Miss Annesley would only be nervous if she knew you had it."

Palmer took out the revolver and examined it anew. "Thanks, awfully," he murmured, his face beaming with pleasure.

"As an expression of confidence I think it really *does* go pretty far," the doctor admitted. "In fact, from this on, I'll probably suffer agonies of remorse. My only stipulation is that you tell your father about it."

"I promise to tell him," said Palmer.

"That's all right then. And now I suppose we may as well go and call upon our friend."

Palmer looked up in surprise. "It's too soon," he exclaimed. "We must wait till it gets dark; otherwise, we won't be able to tell whether he is in or out."

"Can't we ask?"

"Of course; but that won't be much good if he happens to be there. You see, we must call when he's *not* in."

The doctor looked doubtful. "You still keep to that plan?"

Palmer was silent, sitting with lowered eyes. "I fancy perhaps I'd better do it alone," he said at last.

"You think I'm trying to back out of it?" the doctor laughed.

Palmer had once more taken the revolver from his pocket, and this time he laid it quietly down on the desk. At the same moment he got up and looked round for his cap. The doctor placed his hands on his shoulders, and pushed him back into his chair. He felt slightly annoyed, but he also felt—perhaps unnecessarily—that he was in the wrong, and apologized. "Come, you mustn't mind what I said. I undertook this job and I'll go through with it." As a matter of fact, he regretted his undertaking, but he was at the same time young enough to be amused by it, and his curiosity was keen.

Palmer was easily appeased, and very soon, on their former footing, they were talking together, Palmer describing to the doctor a method of reading cyphers of the simpler kind, in which letters are replaced by arbitrary signs. There was, in the lucidity of his exposition, something which gave his companion a pleasure that was almost æsthetic. The exhibition of this fresh young intelligence at work was to him extremely fascinating, and the difficulty he experienced in getting at any conception of the temperament behind it added to his interest.

"Aren't you very good at mathematics?" he asked.

"Fairly good. Not good enough to specialize—at least, I don't want to specialize. There are three or four chaps at school who are probably just as good as I am; and of course they work a great deal harder."

But darkness had crept up while they were talking, and Palmer signified that they might now proceed with what they had to do. "If he is in, there will be a light in his window: if there isn't a light, we can call. I don't fancy he is a person who sits much in the dark when he is alone."

They walked up the street in the direction of the house where Mr. Bradley lodged. This house stood on the extreme outskirts of the town; nevertheless, it did not take them many minutes to reach it. They had chosen the farther side of the road, so that they could see from some distance whether there was a light in the window or not. There was none, and they were about to cross over when Palmer suddenly pulled his companion back into the shadow of a gateway. Simultaneously, the door of Mr. Bradley's house opened, and the organist himself came out. They watched him walk on down the street.

"That was a close shave," Palmer murmured. "I think we'd better wait for ten minutes, just to see if he turns up again. He may only have gone to the post or something, and it will take him about ten minutes to go there and back. If I had been alone I would have followed him till I was sure of not being interrupted. You see, he hasn't taken the direction of the church."

"Oh, he'll not come back," said the doctor, optimistically, as they strolled on. "The shops are closed: he has gone for a walk."

"He may have. He had his stick with him, and he would hardly have taken that if he had only been going to the post. Besides, he hadn't a letter, unless it was in his pocket. Still, I fancy it would be better to give him a quarter of an hour."

The doctor, however, was impatient, and in the end Palmer

allowed himself to be persuaded. They retraced their steps and knocked at the door. Mr. Bradley's landlady informed them that the organist was out, but could give no information as to when he would return.

"Perhaps we could wait for a few minutes?" the doctor suggested.

"Certainly, Doctor O'Neill. I'm sure he'd be sorry if he thought he had missed you."

She took them upstairs and lit the lamp, lingering for a little to discuss the weather and the crops, much to Palmer's annoyance. At last she left them, and the boy, gliding across the room noise-lessly as a cat, opened the door and listened.

"She's gone into the kitchen," he said. "It's all right."

He looked about him eagerly. It was a fair-sized room, with two windows giving on the street, and two doors, one by which they had entered, and another which, as Palmer opened it, they saw led into a bedroom. Between the two windows was a bookcase, and in a corner by the bedroom door was a writing-table, with two rows of drawers. By the wall, facing the bookcase, stood a piano.

With the exceptions of a table and half a dozen chairs and a gilt-framed mirror above the fireplace, this was all the furniture the room contained: there were no pictures, no ornaments of any sort. Palmer went straight to the bookcase and took out an armful of the oldest-looking volumes. Presently he handed one of these to the doctor, open at a page across which Mr. Bradley's name was scribbled; and next he gave him a book which had evidently been bought not long ago.

"They seem to be the same," the doctor murmured, gathering that he was expected to compare the autographs.

"Yes; but the original fly-leaf of the old book has been torn out. It's the same with all of them: it's not a mere matter of chance. He has been pretty careful. It was in a manuscript music book that I saw his full name written: it ought to be about here somewhere." He went to the piano and turned over rapidly a pile of music. In a few moments he found what he was in search of, and brought it to the doctor. "You see, the writing is the same. Only the name was then Clement Bradley Tennant. The two pages have got stuck together. That's why he didn't notice it perhaps; or he may have pasted them together purposely, to keep the music that is written on the other side. If you hold it up to the light you can make it out quite distinctly. It was the pages being stuck together that attracted my attention."

The doctor gazed at the signature. "It certainly appears to be the same," he admitted.

Palmer replaced the books and began to prowl about once more. He approached the writing-table, and Doctor O'Neill, with qualms of conscience, watched him examine the contents of a letter-rack, and then turn over the leaves of a blotter. This last he brought to the mirror and held each leaf of it separately up before the glass, scanning it closely, though the blotting-paper was so much used that very little could have been decipherable. The boy's movements were extraordinarily rapid and silent, and the doctor could only stare at him with a growing consciousness of disapproval. In the end nothing but the recollection of his promise not to interfere prevented him from direct remonstrance.

Palmer, however, apparently did not find what he wanted, for he muttered to himself, and at last replaced the blotting-book and turned his attention to the drawers. Two of these were unlocked, and Palmer searched them swiftly, but it was when he asked the doctor to lend him his keys, and at the same time produced a penknife and a piece of wire from his pocket, that the latter felt constrained to speak. "I say—you can't do that, you know!" And he half rose from his chair.

Palmer paused. "Perhaps it won't be necessary," he answered; and crossing the room he disappeared into the bedroom.

The doctor followed him, and saw him light a candle, and then softly lock the bedroom door giving on the landing. "You promised not to interfere," he whispered back over his shoulder.

"I know I did, but——"

"If you go back to the other room you won't see me. Open the door a little, so that you will be able to hear if anybody comes upstairs."

The doctor returned to the sitting-room, and in quite a short time Palmer rejoined him there. "I've got what I wanted. I think we may go now."

The doctor looked at him questioningly. "I hope you didn't pick any locks."

"No; I didn't want to try the locks if I could avoid it. I haven't got the proper things to pick them with, and I don't want to leave any marks."

"And what have you discovered?"

Palmer slipped past him and closed the door, while the doctor, at the same time, became aware of footsteps approaching along the pavement of the street. The footsteps stopped and they heard the rattle of a latch-key.

"We're in for it now," the doctor murmured, conscious that his own share in the performance was about to begin, and not feeling happy at the thought.

They heard Mr. Bradley running up the stairs. Then the door was flung wide, and he stood on the threshold, gazing from one to the other of his visitors, while the flush on his face deepened. It was obvious that he was more astonished than pleased by this unexpected civility, and the situation was an awkward one, for he advanced no further, nor did he make any attempt to pretend that he was glad to see them. He simply stood there in silence, as if awaiting an explanation.

The doctor had not been prepared for this attitude of immediate hostility, and the words he uttered, as he found himself apologizing, sounded remarkably lame. Palmer, however, had a better excuse.

"Grif has lost the music of that thing he was to sing in church on Sunday. I don't think he'll be well enough to sing, but I thought, as we were passing your house, I would ask you if you had another copy. He was hunting everywhere for it to-day."

"Yes, he can have my own copy. I expect it is down in the hall. I'll just go and see."

He left them and they heard him running downstairs.

"He's gone to ask the landlady how long we've been here," said Palmer.

"It doesn't matter. That was rather a lucky whopper of yours."

"It wasn't a whopper. He *has* lost it, because I took it myself; and he was looking for it all over the place this morning."

"Well, I fancy it might be better for you to cut along as soon as you get the music, and leave me to tackle him alone."

"He'll think it queer if I go, when we came together."

"I fancy he thinks it pretty queer as it is. My idea, you know, was to speak perfectly openly to him, and I can hardly do that if you're here."

"What do you want to speak to him about?"

"About Grif, of course. I shall approach the subject as gently as possible. . . . Do you *want* to stay?"

"Only for a few minutes. Do you mind sitting there? and I'll sit here." He moved the lamp a little, also the chair which Mr. Bradley presumably would take.

The organist came in. It seemed that the music wasn't downstairs after all; he must have left it in the church: but he did not ask how Grif was, which was what Doctor O'Neill wanted him to do.

The doctor was himself obliged to broach the subject, saying that the little boy was not getting on so well as he had expected; but Mr. Bradley's regrets were politely indifferent—so markedly so, that the doctor decided he had better defer any further mention of the matter till Palmer should be gone. Presently he made a sign to the boy, but Palmer appeared all at once to have grown stupid, and merely gazed at the doctor with an irritating blankness of expression.

They discussed music, of which the doctor knew nothing, and Mr. Bradley, with an air of boredom so profound that it must have been assumed, listened to the remarks he hazarded. They talked on, and never in his life had Doctor O'Neill been subjected to such a subtle rudeness. He felt that he should not be able to stand it much longer. Every observation Mr. Bradley now let drop was, he knew, a more or less direct invitation for them to take their departure, and the doctor at last began to experience a certain curiosity as to how far such a conversation could go before it became brutally explicit. He had endeavoured to lead Mr. Bradley to talk about the past, but very soon he had seen the uselessness of such an attempt. Mr. Bradley, he now felt sure, knew precisely what they were there for, and it was only because he derived a mali-

cious satisfaction from the doctor's discomfort that he did not cut
the interview short on the spot. Certainly, if he *had* seen through
them, he was taking an ample revenge.

The doctor felt at present that where he had made a fatal mistake was in bringing Palmer. It was Palmer who had aroused the
organist's suspicions: without Palmer all might have been well.
Meanwhile, the red-haired boy seemed to take no notice of anything they were saying. He had begun to examine the books on the
shelf near him, reading out several of the titles in an undertone.

"*Hallucinations*! My father has that book, I think."

Mr. Bradley glanced malevolently in the boy's direction, and the
doctor asked politely, "Are you interested in the subject?"

"Not in the least," replied the organist, coldly. "Half those
books don't even belong to me—that is to say, I didn't buy them. I
read very little."

"Isn't an hallucination a kind of ghost that isn't really there?"
Palmer innocently inquired, turning to Mr. Bradley.

"Yes, something like that:—an idea that enters the heads of
stupid people, and leads them to make themselves ridiculous."

The doctor laughed. He decided that, since Palmer was evidently determined not to budge without him, they had both better
go. After all, his coming here had probably conveyed to Mr. Bradley the message, or the warning, which was all—considering he
had no definite knowledge to go upon—that at the best he could
have given him.

"Well, I expect it's about time we moved on," he murmured,
preparatory to getting up; but Palmer sat staring at the wall opposite him as if he had not heard. His face had altered, his forehead
was wrinkled up, and a curious, fixed expression had come into
his eyes. The doctor, who had half risen from his chair, sat down
again. If ever anyone had the appearance of being confronted by
an hallucination, it was Palmer at that moment.

The organist was watching him too, and, as he watched, his
long thin fingers all at once began to move nervously. He seemed
on the verge of saying something; his lips parted to speak; but he
checked himself. At last he broke into a thin high laugh. "What are
you staring at?" he asked.

Palmer started up out of a dream. "Nothing," he answered a little confusedly. And then, as if in spite of himself, "I was just looking at your shadow on the wall."

The organist moved quickly, and pushed back the lamp.

"Don't," said Palmer, getting up. "There's a boy at school who can do ripping silhouettes from people's shadows:—some of them are awfully queer! . . . If I had a piece of paper I could do yours."

As he spoke he took a pencil from his pocket, and moved towards the writing-table. Simultaneously Doctor O'Neill became aware that something had happened. A moment previously he had had before him an elderly gentleman, perhaps a little eccentric-looking, but obviously refined, and even distinguished, in appearance. What was it, then, that had taken place; what incredible transformation? For in that white grimacing mask of hate turned towards the back of the retreating boy he saw only the face of a devil.

The impression passed so quickly that had it been less vivid he might have doubted of its reality. Mr. Bradley recovered himself even before Palmer had time to reach the desk. "I'm afraid you won't be able to do your drawing to-night," he said acidly. "I must go now. I want to try over some music before it gets too late."

The doctor rose to his feet at once. "I really must apologize for keeping you."

"Not at all; it has been delightful. I was under the impression you were very busy, otherwise we might have had more of these pleasant evenings together. Does this interesting boy—I hope he will pardon me for not knowing his name?—does he invariably accompany you on your rounds?"

"Oh, we're great pals," the doctor said, with a rather pumped-up geniality. He pushed Palmer out of the room before him, for Mr. Bradley's little bow, delivered with his hands clasped behind his back, was quite sufficient indication that they were dismissed.

The doctor was conscious that all through he had played a subordinate and rather hopeless part, and that he had played it extremely badly. "You're right," he remarked, when they once more found themselves in the street. "The man is certainly insane—I should think dangerously so. I wonder how long he has been like this? At

any rate, steps must be taken at once: in fact, I don't know whether
I oughtn't to warn the people he is with now."

"You saw his face when I got up to draw his shadow? That's the
way he looked when he caught me in the church—only to-night he
was a good deal worse. If you hadn't been there there might have
been developments."

"Perhaps too many developments," said the doctor briefly.

"I was ready for him; I was watching him in the mirror."

"I don't think he'd have given you much time. And at any
rate, if you *had* used your revolver, what would you have felt like
afterwards?"

"I don't know. I don't think I'd have felt a great deal."

"I expect your bark is worse than your bite, Palmer. . . . Well, I'm
coming home with you. I must have a talk with Canon Annesley."

"About this?"

"Yes; something will have to be done. The man isn't safe."

They walked side by side along the road, in the direction of
the Glebe, the doctor a good deal worried in more ways than
one.

"We shouldn't have gone as we did," he said at last. "We ought
to have managed differently. The worst possible thing was to excite
him."

"But if we hadn't gone we shouldn't have known. It was a pity
he came back so soon."

"I might have found out—found out sufficient at all events—
simply by leading him on to talk. . . . That is, if you had given me a
hint. *Your* method, I'm afraid, was rather drastic. Another thing;—
I think you should have told me all you knew. I thought you *had*
done so, this afternoon."

"I did tell you all I knew, sir. This was only a guess—from something Miss Annesley told me Grif had said when he was ill. It was
after I had seen you, just before tea this evening, that she told me.
And my guess might have been all wrong. I wouldn't have risked it
if I hadn't seen he knew what we had come about."

"And what do you make of it now?"

"I can't make very much of it. But *he* did. It had some meaning for *him*. And it was because he thought I had hit on the truth

that he looked like that. It has something to do with his shadow. I noticed once or twice before, when I saw him out walking, that he kept looking at something—something which seemed to me not to be there. . . ."

The doctor grunted; he felt dissatisfied. "What was it you found in his bedroom?" he asked.

"An address for you to write to—to make inquiries."

They walked along in silence for a little way, Palmer from time to time glancing uncertainly at his companion. The road was deserted, and the high hedges, black in the still moonlight, seemed to shut them in. A freshening breeze filled the night with murmuring sound, and blew the scent of honeysuckle in their faces.

"Do you think it is rotten—all I have done?"

The doctor started out of a train of uncomfortable cogitation. "No, no; certainly not. I think it very possible you may have averted some—some disaster."

"You didn't like it, all the same—when we first went in," said Palmer despondently.

The doctor forced a laugh. "Oh, well—perhaps not. You see, a person suffering from delusions isn't exactly a criminal. And then, it was all—rather outside my experience."

Palmer was silent a moment. Then he said in a low voice, "But you don't think I'd do that kind of thing without a very good reason, do you?"

"Of course not."

"I wouldn't, you know," said the boy eagerly.

"I'm sure you wouldn't." He laid a friendly hand on Palmer's shoulder.

Palmer, however, was determined to be honest. "The first thing of that sort I tried was at home. It was long ago, and I was only a kid of about ten or eleven. Mamma had lost some money—two sovereigns had been taken out of her purse, she said. I remembered seeing one of the servants, a girl called Jane, come out of mamma's room, and I remembered that she had hurried past me in the passage. I was sure Jane had taken the money. There was a fuss made, but mamma didn't want to call in the police or anything like that, though when papa laughed at her it only made her more sure than ever that she had been robbed. I waited till I saw Jane by herself, and then I said to her that perhaps mamma had dropped the money, and that it might have rolled under the fender in her room; but I had first looked under the fender to make sure there was nothing there. Jane was quite excited by the idea, and she ran upstairs, while I dawdled behind so as to give her plenty of time. When I came in she was standing in the middle of the floor, and she called out in a queer nervous kind of way, 'You can look for yourself, Master Palmer; I won't have anything to do with it; I won't go near it.' So I lifted up the fender, and there were the two sovereigns; and she was so stupid that she had actually laid one exactly on the top of the other. Then suddenly she began to cry. She put her arms round me and kissed me. I told her she must keep the money; that if she didn't they would know she had stolen it. And in the end she confessed, and told me why she had taken it. It was for one of her brothers, who had got into trouble in some way, and she had intended to pay it back. I promised not to tell, and persuaded her at last to keep the two pounds. She left a little while afterwards, and I never saw her again. But she paid back the money. She sent mamma a postal order nearly a year later, and though they suspected it came from Jane, nobody was ever quite sure."

"Well, I'm glad you didn't give the girl away," said the doctor quietly.

CHAPTER XXII

FIRE!

'The dogs they do bay, and the timbrels play,
    The spindle is now a-turning;
The moon it is red, and the stars are fled,
    But all the sky is a-burning.'

—*Ben Jonson.*

WHEN they reached home the birthday festivities were over. Aunt Caroline, who was alone, put down her book on their entrance, and sent Palmer to Canon Annesley's study to tell him of the doctor's arrival.

The canon listened in silence to what the doctor had to say, but Palmer, watching him, formed the idea that he listened unwillingly. And whether the doctor told his story badly, or whether the canon happened to be in a particularly sceptical mood, the result certainly seemed to be that he took the matter very lightly indeed. Of course, Bradley had always been eccentric and irritable. No doubt he was a little run-down. A holiday, a complete change, was what he needed: it would set him on his feet again in no time: the canon would make a note to talk to him about it.

And that was all! He sank back in his chair with a little smile, and folded his hands. Aunt Caroline, it is true, was more impressed, but what amazed, and then exasperated the doctor, was that neither of them appeared in the least to realize the gravity of the matter in its relation to Grif, or even to admit that it applied to him at all.

"You don't seriously want me to believe the man is mad, do you?" the canon exclaimed at last. He seemed even a little bored by the doctor's persistence: and he slewed round sharply to stare at Palmer, who was sitting very quietly in his corner.

The doctor not only wanted him to believe it, but went over for the third time all the evidence Palmer had managed to collect.

Canon Annesley drummed with his fingers on the table. Apparently he was not yet convinced. He quite frankly, as he said, found it impossible to believe that Mr. Bradley had had anything to do with Grif's illness. No man would do such a thing as deliberately to terrify a child—especially a child he obviously liked. "I really think, doctor, and certainly I hope, you are mistaken. He may have been foolish enough, or thoughtless enough, to tell the boy a ghost-story, not realizing that he had to do with a rather too active imagination: but that there is more in it than that——" He again had a good look at Palmer, whom he evidently believed to be somehow at the bottom of the whole business. He even went so far as to administer to Master Dorset what was, for him, a fairly strong reproof.

"I think, Palmer, it would be better if you did not keep quite so close a watch upon your neighbours. A habit of suspicion is of all things the most intolerable, and it is one which, if you don't try to check it, I am afraid will grow upon you."

A faint flush rose to Palmer's cheeks, but he answered nothing.

Doctor O'Neill, however, replied for him.

"There's no use blaming the boy. I consider that throughout the whole matter he has given proof of the highest intelligence and courage."

"I never for a moment doubted either his intelligence or his courage, doctor," said the canon, mildly, "and of course if he thought Grif was being injured by his friendship with Bradley, it was right of him to tell somebody so:—he might even have mentioned it to us! I was only referring to a bias of mind which may sometimes lead one to brood over things that have not quite the significance we read into them."

The doctor grunted, not very politely. "Well then, the bias is mine," he made answer, "and also the suspicion. The only difference is that I had not the imagination, or the flair, or whatever you like to call it, to get at the facts, till they were shoved under my nose."

The canon raised his eyebrows ever so little. He disliked violence, whether in speech or action, and the doctor struck him as being far too impulsive, both in his manner, and in the judgments he formed. "But my dear O'Neill," he suggested pleasantly, "aren't you basing everything on a theory which has yet to be proved? After all, a man can't be damned even on Palmer's intuitions, brilliant as they may be. I venture to think that in corroboration we require something—well, shall I say rather more solid?"

"Don't you think, papa, you might put off the discussion of Palmer's share in the matter till another time?" Aunt Caroline at this point interposed.

"Oh—er—yes," Doctor O'Neill apologized. "As a matter of fact I had forgotten he was there."

"I don't know what he won't deduce from it," said the canon dryly. "Palmer, accept my apologies if I have hurt your feelings in any way. I shall certainly follow your future career with the liveliest interest:—and I've an idea that 'lively' will be the right word for it."

"All the same, I don't think you in the least grasp the seriousness of the matter," said the doctor obstinately.

"Papa never does," said Aunt Caroline.

The canon protested. "Really, my dear, this is most unfair. I couldn't be more serious without becoming lugubrious, and I refuse to admit that the evidence I have heard demands that of me."

But, even as he spoke, the sound of somebody running quickly up the avenue broke upon their ears, and the canon nodded his head towards Palmer, who had jumped to his feet, and now stood, like a dog straining on his leash, facing the door. "Possibly this is the rest of the evidence," he said.

Palmer sprang from the room, and next moment he ushered in Johnnie, breathless and nearly inarticulate.

"The're a fire," Johnnie gasped, rolling his eyes, "a fire blazin', an' all the doors is locked. An' Mr. Bradley's playin' the organ so that you could hear it in the town!"

"Where is the fire?" asked the canon, while Palmer was already racing upstairs to tell Edward.

"In the church," gasped Johnnie. "An' the organ—you never h'ard the like of it!"

"He's set fire to the church," cried the doctor, knocking over a chair in his excitement. He bundled Johnnie out into the hall. "Run on to the town and call up the fire-brigade. Run like——"

"I'll go on the bike," shouted Palmer from an upper landing, while various small figures, clad in night garments, began to make an appearance, piping innumerable questions at the tops of their voices.

"Children, go back to bed all of you!" Aunt Caroline commanded.

"I must get the keys," said the canon fussily. "Doctor, you had better go on at once; I'll be with you as soon as I can."

The servants, too, had awakened, and confusion reigned in the house. Profiting by it, Edward, Grif, and Jim, hastily pulled on their trousers, and such other clothing as was absolutely essential. Then they rushed down to the hall. Edward and Jim were out of the house before Aunt Caroline could stop them, but Grif, as usual, was captured.

"Grif, you're not to go out. The others are very naughty and disobedient."

"But I've never seen a fire," he begged.

Ann and Barbara at this moment appeared, and Aunt Caroline, feeling that it was rather hopeless to get them back to bed, capitulated. "If I let you go with me, will you promise to keep close beside me all the time, and come home when I tell you to?"

"Yes, yes." The air was filled with promises, and there was a stampede to the door.

"Stop!" screamed Aunt Caroline. "You can't go like that, in your slippers! And you, Grif, must wrap yourself up well. Put on your shoes and your coat, and wait here for me."

The doctor, meanwhile, was hurrying on to the church. When he reached it he found that Johnnie had by no means brought a false alarm. The fire was dancing merrily in the fore part of the building, the old dry timber of the pews blazing and crackling, while a red glare lit up the windows. And in the midst of it, and in a heat that must already be appalling, the organ was thundering and shouting, the whole place seeming to vibrate to its din.

The doctor tugged at the side door, but uselessly, for it was locked. Seizing a stone, he began to smash in one of the windows, while still the organ crashed and sang. The doctor was a powerful man, and to break down the framework of the window was not difficult, though, to do so, he had to climb a foot or two up the wall, and cling to the sill with his left hand. A rush of hot air puffed out in his face, but he could see that it would be some minutes yet before the fire made the chancel untenable. As the prospect of a struggle with a madman in a burning church whose doors were locked, and the keys perhaps flung in the flames, did not, however, appeal to him, he dropped to the ground again, and ran back to meet the canon.

At last he saw him coming, and with him were Edward and Jim. They all hastened to the church together. To enter at the front was impossible, and the doctor, having got the key from the canon, ran round once more to the side entrance, but, to his surprise, he found that the door was now open. Also the sound of the organ had ceased. Mr. Bradley must have found the place too hot for him, and come out.

The doctor took a step or two forward, but on the threshold a blast as from a furnace, mingled with smoke and sparks, swept out to meet him, and he recoiled.

"Keep back!" he shouted to the others, who were pressing close on his heels.

They all retreated, and Edward and Jim were ordered to stand well away from the walls while the doctor made his second attempt. This time he succeeded in getting as far as the chancel, but the heat was terrible, and the smoke almost blinded him. Mr. Bradley was nowhere to be seen.

"He's not there," the doctor cried as he dashed out again. "He must have left the church when I went to meet you."

They moved round towards the road, where a small crowd was beginning to gather. All at once there was a shattering explosion. Two of the windows had burst, and from each a long slender tongue of flame shot up, licking against the wall and reaching to the roof. This explosion was followed rapidly by others, and in a few minutes the whole front of the church was a rushing mass of flames, which seemed to stream up into the sky, to float for a little distance, and then drop down again in a loose, golden shower. The heat grew so intense that they were obliged to retreat, for the walls themselves were now cracking and smoking, and the front door bulged, as if thrust out by an immense force. The crowd was increasing, and at last they heard the fire-brigade.

"They can't do anything," Canon Annesley shouted in the doctor's ears, for he knew there was no water nearer than the river, and hand-pumps obviously would be useless. The firemen themselves admitted this, and simply stood among the other spectators, to watch the blaze.

"Look! Look!" a boy screamed, pointing upward. "The're a man up there!"

All eyes were raised to the tower, and high up, on a ledge, seeming to stand against the bare wall, they saw a black figure. A thrill of horror shivered through the rocking crowd. In the glare of light the dark form was distinctly visible, his face, his wild silver hair, his outstretched arms. He seemed to be shouting, but his voice was drowned by the roar of the flames. There was a simultaneous rush to drag round the escape, but when it was reared against the wall it proved too short by nearly fifteen feet. Nevertheless, one of the firemen began to swarm up it, but the heat was too great, and he was forced back again. There followed a dull crash, and the flames momentarily died down, only to spring up again with redoubled power:—the roof, or a portion of it, had fallen in. And still the figure on the tower stood there, his arms outspread, as if nailed to the stones, in the attitude of crucifixion. Then, all at once, they saw him lean forward and dive. For an instant a dark body was visible hurtling through the air, and a scream of dismay rose from the women.

The body was borne over the grass and laid down by the churchyard wall. This culminating tragedy quelled the excitement of Jim and Edward and Palmer, who up till then had been dancing about, half intoxicated by the splendour and beauty of the flames, the fact that it was grandpapa's church which was burning never even entering their minds. Now they remained silent and awestruck, and in this sudden passivity were discovered and seized upon by Doctor O'Neill, who brought them over to where the canon stood at the edge of the crowd.

"I shouldn't advise you to wait any longer, sir," the doctor said. "It's fortunate that Miss Annesley and the other children left before this last scene took place."

"Yes, I'll go now," the canon murmured in a half-dazed voice. "Poor Bradley! I suppose we may hope that he was at least spared the horror of realization?"

"Yes, I think so. And I don't think he suffered; the body is not burned. . . ."

The canon laid his hand on Edward's shoulder. "Come, boys," he said. "We may as well be getting home. Are you going to stay, doctor?"

"No; I'm coming too."

The canon walked on, a grandson on either side of him; while Doctor O'Neill followed with Palmer.

CHAPTER XXIII

THE GLITTERING NET

'O Rose, thou art sick!
The invisible worm,
That flies in the night,
In the howling storm,

Has found out thy bed
Of crimson joy;
And his dark secret love
Does thy life destroy.'

—*Blake.*

'And all my days are trances,
And all my nightly dreams
Are where thy dark eye glances,
And where thy footstep gleams—
In what ethereal dances,
By what eternal streams.'

—*Edgar Poe.*

IF, as he walked home that night, Doctor O'Neill felt any misgivings concerning the part he and Palmer had played in relation to Mr. Bradley, and the possible effect their action might have had in bringing about the subsequent tragedy, he kept them to himself; yet undoubtedly he was relieved when, two days later, he learned that the boy's reading of the case had been singularly accurate. A telegram to the address discovered by Palmer had brought over a friend of Mr. Bradley's by the next boat, and the whole story was then revealed. It was an unpleasant story, in substance very much what Grif had listened to on that Sunday afternoon when he lay sick in bed, but the fact that it so justified himself and his young companion made it welcome to the doctor.

Only he and the canon heard the full details, though the doctor afterwards shared them with Palmer. They now learned of the homicide, which had been followed by Mr. Bradley's detention for a period of several years in a lunatic asylum. Then, apparently cured, and on his father's guaranteeing to look after him, he had been released; but after his father's death, possibly fearing that he might be put again under restraint, possibly only to escape from those who knew his story, Mr. Bradley had disappeared. It was now that he dropped the name of Tennant, keeping only his two Christian names, and that he came as organist to Ballinreagh church. The only person belonging to the past with whom he kept in touch was this friend who related the history. Sometimes they met and stayed for a week together, but Mr. Bradley would never visit at his friend's home, nor allow him to come to Ballinreagh. And of late certain rather ominous signs, which might prelude a relapse, had begun to loom like warning lamps through the darkness:—for instance, that matter of mysterious letters, letters which never arrived, letters which would confirm a claim to some fantastic title or fortune. . . .

Doctor O'Neill at this point could not help casting a meaning glance at the canon, but the canon was absorbed in the story, and though, later on, he admitted that he had judged Palmer over-hastily, both he and Miss Annesley, to the very end, refused to believe that the organist had been in any way responsible for Grif's illness.

The doctor threw out a question or two on the subject of Mr. Bradley's delusions, and himself described Palmer's curious experiment, while the canon fidgeted uneasily. . . .

And the matter dropped. . . . It cannot be denied that, as time passed, the progress of a fund for rebuilding the church occupied more of Canon Annesley's thoughts than the memory of his organist; and those with whom that memory remained greenest were Grif and Doctor O'Neill.

But for very different reasons. The doctor was interested entirely on Grif's account. That is to say, he still puzzled over the unfortunate Mr. Bradley, because he was still puzzled as to the nature of the hold he had obtained upon his patient. Nothing had been revealed as to that, and nothing now seemed ever likely to be revealed. What caused the matter to linger in the doctor's mind was the simple fact that Grif was not making the progress he had expected. The little boy had been what was called 'better' for some weeks now, but the doctor did not believe he was well. He ran about more or less as he had done before his illness; Miss Annesley and his grandfather seemed quite satisfied as to his health:—and in spite of this the doctor knew, and Palmer knew, that he was not the boy he had been. . . .

August crept on, and with September the deeper golden tones of autumn began to steal into the summer. Here and there a fallen leaf, here and there a sign of over-ripeness, betokened that approaching weariness which, once a year, drops slowly down upon nature, as sleep, once a day, upon the eyes of a tired child. And Grif, to the doctor's keen vision, seemed a little weary too. He watched him closely; watched the bright eyes and sallow face, the slender form and listless movements; and a deep pity for this strange, quiet, little chap grew up within him.

One morning Aunt Caroline spoke to him about Grif's going to school, and the doctor stared in sheer amazement. He could hardly believe his ears. "But the thing's absurd!" he said, trying to keep the irritation he felt out of his voice. "Can't you see that it is?" And when Aunt Caroline did not see, he shrugged his shoulders impatiently. In the end he got angry. "It would be a positive cruelty to send him as he is now. I never saw a boy less fitted for a public school in my life. You're simply condemning him to a life of misery."

"Misery?"

"Yes," snapped the doctor, "misery:—none the less real because he won't be able to account for it satisfactorily, and I dare say won't mention it at all. He's *bound* to be unhappy, and if he is unhappy he won't live. You may think that a ridiculous exaggeration, but I'll stake any medical reputation I may possess on its truth."

Aunt Caroline said she would write to her sister, though there was hardly time to get an answer now. Grif's father, in particular, was very keen that at the beginning of the autumn term he should go to school with Edward. "It's not as if he were to go alone," Aunt Caroline added. "He will have his brother there to look after him, and Palmer."

"His brother can't look after him," replied the doctor bluntly. "Palmer might be able to do a little, but you must remember that at school it's quite impossible for big boys and little boys to chum together. What's more, they are utterly different in temperament, in everything. Even if they were of the same age, it would be impossible for Palmer to make a close friend of Grif."

Aunt Caroline was nettled. "You seem to have a wonderful opinion of Palmer—especially in contrast to my nephews!"

"I *have* a good opinion of him," the doctor answered. "Do you think I am mistaken?"

"I should be sorry to say that."

"I really believe—considering all things—that you ought to be. . . . But I should like to know just this. Will you ever ask Palmer to stay here again?"

Aunt Caroline shook her head. "I didn't ask him this time," she mentioned quietly. "He came as a friend of Edward's."

"And what have you against him?"

"I have nothing at all against him." She paused, and then went on: "You have evidently formed an idea, doctor, that papa and I have taken a dislike to Palmer. Papa *does* dislike him, I admit; but for myself, all I can say is, that he is not a companion I should naturally choose for the other boys. I may be wrong:—if I am, you will at least give me credit for not having interfered up to the present. What it really amounts to, I suppose, is that somehow I don't feel perfectly sure that he is a *good* boy. Don't look so disgusted! After all, you asked me what I thought. I don't know Palmer; none of us do:—I don't know a thing more about him at this moment than I did on the day he arrived here; and I can't look upon that as an encouraging sign."

She smiled a sort of challenge, which the doctor failed to take up.

"I know what *you* like about him," she went on, "and of course all the children like him too:—Ann simply says her prayers to him. But do you think he likes *them*? He likes Ann, I dare say, and, though you mightn't expect me to admit this, I also think he likes Grif a little, in his own way. But do you really believe he cares for Edward, who is his particular friend? . . . . Not one little bit. Nor for any of the rest of us. Oh, I know: I am quite sure. He could watch us all drown without raising a hand to throw us a rope that might be lying at his feet."

"I'm sorry you find him so vindictive," said the doctor, taking up his hat.

"I don't. He doesn't strike me as being in the least vindictive. I simply think he is callous. All you imagine to have been done for Grif was really done for sport. I'm quite willing to grant that he is very clever and brave:—but I doubt if he has any conscience, or any moral sense."

The doctor was silent. He knew that to argue would be only waste of breath. But his own opinion of Miss Annesley dropped there and then to zero. Her whole attitude, where Palmer was concerned, seemed to him, like her father's, stupid, ungrateful, unfair. To the doctor's mind, Edward was just an average boy, perfectly commonplace; Jim was simply mischievous, though a nice little chap, and quite bright and intelligent; while Grif was intelligent too, and rather babyish for his age. To compare any of them with Palmer was ridiculous. From a Sunday-school, or an 'aunt' point of view, they might be better or they might not; but, considered as the stuff of which a man is made, they simply, in comparison, did not count.

So he put it to himself, disgustedly, while he drove down the avenue, and along the road, in the direction of the now ruined church. As he passed by the graveyard he caught sight of Grif and stopped the car.

"Like to come for a drive?" he suggested. "I'll be able to bring you back in time for lunch."

Grif got in beside him, but his action was marked by that strange docility which the doctor did not care to see, for he could not help feeling that any other suggestion he might have made would have been followed in exactly the same way. In the doctor's eyes such amenability too nearly resembled apathy.

They drove in silence, and as the little boy sat there beside him, bare-headed and bare-kneed, Doctor O'Neill was struck anew by that peculiar expression of a kind of patient sweetness in his eyes, and by the lightness and slenderness of his body. It somehow touched him acutely, and he swore below his breath as he recalled Miss Annesley's remarks about school. The doctor liked Grif. Since he had begun to look after him professionally he had even grown fond of him; but the interest he felt was very different from the interest he took in Palmer, and that difference seemed accounted for by the way Grif sat beside him now, sat there as quiet as a little mouse, not saying a word, but just nestling up to him confidingly. He felt really an affection for the little fellow, but his affection was mingled with, if not based on, pity, and the doctor was a man who naturally preferred those whom there was no need to pity.

It was after he had paid his call, and when they were on their way home, that he said, "Why don't you ever go to see Captain Batt and Miss Nancy now? They were asking me about you the other day, and saying you hadn't been there for ever so long."

Grif coloured. "I'll go and see them," he answered softly.

As a matter of fact, he felt rather guilty towards the Batts. He did not understand why it was that he should no longer be eager to go there; he even felt ashamed of his lack of enthusiasm; but some shadowy barrier seemed to have grown up between him and his friends. He had been conscious of it the last time he had gone. The place had not been the same, nothing had been the same; he had lost touch, he was a stranger there; and as he had wandered about, blind and baffled, turning this way and that in a fruitless endeavour to get back, he had known that it was useless. Something had happened; he had been cut off; he was like a dog who has lost a scent; and he had wanted to run away and be alone with the tears which kept rising to his eyes. . . .

He had lost touch with everything now. All the things he used to care for were fast slipping from him—even their meaning. Sometimes, in a kind of reaction or despair, he would rush back into the past, enter feverishly into what the others were doing; but these reactions grew from day to day more feeble, and he seemed, like a sinking ship, to be settling down before the final plunge, that would carry him into the darkness and the cold.

And the doctor, though dimly, was aware of all this. He was aware, for Palmer had told him, that Grif, who used always to be singing about the house and out of doors, now never sang; he knew there was something against which his tonics were of no avail; and from Grif himself he could get no guidance as to what it was, for the little boy's very gentleness made it but more difficult to do anything with him.

What the doctor did not know was that the sound of the Spring Song sang now in Grif's ears from morning till night. What he did not know was that it sang through his dreams, and that Grif, awakening, would sit up in his bed to listen to it. And he would wander off alone to listen to it; he had been listening to it to-day when the doctor had driven up in his car. And sometimes he felt that the player on the flute was very near, sometimes he seemed to see him. Mingled with this fascination was a fear. He had hours now when he saw, with a curious and terrible insight, whither he was being drawn. He had written down pledges on paper, and signed them—only to break them: and his will was getting weaker. He knew that in yielding to this half-dreaded, and of late more than half-dreaded spell, he was injuring himself and all those who loved him. He could hear, far away, the low roar of the whirlpool into which he was being sucked; he could feel the overpowering drag of those dark frozen waters.

He knew that the things he had once cared for were becoming less and less able to hold him, even for a moment. He knew that he was becoming more and more absorbed in one feeling, one languid listless passion, which seemed strong now only because all other things were weak, which was able to fascinate him without bringing him happiness, or even a passing pleasure. At times he longed, with a hopeless despairing crying of his soul, to tell somebody, to ask for help; but he felt there was no one he could speak to, no one he could tell.

He could not tell Aunt Caroline. He knew that if he did she would not be able to do anything for him; he knew just what she would say, how she would get him to make a promise. A promise! He had promised so often already, and had so often broken his word. . . .

The doctor set him down at the Glebe gate, and Grif thanked him. Then he turned and walked up the avenue to the house. He walked slowly, listlessly. And the doctor knew that three months ago he would have been running and shouting, shouting to the others, beginning to tell them about his drive while he was still fifty yards off. To-day he doubted very much if he would even mention the matter.

CHAPTER XXIV

GRIF FALLS ASLEEP

'What peace doth now
Rock him asleep.'
—*Vaughan.*

OWING to what the doctor had said it was decided that Grif was not to go to school till an answer should have been received to Aunt Caroline's letter:—Edward and Palmer would be returning next week.

It was on a morning towards the end of September that he wandered away by himself, and his feet of their own accord seemed to take, as they very often did just now, the direction of the churchyard.

The rebuilding of the church had not yet been begun, though the canon hoped to see it well in progress before the year was out. Grif's head was bent, and there was a certain drag in his walk, as if all volition had gone out of it, and he were merely obeying a summons. As he reached the low wall he paused and a look of aversion came into his eyes.

Pouncer was with him, and Pouncer, too, appeared to feel his master's depression. A heaviness of autumn was over them, and in the grey stagnant air each sound—the rattle of a passing cart, the cry of a boy driving sheep—dropped like a stone into a pond, became lost in the silence which spread above it again, sending only a faint ripple out to some eternal shore.

He looked at the reddening blackberry-leaves; he stroked them softly: and, had anyone been there to see it, there must have seemed something peculiarly pathetic in that simple action. Then, in the distance, he heard the hoot of an approaching motor. It told him that the doctor was coming, and for some obscure reason he was seized by a desire to hide. He climbed the wall and crouched down below it on the other side, holding Pouncer close to him till the car had passed. Then he wondered why he had hidden. He did not know why; only from day to day the instinct was growing stronger and stronger within him to hide from everything.

The passing of the doctor reminded him of the drive they had taken together, and of the promise he had then made to go to see the Batts. He had not kept his promise: he had not been able to keep it; for it seemed to require an almost impossible effort of will now to do even the simplest things.

At length he conquered his listlessness and climbed back into the road. He actually ran for a little way, trying to get out of sight of the churchyard as quickly as possible, as if he feared to walk on and on, as he sometimes did in a nightmare, and still find it close beside him. Even Pouncer appeared to be affected by the same idea, for he raced ahead, barking and puffing, spreading out his legs in a clumsy gallop.

Gradually Grif's feet began to move more slowly, and at last he came to a complete standstill in the middle of the road. Pouncer looked back at him anxiously, still keeping a little in front, but the boy remained motionless, his eyes half shut. He wanted to go on, yet something called him back. In a vague way he realized that he had reached a sort of crisis, and that defeat, should it occur again, would this time be permanent. . . .

He felt Pouncer beside him, licking his hand. He moved on blindly. A dead stillness seemed to have fallen over everything, and the very air appeared to push him back, to bar his progress, to be like the dense and clinging weeds which thicken a stagnant pool.

He stumbled on, and presently the old garden wall rose before him, and with that his pace quickened. He reached the gate and pushed it open.

He found Captain Narcissus at work, clipping one of the box-trees, which was cut into the shape of a bird; but Grif did not stay long with him, for the captain told him to run on in and see Miss Nancy.

Leaving Pouncer outside, he entered the house, and there a ser-

vant told him that Miss Nancy was up in her own room. He went
upstairs, and as he pushed open the door he saw her seated near
the window, hemming curtains; but as soon as he entered she put
down her work and caught him in her arms. She did not ask him
why he had not come to them for so long; she did not ask about his
illness, though she was shocked at the change in his appearance;
she simply accepted him as he was. After a little she took up her
work again, and Grif, sitting on a stool at her feet, leaned against
her knee. And presently of his own accord he told her why he had
not been, or tried to tell her, for his chief explanation was that
something had prevented him from coming. "I have not been very
well," he said.

"But you must get quite strong before you go home," Miss
Nancy smiled.

She looked down at him, as he sat gazing far away out of the
window, and a dimness rose in her eyes as she stroked his hair.

"Yes. I think—I think I could get well here."

The dreamy words seemed to her to have a strange meaning,
and she bent a little lower. "What is it, Grif?" she asked gently.
"Won't you tell me what it is?"

He tried to tell her, but the story, which had never passed his lips
till then, seemed loth to pass them now.

She listened, but it was not at once that she understood the
meaning of his words. When it did come to her, it came in a single
illuminating flash, and she saw it all from the beginning. She saw
it, and she saw its horror; and what made its horror was that he
himself did not, or could not, perceive it in the light of delusion.
She felt an infinite compassion for him, but she said nothing, letting him finish out his tale to the end.

His head leaned against her lap, and his eyes were nearly closed.
She held his hand in hers, his brown thin hand, which seemed dry
and fragile as a winter leaf.

"But that was not Billy," she said to him, in a low voice. "He was
not like that: he never could be like that. It is some cruel falsehood
which has been dropped into your mind, and grown up there. . . .
Come with me to Billy's room now, and I will show you his things,
and tell you about him."

She got up, and, holding Grif's hand, took him into a bright still room overlooking the garden. A robin was chirping on the window-sill, but he did not fly away when they entered.

"See, these are his toys," she said. "He was just an ordinary boy. This is his stamp-book; this is the museum he made with things his grandfather gave him; these are his soldiers, and this is the boat he used to sail on the pond and on the river. These are his skates, and these are his books—I expect you have read most of them—*Huckleberry Finn, Twenty-thousand Leagues under the Sea, The Young Fur Traders, Nat the Naturalist*. . . . And this is his picture hanging on the wall."

Grif looked at the laughing, merry face, and as he did so something which had been coiled about his mind ever since the afternoon before his illness, seemed to drop away. It was as if a window had been opened into his soul, letting in the fresh clean air and the sunshine, letting in the song of the robin and the blue sky and the wind. He shuddered for a moment, as a kind of ecstasy of relief swept up through him. He gave a little sharp cry as he buried his face against Miss Nancy. "I know now—I know now," he whispered. "It is all different."

The rapture of freedom, of happiness, seemed to beat upon his heart, and he sobbed with the joy of its healing, cleansing waves, which rushed over him and through him. He had turned very white, and Miss Nancy, leading him to the big rocking-chair by the window-seat, sat down there and drew him to her. He was so light that she scarcely felt his weight as she held him in her arms, held him closely, his dark head pillowed on her breast. The white face sank lower on her shoulder, and in a little while he became very quiet, so that she knew, looking down at his shut eyes, that he had fallen asleep. "He will get well now," she whispered to herself. "He is well already." And her lips moved in a silent prayer. "When he wakens up he will be happy. All this will have passed from him, and he will be well and strong."

Outside, the robin continued to sing, and a low, sweet, humming noise told her that Captain Narcissus had begun to cut the grass. The sound of the lawn-mower rose, monotonous and pleasant, a pleasant soothing music, which seemed to bring back the spirit of the dying summer. She sat on, listening to it, and thinking of the boy lying so quietly in her arms. At last the noise ceased, and she guessed that the Captain was coming indoors. Probably it was nearly lunch-time.

"Shall we go downstairs?" Miss Nancy whispered, for Grif was sleeping now so lightly that she could not hear his breathing, could not even hear it when she bent her head till her lips touched his hair.

But Grif slept on.

THE END.

NEW & FORTHCOMING TITLES FROM VALANCOURT BOOKS

R. C. ASHBY (RUBY FERGUSON)	He Arrived at Dusk
FRANK BAKER	The Birds
WALTER BAXTER	Look Down in Mercy
CHARLES BEAUMONT	The Hunger and other Stories
DAVID BENEDICTUS	The Fourth of June
JOHN BLACKBURN	A Scent of New-Mown Hay
	Broken Boy
	Blue Octavo
	Nothing But the Night
	Bury Him Darkly
	The Household Traitors
	Our Lady of Pain
	A Beastly Business
THOMAS BLACKBURN	The Feast of the Wolf
JOHN BRAINE	Room at the Top
	The Vodi
BASIL COPPER	The Great White Space
	Necropolis
RONALD FRASER	Flower Phantoms
STEPHEN GILBERT	The Burnaby Experiments
STEPHEN GREGORY	The Cormorant
CLAUDE HOUGHTON	I Am Jonathan Scrivener
	This Was Ivor Trent
GERALD KERSH	Nightshade and Damnations
FRANCIS KING	To the Dark Tower
	Never Again
	An Air that Kills
	The Dividing Stream
	The Dark Glasses
	The Man on the Rock
C.H.B. KITCHIN	Ten Pollitt Place
	The Book of Life
HILDA LEWIS	The Witch and the Priest
KENNETH MARTIN	Aubade
	Waiting for the Sky to Fall
MICHAEL McDOWELL	The Amulet
MICHAEL NELSON	Knock or Ring
	A Room in Chelsea Square

BEVERLEY NICHOLS	Crazy Pavements
OLIVER ONIONS	The Hand of Kornelius Voyt
DENNIS PARRY	Sea of Glass
ROBERT PHELPS	Heroes and Orators
J.B. PRIESTLEY	Benighted
	The Other Place
FORREST REID	The Garden God
	The Tom Barber Trilogy
	At the Door of the Gate
	The Spring Song
HENRY DE VERE STACPOOLE	The Blue Lagoon
RUSSELL THORNDIKE	The Slype
	The Master of the Macabre
JOHN TREVENA	Furze the Cruel
	Sleeping Waters
JOHN WAIN	Hurry on Down
	The Smaller Sky
HUGH WALPOLE	The Killer and the Slain
KEITH WATERHOUSE	There is a Happy Land
	Billy Liar
ALEC WAUGH	The Loom of Youth
COLIN WILSON	Ritual in the Dark
	Man Without a Shadow
	The World of Violence
	The Philosopher's Stone
	The God of the Labyrinth

Selected Eighteenth and Nineteenth Century Classics

ANONYMOUS	Teleny
	The Sins of the Cities of the Plain
GRANT ALLEN	Miss Cayley's Adventures
JOANNA BAILLIE	Six Gothic Dramas
EATON STANNARD BARRETT	The Heroine
WILLIAM BECKFORD	Azemia
COUNTESS OF BLESSINGTON	Marmaduke Herbert
MARY ELIZABETH BRADDON	Thou Art the Man
JOHN BUCHAN	Sir Quixote of the Moors
HALL CAINE	The Manxman
MONA CAIRD	The Wing of Azrael
EMILY FLYGARE-CARLÉN	The Magic Goblet

MARY CHOLMONDELEY	Diana Tempest
MARIE CORELLI	The Sorrows of Satan
	Ziska
CAROLINE CLIVE	Paul Ferroll
BARON CORVO	Stories Toto Told Me
	Hubert's Arthur
GABRIELE D'ANNUNZIO	The Intruder (L'innocente)
JOHN DAVIDSON	Earl Lavender
THOMAS DE QUINCEY	Klosterheim
ARTHUR CONAN DOYLE	The Parasite
	Round the Red Lamp
BARON DE LA MOTTE FOUQUÉ	The Magic Ring
SARAH GRAND	Ideala
H. RIDER HAGGARD	Nada the Lily
ERNEST G. HENHAM	Tenebrae
CHARLES JOHNSTONE	Chrysal (2 vols)
CAROLINE LAMB	Glenarvon
FRANCIS LATHOM	The Castle of Ollada
	The Midnight Bell
	The Fatal Vow
	Astonishment!!!
	The One-Pound Note
	The Impenetrable Secret
	The Mysterious Freebooter
SOPHIA LEE	The Two Emilys
SHERIDAN LE FANU	Carmilla
	The Cock and Anchor
	The Rose and the Key
M. G. LEWIS	The Monk
ELIZA LYNN LINTON	Realities
EDWARD BULWER LYTTON	Eugene Aram
FLORENCE MARRYAT	The Blood of the Vampire
	There is no Death
RICHARD MARSH	The Beetle
	The Goddess: A Demon
	A Spoiler of Men
	The Seen and the Unseen
	Both Sides of the Veil
	Curios
	A Second Coming
	Philip Bennion's Death

	The Complete Sam Briggs Stories
	The Complete Judith Lee Stories
BERTRAM MITFORD	Renshaw Fanning's Quest
	The Sign of the Spider
	The Weird of Deadly Hollow
	The King's Assegai
	The White Shield
	The Induna's Wife
JOHN MOORE	Zeluco
OUIDA	Under Two Flags
	In Maremma
ELIZA PARSONS	Castle of Wolfenbach
	The Mysterious Warning
WALTER PATER	Marius the Epicurean
ROSA PRAED	Fugitive Anne
FRANCIS PREVOST	Rust of Gold
ANN RADCLIFFE	The Italian
	The Mysteries of Udolpho
	Gaston de Blondeville
CLARA REEVE	The Old English Baron
GEORGE W.M. REYNOLDS	The Mysteries of London
	The Necromancer
REGINA MARIA ROCHE	The Children of the Abbey
	Clermont
JAMES MALCOLM RYMER	The Black Monk
PERCY BYSSHE SHELLEY	The Cenci
M. P. SHIEL	Prince Zaleski
CHARLOTTE SMITH	The Story of Henrietta
BRAM STOKER	The Watter's Mou'
	The Mystery of the Sea
	Lady Athlyne
	The Lady of the Shroud
	The Snake's Pass